REVELATION

REVELATION

A Novel

Bobi Gentry Goodwin

SHE WRITES PRESS

Published 2019
Printed in the United States of America
ISBN: 978-1-63152-606-0 pbk
ISBN: 978-1-63152-607-7 ebk
Library of Congress Control Number: 2019909105

For information, address:
She Writes Press
1569 Solano Ave #546
Berkeley, CA 94707

She Writes Press is a division of SparkPoint Studio, LLC.

To all who have struggled to find the way.

PROLOGUE

The sound of the gunshot reverberated in his head. The gunshot rang out and shook the antenna. The picture tube was fuzzy and the sound inaudible. Robert gazed into his younger brother's frightened eyes. He was scared to go downstairs but aware of what he had to do. He stood strong. At only ten years old, he knew he had to be the one to face the unknown. He was the oldest.

The first step down the staircase almost buckled his legs underneath him. He called out to his mother and listened for her reply. The third call left his mouth in a whimper. His saliva was gone by the fifth beckoning. His family had escaped much. He wondered if the past was catching up to them.

He walked past the telephone, never once glancing in its direction. He could hear his well-meaning neighbor Big Mama Angela Tee on the other line. *Boy, you should have picked up the telephone and called me.* He knew there was no time. Robert tiptoed toward the kitchen, which remained in disarray as if nothing had changed. But his stomachache told him something had.

Robert's mother had told him hours before to go upstairs and not come down. She had business to tend to. Robert hated the businessmen who entered their home all hours of the day and night, leaving money for her and trailing behind them more drugs. The children at his school often identified their dreams for the future. Doctor, lawyer, businessman. Robert swore that when he became an adult he would never become a businessman. All the businessmen he knew only caused his family a familiar pain, like playing hot hands. Robert always knew what was coming, but he was never quick enough to change the outcome.

Big Mama Angela Tee had tried to change things. She was a constant source of dinners when they didn't have food. Clothes when they had none. A bed when he and his brother were left home alone. She provided love where it was missing. Although she was the strongest woman he'd ever met, she still couldn't do anything about the reunification. She'd hated to return Robert and Randy back to their mother, but as their neighbor, she had no other choice. She was only a do-good church mother. The state had rendered a decision. Big Mama wasn't a relative, and his mom was. Besides, the social worker said, his mother had fought tooth and nail to get them back. The boys were all she had left, and they belonged to her. Possession was nine-tenths of the law.

Robert had swallowed his tears when his mother arrived to pick him up. He greeted her with a plastered-on smile and a lifeless hug. He loved her, but he didn't want to live with her. Living with her was not like living at all. Living with her was dying—slowly. Before Big Mama was granted temporary custody, there was only one way, his mother's way, but Big Mama Angela Tee had shown them another life. The life he'd always longed for. A world full of colors that was safe and secure. He was once blind to it, but now he could clearly see.

His new vision had become the problem. He could no longer close his eyes. The past separations from his mother had led to small reunions with the hope of change; but the last time he was different, his eyes were different. He knew that nothing had changed. His mother was sober, smelled good, and was smiling. She had followed the directives of the court. Everyone was happy, but they didn't notice. How could they not notice that her lips were painted red?

The red lips had approached him and kissed him on the cheek, staining his face with the anger he felt inside. His blood had boiled. His ears and face had warmed. The adults said he was flushed. His social worker, Sharyn Melrose, laughed, saying it was written all over his face. She was well-meaning and kindhearted but couldn't comprehend his truth.

Robert's feelings were written all over his face, but no one saw them except Big Mama. She knew. She had walked over and hugged her foster son and spoke softly in his ear, "I'm just a phone call away." He knew she always was, but right now he couldn't call.

Robert walked slowly past the dirty dishes stacked on the kitchen table. "Mom?" he called. He could see splattered polka dots on the carpet as he sneaked past the refrigerator; it stopped him in his tracks. His mind was conflicted. Part of him wanted to go forward. Part of him wanted to run back. His stomach was the first part that reacted. The blood-stained carpet mixed with his vomit. He fell to his knees with his insides spewing out. He stood and turned his head away from the vomit. The smell startled him.

Robert saw her red lips first. At first he thought her lipstick was smeared, but under closer inspection he could see the blood had trickled down. He could not scream. He could not cry. He looked at his mother's body. The gun had fallen from her hand. Robert initially wanted to pick it up and join her in the great escape. He looked at her and looked at it. Slowly he took a step toward the gun, carefully glancing at his mother. He didn't want her to see him playing with it, but he knew in his heart she couldn't. He once again noticed her red lips—the red lips that had kissed him gently that day at the reunification center. He turned swiftly away from the gun and walked to his mother. Kissing her on the lips, he thanked her for freeing him to see other colors once again.

1

Angela

"Five-o, Mommy. Mommy, five-o." The six-year-old boy shook his mother frantically, attempting to warn her of the police officer's arrival. His eyes filled with tears as the burly police officer guided him away from the corpse. Angela Lovelace stood silent, unable to engage in her job duties. It was the first time she had frozen.

Coworkers often reminisced about their first time freezing. They laughed about the dreaded stillness that results from an overwhelming emotional response that takes the body hostage. Some bragged it never happened to them. Social-work supervisors reported that it happens to almost everyone. Angela stayed silent in those lunchroom debates. She distanced herself from the banter and callous joking of her colleagues.

Nothing was funny about removing a child. Nothing was lighthearted about their life situations. And now it was happening to her, without warning. She wished she could travel back to the past and listen to her colleagues. Hear the advice they gave to green workers fresh out of school. She needed advice now. She needed to thaw.

When the report came in about a boy who hadn't shown up for school, no eyebrows were raised. But when the mother's name showed up on six other Child Protective Services reports, an investigation began. Angela didn't have time to conduct a home visit before her supervisor pulled her in on a conference call with neighborhood police. The downstairs neighbor had called, hearing the kindergartner's cries coming from upstairs. The neighbor knew the boy's mother used drugs. Almost everyone in the building used drugs. Section eight low-income housing had provided the means; a slumlord had provided a roof.

The joint response team prepared to meet at 1:00 p.m. Angela treated herself to a cup of coffee before the meeting. She knew this was going to be a long day. She followed the officers to a run-down, cluttered street in the Excelsior district. Free signs attached to a couch and two worn bookcases obscured her full view of the dilapidated building. As she exited her car, she stepped over a pile of curbside rubbish. She followed the officers up the narrow staircase as the team slowly approached the second floor leading to the door. Angela's senses were almost immune, but the litter-filled hallway reeked of urine. She looked around at the dark doors and graffiti-filled walls, saying a quiet prayer for safety.

The police knocked softly at the door, careful not to arouse suspicion, but to no avail. The knocking led to forced entry as Angela stood down the hallway a safe distance from the trained officers. Finally she received the officer's signal. Her afternoon was booked.

Angela was aware of her surroundings as soon as she entered the neglected apartment, but she couldn't move. Her attention was drawn away from the dead body by a tattered picture of her own father on the wall. Her mind filled with a million unanswered questions. The foremost one was why her father's picture would be in the apartment of a dead junkie. Looking again at the young face of the mother, she searched for truth but found nothing there.

Angela finally wrenched her attention to the rest of the surroundings. She suspected an overdose as she noticed the pipe on the table. She could barely hear the officer talking to her. His stern words were muffled by the sound of her heartbeat. His hand pulling on her arm was dulled by the tingling in her extremities. She waited for the sting of reality to hit. Time stood still as the police officer addressed her. Her feet were glued to the floor. Her mouth wouldn't open. She couldn't reply. She stood paralyzed from reality. The police officer forcefully escorted her out the apartment door. It wasn't until Officer Johnson clapped his hands that she came alive again. The young boy restrained by another officer was still kicking, trying to get to his mother. Constant crying and screaming beckoned the other neighbors from their doors.

"Five-o. Five-o," the boy whimpered. "The police are here!" he screamed. Angela waited for the child to calm, aiding the police officer in informal de-escalation tactics. The vacuum-cleaner effect used soothing, calm voices humming steadily underneath the boy's cries until his tone mirrored theirs. Angela ushered the child into her arms and took him outside of the building.

"Where's my mommy?" the child asked innocently.

"What's your mommy's name?" Angela replied, avoiding the difficult question while seeking her own answers.

"Samantha," the boy answered, trying to look up the stairs and into his crowded apartment.

"Samantha is a pretty name. What's your name?"

"Tre Mason," he responded, trying to push his way out of her arms. Angela scanned her memory, searching for a cousin, a neighbor, a family friend who lived in this neighborhood. Where did his mother get a picture of her father? Thinking on her feet had always been one of Angela's strengths. She patted the child's back to reassure him as she searched her past, frantically looking for a Lovelace connection to this child's surname.

"Mr. Mason. Huh. Do you have any brothers and sisters?" Angela clung to him tightly as the coroner's van pulled up next to the fire engine.

"No. Just me and my mommy." Tre looked at her strangely. As

the coroner's representative passed by Angela, she could see the truth register in the boy's eyes as they welled with tears. The small child knew the result of the white truck. He had seen the dance of death before. Tre began screaming once again as the reality of his mother's fate engulfed him. Hitting her was the only way he could voice his anger. Embracing him was the only way she could voice her sorrow.

Robert

The familiar smell of freshly brewed coffee, mixed with the aroma of ripened lemons, comforted him. Robert Lovelace sat in front of his kitchen window, peering through the mini blinds. In the dusk of the night he could only see the shadow of the lemon tree planted in her honor years ago. Lemons were sour but could enhance any meal when paired with the right ingredients, as she'd done in his life.

The plaid shirt he'd pulled from his closet hours earlier was snug around his midsection, but he was grateful it still fit. She made it a point to know his size, and at Christmas had gifted him with his favorite color. Last year, she'd laid the gift at his doorstep, and he was thankful she did. The black-and-red shirt provided a relief he couldn't find anywhere else today.

Robert took a sip of coffee to steady his trembling hands. The churning of instability, mortality, and powerlessness curdled heavily in his gut. Death always made his stomach ache. He grabbed the crowded ceramic fruit bowl in search of overripe fruit. Like the fruit, she had been tossed about, bruised, and exposed to the elements so long that she ended up discarded. Robert tossed a spongy lemon into the nearby trash. His stomach plunged as he recalled her face.

His hands warmed as he wrapped them around his coffee mug and savored a sip of his beloved French roast. He grabbed his Bible from the chair nearby and turned to Psalms in an effort to put a praise on his lips. Time alone to hear from the Lord was exactly what he needed, especially after this afternoon's phone call.

Robert heard the faint rattle on the door like the foreshadowing of something ominous occurring in a horror film. He rubbed his hands on his blue jeans and reluctantly closed the Bible, pulling himself up by the round kitchen table. He pressed his chair back with the heel of his hiking boot and labored to the front door. Robert expected his neighbor with another complaint. He'd forgotten to move the trash bins from the sidewalk this morning.

The porch light flickered as Robert squinted in front of the peephole. Startled, he took a step back as he realized that pretending he wasn't home might still be an option.

Robert rubbed his temples, laid his calloused hand on the dead bolt, and snuck a peek out of the nearby window. Parking in the driveway was a mistake. He wished he'd cleaned out the garage like he'd planned. The adjoining edifice was still filled with boxes of canned goods awaiting the sixth annual food drive he sponsored as a memorial to honor the life of his Big Mama.

The dead bolt flipped back with ease, but his hand still felt bonded to the door. Robert didn't want to see her, especially now. He took a deep breath, slid the door open, and rested on his heels. His ex-wife, Rose, gazed at him. He bit his lip and stood silent.

"Well." She adjusted the designer handbag on her shoulder. "Are you going to let me in?" Rose questioned. Robert tilted his head as he heard the condescending voice of his own mother. His mother was guilty of staying away for days at a time, but his ex was guilty of never showing up. He placed his hands on his hips, refusing to move away from the door's entry. "Robert!" she hissed.

Robert reluctantly stepped to the side and allowed her into the foyer. He knew he had to be careful with her. She was like a log crackling in the fireplace; standing close produced warmth, but too close, fire. "Sorry, I was preoccupied," he said, following her into the living room.

"Story of my life," she snarled. "I know *you* were the first person they called," she said, pulling a handkerchief from her purse.

"I received the call." He evaded her eyes and plopped down into the suede oversized lounge chair she had forbid him to purchase.

"When were you going to tell me?" she questioned, fanning herself with the white cotton as she leaned against the wall.

"I hadn't even processed it myself, Rose. It's hard to deal with. I didn't know what to do." He scratched his head.

"Do?" Rose marched up to him and squared her shoulders. "What are you thinking about doing?" she accused.

Robert's hands windmilled. "Rose, someone *I* love passed away, and right now your agenda is the least of my concerns." Robert stood up, pushed past her, and inadvertently bumped into their son exiting the stairwell.

"Who died?" Kevon asked, staring at both his parents.

"Nobody," they barked in unison.

2

Sharyn

Sharyn Lovelace Sanders slammed her husband's dinner plate on the table, almost knocking over his empty glass. Her irritation bubbled over like a fountain. "You want something to drink?" Sharyn spit out the only communication they'd had today.

"Yes." Michael looked up and nodded cautiously, half questioning yet agreeing. Sharyn placed her hands on her hips and tilted her head to the side. She glared at him, trying to identify this stranger. The brown corduroys were the same pants she'd purchased online. The blue cotton button-down shirt was identical to the gift her mother had presented to him on his birthday. The dark brown eyes, chiseled face, and dimpled chin were all familiar, but he'd changed. The affection was different between them, like falling out of love. The exact moment it had happened was a mystery, but it had changed everything when it did.

Sharyn snatched his glass off the table and headed toward the refrigerator. She pulled open the stainless-steel double doors, grabbed the apple juice, and poured almost to the rim as she tried not to look in his direction. She refused to fill his glass with crushed ice, the way he liked it. Looking at him perched on his seat like a king on the throne, she felt tempted to leave the tumbler on the counter.

Sharyn refused to move. He didn't deserve any special treatment.

She was the one wronged, not him. Michael was keeping his distance, and it annoyed her. Usually he'd try to comfort her when she was irritated. He'd make dad jokes to produce a smile. He was her handyman, using every tool in his arsenal to cheer her up; but today, he sat stone-faced, like a judge waiting to swing his gavel.

"Am I going to get that juice?" Michael crinkled his forehead.

"Oh, yes, sir." Sharyn pulled out the sides of her brown peasant skirt and bowed like a servant, her bangs nearly covering her eyes. "I mustn't keep *you* waiting." Sharyn tossed her head back and shuffled her feet defiantly. The ruffles on her white rayon blouse leaped in the air. Sharyn's anger was fanned by Michael's rigidity. Whether it was crushed ice, pressed handkerchiefs, or his refusal to visit an infertility specialist, once he made up his mind, there was no way to change it. The hierarchy was clear, and she would never be promoted.

"Okay, Uncle Remus!" Michael poked out his lips.

"I was figuring out what *I* was going to drink after I *serve* you." Sharyn moved in slow motion toward the table.

"Serve me?" Michael questioned. "You haven't served me in a while."

Sharyn refused to bite. She didn't want to argue anymore; she wanted a resolution. "Forget you, Michael." Sharyn rolled her eyes as she placed the juice next to his plate. She was doing her part—why wasn't he doing his? They'd been trying for two years, and she still wasn't pregnant. They could see a reproductive endocrinologist tomorrow to get the help they needed, and she was willing to spare no expense. Sharyn pulled out her chair, sat down, and was immediately reminded of when she tried to explain to her father that she needed tampons to go swimming instead of the lower-priced sanitary napkins. She felt the heat of anger flush her face. "You don't get it." Sharyn's shoulders tensed.

"No, I don't," Michael snapped. "Where is my ice?" He tipped his glass toward her.

"No ice," Sharyn barked, as she sat down and stuffed corn kernels in her mouth. The muffled sounds of chewing echoed in the gulf that was beginning to separate them. She couldn't even bring herself to look at him.

"I guess I'll get it myself." Michael headed toward the refrigerator. Sharyn looked down at the bland plate. Meatloaf, mashed potatoes, and sweet corn prepared with no effort or energy. She hadn't even made a gravy. The plate reminded her of their marriage. No pizzazz.

"Go ahead, serve yourself." Sharyn glared at him as she shoved the stiffened potatoes around her plate. A lump formed in her throat as she fought back tears. She loved God like Michael did, but he was a fanatic.

"Never mind, I don't need any ice, it's been cold enough around here lately." Michael smirked, returning to the table.

"Below the belt," Sharyn growled, as Michael settled in his seat. She was sick of his pious attitude. Like a doctor relaying bad news, he was well guarded and obstinate, and refused to take into account any opinions other than his own.

"Any more corn?" Michael asked, looking at his plate with vacant eyes.

"The corn is gone," Sharyn snarled, referring more to her trust than to the starch. She swallowed her food down as fast as she could, anxious to excuse herself.

Sharyn gathered her plate, walked over to the large double sink, and shoved her glass into the dishwater. The sudsy white water turned pink as glass fragments floated to the surface. She lifted her hand gently out of the highlighted water. A large shard of glass stood wedged in her hand as bright red blood squirted in different directions. Her knees buckled.

Angela

Angela's caramel eyes stared blankly at her laptop as she reviewed the email again. She ran her fingers through her thick brown shoulder-length hair, swallowed hard, and grabbed the goblet of white wine. The sip caught in the back of her throat. Coughing reminded her that she didn't drink, but tonight she was grateful for the bottle Jonathan had gifted her last week. It had been a tough day, and she was unsure of what to do next.

Scrubbing herself from the shrapnel of traumatic debris that her job readily supplied was non-negotiable. Angela had developed a ritual years before to wash off the heaviness of the pain that she witnessed daily, to flush the unseen wounds. After work she grabbed powder, baby oil gel, and her signature floral scent that she found at a small boutique in Calistoga and layered the products like bandage dressings. She meditated for five minutes and then tried to return to her life, unscarred as she usually did—but tonight was different. The cries of the boy still radiated in her ears, and the smell of death hung at her nose.

An hour later, Angela still hadn't been buffered. Fingernail shavings were tossed about her computer from constant biting as the dead woman, the young boy, and her own father, Robert, occupied her mind. Her cell phone beckoned. Should she call her date to cancel, or should she call her father and confront him?

She glanced at the tattered picture of her father on the coffee table. Angela had never taken anything from the home of a client. She prided herself on her social-work ethics, but this was different. Somehow he was involved in this case.

Angela took another gulp of wine. It went down easier this time, and like a second teaspoon of cough syrup, she hoped it would soon cure her ailments. She reread the email she'd scripted to her supervisor highlighting her desire to be removed from the case, took a deep breath, and pressed the delete button.

Angela leaned back on her couch, closed her eyes, and surrendered. Her math teacher always had told her that when she couldn't find a solution to a problem, she should take a break to recalibrate her brain. Tre Mason was a problem that she wasn't going to solve tonight, and her mind needed a diversion. Angela opened her eyes, sat straight up, and grabbed her cell phone, opting for a familiar equation. She dialed his number instinctively.

"I was wondering when I'd hear from you. It's been days," Martin said, before she could speak.

"Someone's been counting again." Angela placed the glass on the edge of the table, grateful for the deviation.

"Always. You miss me?" he asked. Angela sat silent for a few seconds, hating to expose her feelings.

"I've been thinking about you," she murmured, as she stationed her laptop next to her on the couch.

"How much?" he pushed.

"I've been thinking about you for the hundredth time." Angela grabbed the goblet, took a swig, and returned it to the table.

"You better have."

"Pushy! I thought ministers were supposed to be kind *and* humble."

"I thought I was kind and humble. I miss you is all. I've been to conference after conference and haven't had any downtime."

"I'm sure it hasn't been all that bad." Angela felt her inhibitions waning. The wine bottle was still cold as she refilled her glass.

"The only thing I was able to do in Dallas was visit The Sixth Floor Museum, which is some American history I wish we could've experienced together. Plus, while I've been down here the rumor mill has been churning up there. I've been getting ample feedback about your social life." Martin scoffed. "Talk about being assassinated."

"Assassinated? What have the local reporters been telling you now? My business is not *your* business. You're not my daddy."

"Not yet," Martin teased.

"Is that right? Says who? I already have a daddy." Angela giggled haphazardly, twirling a loose curl around her finger.

"Not one like me. I'm sitting here thinking about you when I should be studying the Word," Martin admitted.

"Well, I should be working on the new case I received today, but I'm sitting here talking to you. What were you thinking, Reverend? Care to have confession?" Angela examined her bare left hand as the warmth from the alcohol found its way to her extremities.

"Well, not yet, Angela, but in due time. God's time. You're gonna know exactly how I feel about you when God says the same. You're a special woman, and any man would be lucky to have you," Martin declared.

"I know, I know. Lucky," Angela lied, feeling disappointment cement in her stomach like a boulder. "I have to go." She was tired of him dangling himself in front of her and then closing himself off like a jack-in-the-box. "I have to get ready for dinner."

"Alone?"

"I have a suitor." Angela smiled, hoping her truth stung him.

"So I've been hearing," Martin said sarcastically.

"There you go, Martin. You know my intentions. I've been open with you. I don't have any brakes on. You're the one driving, and I've been willing to go where you take me." Angela smacked her lips as the familiar feeling of regret resurfaced. No matter how she changed the variables, their calculations always remained the same.

"But are you willing to go at my pace?" Martin asked.

"Look, I've been riding at your speed for the longest. Don't sit there all self-righteous and get upset when I get tired of riding solo." Angela sat straight up and eyed the clock.

"You're special to me, and I want to keep it that way," Martin said.

"I bet you say that to all your women," Angela hissed.

"Funny. You know me better than that."

"I gotta go. Study your Word, and I'll talk with you later." Angela disconnected him from her phone and her heart. She stood up, brushed off her jumper, closed her laptop, and dialed ferociously.

"Jonathan, can you get here any sooner?" she asked, giggling as she guzzled the last swig of wine.

3

Sharyn

Sharyn fought back tears. She hated the sight of blood. The ruby red reminded her of the pain she'd felt the day she'd said goodbye to her unborn child. The stench of soaked sanitary napkins that she'd never forget. The prescribed ibuprofen barely numbing the ache that arose in her after the procedure. The medicine had taken care of her physical pain but hadn't touched her emotions. It had taken her years to forgive herself. She knew she wouldn't have survived except for her grandmother, Big Mama, drilling in her head that God knows and cares. Sharyn wondered if she could ever be like the Jesus her grandmother told her about and forgive her spouse.

Michael fussed over her at the sink after he pulled the glass protruding from her hand. "It doesn't look that deep, but keep pressure on it." He grabbed her hand, placed a white dish towel over it, and squeezed. "I'm going to run upstairs and grab the first aid kit. Stay right here and keep applying pressure," he instructed. Sharyn pushed down hard on her laceration. Her stomach turned as blood began seeping through. She turned away.

Michael's corduroys and blue shirt were now speckled with blood as his six-foot frame disappeared up the stairs. She glanced down at the towel and her ruined blouse. Sharyn felt tears flooding her eyes as both her palm and her heart ached. Michael returned with their first aid kit, removed the dish towel, and covered her hand with clean gauze. He wrapped his arm around her waist and guided her slowly to the leather couch stationed in the family room.

"Sit down." Michael sank down beside her and prepared to survey her injury. Sharyn winced as Michael unwrapped the gauze. She turned her head in disgust as he gently cleaned her wound with a wet cloth and carefully applied peroxide to the cut.

"Thank God it isn't as bad as I originally thought." Relief registered across Michael's face as he dried her hand and placed a large bandage over her cut. It made her feel better instantly.

"But you said it wasn't deep." Sharyn eyed the bandage as blood pooled underneath. Michael lifted Sharyn's hand to his mouth and gently kissed it, reminding her of how gentle he could be. He was the kindest man she'd ever met. She placed her healthy hand on his broad shoulder and squeezed for reassurance, the way she used to when they attended the concerts he liked instead of her favorite bands, or viewed the movies he didn't want to see but she did.

"I didn't want to scare you. Are you okay?" Michael asked. Sharyn exhaled; she hadn't seen the tender side of her husband in months. She missed the softness that welled in his deep brown eyes.

"Thank you. I'm better now," she said, leaning into him. "You know, Michael, we can't keep going on like this. If you'd listen to me, I think you'd understand. I'm not trying to hurt you. I want what's best for us." Sharyn jumped through the window of opportunity.

"And I don't?" Michael retorted, letting go of her injured hand and her hope for reconciliation. His shoulders tensed underneath her touch.

"Honey, we have two separate views on God's role. And we need to come to some understanding because this is tearing us apart," Sharyn whispered softly as she gathered her hands on her lap and played with the border of the bandage. The beige dressing fixed to her brown skin mirrored the stark contrast of their opinions.

"Wait one minute!" Michael protested. "Don't try to blame this not-talking crap on barrenness."

"But—" Sharyn interjected.

"But nothing, Sharyn, this attitude you have is unacceptable. I love you and we've been married for a long time, but you've always struggled with respecting my authority. I'm the man of this house, and my house will be in order." Michael stamped his foot. "I decided that we weren't going to seek out a physician, and that's final."

"I never made a decision, Michael." Sharyn's lips tightened as she was catapulted back to her childhood. Her father, Robert, always encouraged her to make her own decisions, preaching that every action she took was a choice. If she didn't do her homework, she was deciding to fail; if she didn't clean her room, she was deciding not to be awarded privileges; if she helped her siblings, she was choosing responsibility. "And I have a right to."

"You have a right to your opinion, but it's not up to you to make *the* decision, Sharyn." His voice softened. "We talked about it, and I made the final call. Now as the church submits to Christ, so also wives should submit to their husbands—in everything. Not in the things they want to, Sharyn. In everything."

"Please, Michael, church is on Sunday!" Sharyn leaned back into the couch, shaking her head.

"I know you feel hurt, but God is the head of our lives, and we must have faith in the things He decides to do. I'm trying to follow Him and do what's best. I can't do things to please you—or me, for that matter. All I can do is what I'm led to do." Michael's face went emotionless, like a cement statue. She had seen this look before. She'd lost this battle.

"You're right, Michael. Do what you want. You're the mighty husband, and whatever you say is how it's going to be. I suppose I'll tuck tail and go with it." Sharyn rolled her eyes.

"It's called submission, Sharyn," Michael corrected.

"Submission or slavery?" Sharyn lowered her head.

"Slavery, really! Now you're being ridiculous." Michael threw his hands in the air.

"No, I'm not, but I guess this is my life. Lying awake at night. Avoiding children's departments. But you'll never get it. You don't know how it feels to see mothers with their children and face my period every month." Sharyn's face reddened.

"You don't think I feel anything," Michael snarled, and slammed the first aid kit on the table.

"You aren't a woman waiting for a magic line to appear." Sharyn grabbed her forehead. The throbbing matched the pain in her hand, a steady beat of anguish. Her shoulders jerked like a car running out of gas as tears fell from her eyes. Michael cupped her face.

"You know I love you, Sharyn, and I'm sorry you are in pain, but let's cut through all the drama and little temper tantrums, shall we?"

Robert

Robert wiped his forehead with his favorite handkerchief, refusing to succumb to the emotions welling inside of him. He dangled the phone between his shoulder and his ear, trying not to drop it. It reminded him of what he'd always done: juggle.

Robert had learned to juggle by the time he was in middle school. He'd played hot potato at school and at home. Purchase groceries, pay the electric bill, or do laundry had been common choices. When his birth mother had come home at night, she'd hand him wads of cash, but it wasn't until he was eleven that he'd learned to keep multiple balls in the air. Pay a little here, spend a little there, and save a little. Stretching himself thin was nothing new, but with his ex-wife, he was about to break. Robert rolled his eyes as he spoke.

"What am I supposed to do? You seem to have all the answers!" He cradled the phone, now slippery with sweat from his tightened grip. Kernels of anger and resentment exploded in him like popcorn placed over a hot stove.

"There's nothing you can do, Robert. Your hands are tied, and I mean it." Rose's tone was smug. He sucked his teeth, tiring of trying to find a foothold with this obstinate woman. She was tough, guarded, and vulnerable all at the same time. He'd spent the better part of their union trying to keep peace and protect her all at the same time. He was the negotiator who always seemed to lose in the end.

"But he is my family," he pleaded with his ex-wife. Robert stood and leaned against the counter. He kicked his foot against the sturdy kitchen cabinets, something he hadn't done in years.

"He's not my family, nor my concern. I refuse to let something like this interrupt *our* family. I forbade it back then, and I forbid it now. This could destroy our children. What I worked hard to build."

"What *you* worked hard to build?" Robert snapped. The frustration building in his chest reminded him of their embittered marriage. He refused to escape now, unlike he did way back then. No more driving up to Twin Peaks and falling asleep in the car, underneath the stars, too irritated to go home. He was stronger now, mature. He clenched his jaw, ready to take on this forceful woman. She had her life, and he had his.

"Don't you forget our agreement, Robert. Even though our vows have been broken, the commitment to *our* family remains the same. I know you know that, that's why you lied to Kevon. We must stay united on this."

Robert was glad she'd left his home days earlier when Kevon arrived. He'd felt the heat rising between them like a teakettle about to percolate, and he didn't want Kevon to hear the whistle. Robert had watched his own mother fight with scores of men. Language that should never be heard by children flew around their home like darts.

Sleepless nights became the usual until Robert decided to hide a knife under his pillow, half waiting and half hoping he'd have to use it.

"Rose, it happened years ago; let it go. This is a new day, and the circumstances have changed." Robert paced from the kitchen to the dining room of his Victorian. "I'm going up to the police station, I need information."

"No, you're not! I warned you back then to stop, but you didn't listen. You kept right on seeing her. I warned you to let this thing be. I didn't want it at my doorstep then, and I don't want it now."

"So you're going to sit back and do nothing?" Robert questioned, grabbing the brown leather bomber jacket draped on the back of his white dining room armchair. The distressed paint mirrored his heart. "I'm too old for this. I have to . . ."

"Robert, stop walking the floor and listen. Remember our divorce. If you fight this fight, you're going to lose. Now, I'm not gonna do a thing except pray and put me on another cup of coffee, and you are too. You owe me that."

"What if I won't?" Robert's love for her was beginning to sour, like old clothes left overnight in a washing machine. He was tired of his feelings being forgotten about.

"Don't write a check that you can't cash. Have you seen your children recently? I mean *really* looked at them," Rose demanded.

"What are you talking about, woman?" Robert threw his hands up in the air, surrendering to her manipulation.

"Angela is fraying at the edges, Kevon's always teetering off a cliff, and Lord, don't let me bring up Sharyn. You cannot give them one more thing. It's too much. What's done is done, let it be."

"I can't believe you." Robert threw his jacket onto the floor.

"Believe me, this has caused me too much pain as it is. I'm upset about the whole situation, but I made my choice years ago, and I'm sticking with it. I honor my commitments, and I thought you would've learned by now, so should you," Rose snapped.

"Okay, Rose, have it your way. But I want to go on record and let you know, it ain't right. It simply ain't right." Robert slammed his fist on the table, hung up the phone in her face, and grabbed his jacket off the floor. He fiddled in the pocket for the keys, and with a few quick strides he exited his house, jumped in the car, and headed toward Oakland. Lake Temescal Beach House was the last place he saw them. The memory was his alone. Rose could tie his hands, but she would never sever his heartstrings.

4

Kevon

Kevon winced as the pizza cheese skirted down his lip. He knew he should've waited until it cooled, but it looked good. He was ravenous, and it had been a long day. He knew he should've eaten something before he started slamming cocktails, but his appetite had gone weeks ago.

Kevon juggled the hot pie in his mouth. *Where's Michael? He was supposed to be here an hour ago.* Kevon took the clear water bottle the bartender gave him and took a gigantic swig, creating a water slide for the blistering dough. Scarfing down another bite, he grabbed his cell phone to see if Michael had called. No missed call.

Kevon glanced at the clock on the table. It was now after midnight, and he was anxious to get home. The small office was dark and smelled of mold. The dimly lit space was covered in dust and reminded him of an abandoned basement. The small, yellow sticky rat trap in the corner was a reminder of the status of this relic of a bar in revitalized San Francisco. He was thankful the trap was empty. He didn't want to see anything imprisoned, a feeling he knew all too well. Kevon tossed his phone on the table.

"Your ride coming?" James asked forcefully, as he peeked in the office from behind the battered wooden door.

"Yeah, he's on his way. Hey, James, thanks again for not kicking me out of here. I don't know where I would've gone." Kevon tilted the water bottle toward the undersized bartender.

"To jail. Now, the next time you start a fight in here, that's exactly where you'll be going. You're lucky I knew your grandmother. God rest her soul. She helped people in this community. I did it for Big Mama, not for you. Plus, I've had these cans sitting around here for weeks." James pointed to the pile of various canned goods tossed in plastic bins tucked in the other corner. "Remember to take them when your ride gets here." James nodded his head and shuffled back up toward the front of the bar.

"Thanks, man," Kevon replied, taking another bite. He slouched in his seat as the throbbing in his back intensified. He'd hardly felt the blows to his stomach, but the blows to his back had left a lasting impression. Kevon didn't remember how the fight had started, but he knew how it had ended. James had tossed both of his assailants out of the bar and shoved Kevon toward the office in the back of the building. The aged bartender had pumped him with water to help him sober up. Kevon was sure he could have driven home, but James had refused to let him leave. This was the sixth time James had kept him hostage, and Kevon was beginning to consider finding another bar.

"Not you again," Michael said, sauntering into the back room. "Now, you're a sight."

"Thanks for coming, bro, I couldn't call my dad." Kevon stood up but immediately fell back in the chair. Pizza and Hennessy didn't mix.

"Don't thank me, thank this dude." Michael pointed to Martin, who now stood in the doorway.

"You brought the preacher!" Kevon threw his hands up and rolled his eyes.

"Yes, he brought the preacher. Looks like I should have given you a lesson on Proverbs 23:29." Martin smacked his lips.

"Look, Kev, I wasn't going to come, but Martin said I should. He gave me an excuse to get out of the house *and* away from the watchful eyes of your sister," Michael said, pulling out an empty chair.

Kevon plopped his head on the table despite the visible sticky residue garnishing it. His stomach had gotten queasy; he thought he was going to vomit. He gagged slightly, responding to the sensation of regurgitation. Martin picked up the trash can from near the door and plopped it down alongside him.

"Better out than in," Martin said, grabbing the other empty chair. Kevon lifted his head slightly, eyeing the two men who looked like investigators ready to pounce. "Let's get out of here, bro. I got to get home."

"We not going nowhere yet. My car and vomit don't associate. What happened, dude?" Michael questioned.

"Nothing. I was chillin' and these two dudes tried to swell up on me."

"And?" Martin pushed.

"And what? I wasn't trying to hear that." Kevon grabbed the garbage can and spit. He grabbed the leftover pizza off the table and discarded it.

"And?" Martin probed.

"And nothing." Kevon's pitch heightened.

"I guess he don't need a ride," Martin declared, raising from the table.

"Guess not." Michael saluted Kevon like a general in the army.

"Hold up, I mean, there was an altercation, that's it. I saw this honey, and I stepped. I didn't know it was their chick. Next thing I know, they're all up in my face."

"I see." Martin eyed Kevon suspiciously. He sat back down and stared at him straight on. "Did you apologize?"

"No way. I didn't do anything to apologize for." Kevon rolled his neck and leaned back in his chair. "I was here minding my own business."

"Do you sense what I'm smelling?" Martin looked Michael directly in the eyes.

"Bull." Michael laughed. "Let's get out of here. I know someone else that'll pick him up."

"Wait, wait," Kevon interjected, fearing that they would telephone his father. "Truthfully, I don't even remember what happened. All I know is that I was fighting. I mean, I can only remember bits and pieces."

"Now, that sounds more like it," Michael replied. "And where was your boys during this?"

"I came here alone." Kevon sat straight up. He liked coming to James' Place. It was the only bar in Hayes Valley that didn't hassle him for identification. He was above the age to legally purchase alcohol, but his face still appeared youthful. His dimples and lack of facial hair seemed to make people think he was a teenager, and sometimes they treated him that way.

James' Place made him feel like a man. It wasn't a college bar, or a dive bar, it was a grown man's establishment. He could sit alone, talk to a lady, and have a whiskey or brandy all by himself. No crowds, no loud music, and no fanfare. Just him and the bottle.

"You hitting bars by yourself now, my dude?" Michael's eyebrow raised.

Martin shook his head. "Naw, Mike, it looks like the bars are hitting him."

Angela

Angela tried to focus on the breeze. She closed her eyes and inhaled deeply. Her chest rose slowly underneath the blankets. The comforting sound of swaying tree branches outside her window reminded her of fall. The cool wind slipped into her bedroom and glided across her face like a soft cotton ball. She opened her eyes and tried to distance herself from the image of fear testifying through the boy's eyes that had plagued her ever since they met. Outside her window, the bustling morning traffic on Fell Street provided the needed energy to begin her day. The yelling, car horns, and constant chatter were the soundtrack to her morning.

She didn't mind the traffic noise, the garage rental, or the busy liquor store on the corner as long as she was in the heart of the Western Addition. She vowed not to leave despite massive gentrification. She planned to keep herself planted in the soil from which a majority of blacks in San Francisco toiled. Where black-owned businesses once thrived, jazz came alive, and Maya Angelou once played outside.

She loved the small restaurants on the corners, the bicyclists who entered into verbal arguments with car drivers jockeying for parking spaces. She would never give up her quick jog to the metro station on Van Ness Street on nights she did not want to take her car. The City by the Bay was like a deliciously cold, frosty root beer. It bubbled over the top, tingled going down, and left a sweet taste that lingered. San Francisco was the perfect complement to all things it was paired with.

Angela sat up and leaned back on her bed pillows. The gray polyester comforter fell off her shoulders. Angela rubbed her eyes and focused in on her leather satchel in the corner. The brown bag stood out like an unruly gray hair amidst a sea of black. The case was a gift two Christmases ago from her father, a man she thought she knew better than the V-shaped scar on her hand that she had gotten when she fell off her bike in the third grade.

At eight, Angela had barely been able to see the rock lying in her pathway; but as she'd ridden closer, it had grown. She'd convinced herself it wasn't dangerous, that she could avoid it with a small shift of the handlebars. It wasn't until she'd flown over the handlebars that she realized she'd misjudged the danger and made a horrible mistake. Ever since that day, Angela attempted to sidestep the unknown. She desperately wanted to avoid the start of the investigation that directed her back to Tre, with his sad eyes, and the daunting picture of her father displayed in the apartment that reeked of death. She desired to make a small shift in another direction. But as her bike had come face to face with the rock, Angela had been aware then of what she knew now—there was nowhere else to go. Tre and the California Department of Social Services were waiting.

Robert

Retirement may have been a bad idea. Since leaving the post office two years ago, Robert's body required a gentle start to the introduction of the day. Like an old, cold car, he had to be warmed up.

Robert rested his neck against the back of the padded seat cushion. His head throbbed like he'd been to a Stones concert last night. Squeezing his shoulders toward his ears, slowly lifting his eyes, and stretching his arms gave his body some relief. Like the Tin Man, he needed lubricant. Eyeing the steam emanating from his coffee mug, he knew he had to wait longer to enjoy his favorite beverage.

The toppled-over trash can seized his attention. He knew Kevon was milling about in the middle of the night, but Robert refused to confront him again. He had experienced enough confrontation for the week. An empty gin bottle, a bag of chips, and an orange peel lay strung across the kitchen floor. Like his father, Kevon had left a mess in the dark.

Robert rubbed his temples, but the mistakes he'd made still lingered about his senses. Dirty laundry, Big Mama called it. The more he tried to forget, the more he remembered. He secured his mug, sipped his coffee, and grabbed the morning paper, but he was distracted by the music blaring from upstairs. The walls rattled. He groaned, peering at the clock on the microwave. "Kevon, you're going to be late," he yelled, tired of timing his son's entries and exits. It was a quarter after nine, and Kevon still hadn't left for school. "I know you hear me!" Robert screamed.

"Hey, Pops, can I borrow these socks?" Kevon entered the kitchen wearing only basketball shorts, walking like a tiger feeling his power. His muscles rippled as he held up his father's white cotton tube socks. "Mine are dirty."

"Boy, stay out my room!" Robert pursed his lips and rested his hands across his stomach. Kevon was twenty-four years old, and he still hadn't graduated from college, holding permanent residence in his home. After six years, next year his son would be responsible for his own education. The Bank of Robert would be closed. His retirement was dwindling away fast, and he couldn't afford another withdrawal from his 401K. Besides, the fees over at the University of Technology, San Francisco, had gotten ridiculous. The more advanced technology became, the more expensive UTSF turned out to be.

"C'mon, Pops." Kevon winked.

"You'd be on time if you weren't wasting your time on that fraternity mess. Look at your sisters Angela and Sharyn, they handled their business *and* made it home at a decent hour. What time did you get in last night?" Robert asked. He was growing more and more concerned about his only son, who seemed to toggle between partying and sleeping.

"I don't remember, Pops, but you were asleep though. Truthfully, I wasn't even out partying. Fraternities aren't about partying, they're about service. We focus on helping people like Big Mama did. I even brought home a ton of cans that I collected for Big Mama's Faith Feeding Families Memorial Canned Food Drive." Kevon crossed his arms defiantly. "Besides, fraternities have been around forever, since like the early 1900s, like when you were a boy." Kevon laughed and patted his father's back.

"And so has graduating!" Robert snapped back. "It's called commitment, son. Perseverance." Robert had worked at the post office for thirty-one years before retiring, and he still picked up shifts at a local market for extra income. He was able to put his two daughters through college, and he was trying to do the same for his son. He thanked God that the property values in San Francisco had risen with time, like antique jewelry.

Robert leaned forward in his favorite kitchen chair and added more French vanilla creamer to his coffee. "And why didn't you clean up this mess?" He signaled to the trash on the floor, a remnant of the clutter Kevon seemed to leave all around the house. Robert was unsure when it had happened, but the tidy young man who used to encourage the entire family to clean up after themselves had disappeared.

"It was dark, Pops, I didn't see it." Kevon stuffed the socks in his back pocket and grabbed the empty gin bottle off the white tiled floor.

"Boy, you knew you made a mess, and don't think I didn't see that liquor. Remember, son, what's done in the dark always comes to light." As soon as it escaped Robert's lips, his own truth echoed in a distant area of his heart—the space no one was supposed to see or touch, where all his secrets had taken residence.

5

Angela

Angela could no longer sit with her guilt. She skipped her morning debriefing meeting, fell back into bed, and successfully avoided Trevion's case. Angela looked over at Jonathan as he slept peacefully. She wanted to yell, "Get up and get out!" Yet earlier all she'd wanted to do was to be with him. Now she had to take out the trash.

Angela shuffled her legs underneath the bed covers, trying to wake him. He lay motionless. Rubbing her legs against his also proved fruitless. It was getting late, and she wanted him to leave. She was tired of his face.

She hadn't been looking for a steady partner six months ago, but Jonathan had taken her by surprise. When he'd breathed so near her ear that his breath skirted across the nape of her neck, she'd known it wouldn't be too long before she got to know him better. His gentle touch at the small of her back was like jumping into a cold swimming pool on a hot summer day. This guy was destined to stay a while.

But in the calm of the moment, her anxiety had set in. The rearing up of her flesh taunted her. She wanted him to leave as soon as possible so she could tuck away her guilt, nice and neat in a place where she could get it out only when she wanted.

Her stomach danced as her breath labored. She pulled the covers over her chest in an effort to calm. Her eyes scanned her room for a focal point. The flat screen television mounted high on the wall was turned off. Her cherrywood dresser was cluttered with mail, and her accent chair was piled high with clean laundry. Angela turned her head to focus on her four bronze elephants strategically placed on floating shelves. Strength and power were what she needed now.

"Baby, what's that look about?" Jonathan mumbled, startling Angela out of her blank stare.

Angela feigned calm and winked her eye as she turned to face him, licking her lips and shooting him a sexy grin.

"I was thinking about you, that's all," Angela replied, smiling. She had concluded she was done with him, and like a worn-out toothbrush, he had outlasted his usefulness. It was definitely time to secure a replacement.

"I know, we're good together, but we could always be better. You know practice makes perfect," Jonathan said, staring straight into her eyes.

"Hold up." She pulled the comforter down tightly around her bare torso. "I'm already late for work."

"I asked you to call in," Jonathan rebutted. Angela and Jonathan had begun dating after meeting at County General. She was there to secure a newborn she'd placed on hold. The newborn had been accidentally released into the custody of the mother, and instead of visiting the baby, Angela had ended up visiting Jonathan in the hospital administration offices.

"I did call out for the morning, but I have to be in the office by this afternoon. There is an important case waiting on my desk. Plus, no one told you to come over here this morning anyway," Angela barked.

"You don't like surprises?" Jonathan grinned, relaxing back into her pillows.

"I love surprises, but I also love my paycheck. Don't you?" She grabbed his shirt off her nightstand and tossed it in his direction.

"Certainly, but there are some things I like even better." Jonathan raised his hands in surrender. "I get the hint though, gotta love a direct woman." Jonathan leaned forward, then slipped his arm into his shirt.

"Well, next time call first." Angela laughed, leaped out of bed, and headed toward her bathroom.

Kevon

"I'm on my way." Kevon gritted his teeth, regretting calling instead of sending a text message. He plopped down on his full-size platform bed, and the headboard saluted the wall. His framed 2Pac picture shook. He only had three framed pictures that adorned the walls of his room. The three people who'd had the heaviest influence on his life: 2Pac, Magic Johnson, and Big Mama. The late rapper helped him to love himself, the basketball great provided him with hope, and his grandmother had given him love. He'd hung the pictures on his sixteenth birthday, a day he thought symbolized his rite of passage. But he soon discovered things didn't pass, they lingered.

Kevon balanced the phone between his shoulder and his ear while sliding on his father's fresh, white tube socks. He'd wanted to ask his dad if he could borrow one of his freshly bleached white T-shirts, but the cynical tone in his voice let Kevon know he shouldn't ask for any more favors. Kevon had learned to read his father's mood long ago, a trick Big Mama had taught him. Always watch his eyes, she'd instructed, reminding him that his father was not a liar, and the truth could always be found in his stare.

"I could've rode with Therie," Niche snapped.

"Well, why didn't you? I have better things to do than worry about babysitting you." Kevon opened his side table, grabbed a pack of gum, and then turned off his radio speaker. He wondered how long he would stay in this relationship. "I'm not coming." He abruptly hung up the phone without giving her a second thought.

Kevon replaced his basketball shorts with knee-length khakis, and slipped on his sandals and a white tank top. He threw his quilt back on the bed and headed toward his bedroom door. The last scab on his new tattoo had finally come off, and he wanted to show it off. He smiled coyly as he glanced in the floor-length mirror that hung on the back of his door. The snarling black dog that adorned his left calf resembled his uncle's pit bull. He couldn't wait for his fraternity brothers to see it.

"Looking good." Kevon shook his head and grabbed his navy book bag off the pristine hardwood floor. Kevon cracked his door and listened for signs of his father scurrying about. *All clear.* He headed downstairs toward the silence, attempting to go unnoticed.

His father was domineering. An in-house drill sergeant that he wanted to avoid. His mother was more relaxed. Kevon wanted to move in with her, but she always had an excuse. He knew that his persistence would wear her down sooner or later. There was no way she could keep resisting his charm.

"Bye, Pops." He rushed out the front door, jogging to his black pickup truck parked in the driveway. Kevon reached into his front pocket and grabbed his car keys and wallet. He opened his wallet, his eyebrows raised. *Two dollars?* His shoulders slumped. Kevon searched his memory, trying to remember what happened last night at the bar. He remembered the first two hours, but he must have blacked out after that. He glanced back toward the front door.

Kevon popped open the glove compartment, seized his silver flask, and took a quick swig. He shook the bottle, concern registering at the almost-empty sound. He didn't want to deal with the shakes today. Carefully he placed the flask back into the glove compartment and gently closed the truck door. Pulling his house keys from his pocket, he walked slowly up the walkway back toward the house and delicately turned the key.

Kevon sneaked past the kitchen like a tardy employee tiptoeing past his boss's office.

"What'd you forget, boy—your brain?" Robert said sarcastically.

"I left my book on the dresser." Kevon floated up the stairs. He needed cash for the pub, and his father always kept money in his wallet.

Kevon crept past his father's king-sized poster bed. He eyed his father's Ben Davis work pants lying on the black leather recliner next to the bay window. Slowly he moved to the chair, scooting behind it so he could extend his hand into the pocket without picking up the pants. Carefully he extended his hand into the dark gray trousers as his fingers tickled the keys. Moving his hand deeper into the pocket, well beyond the keys, he touched the leather billfold. He wrapped his hand around the wallet and gently pulled it out. *Success.* Kevon opened the wallet and eyed his freedom in twenties. Kevon counted six twenties. *Perfect. Dad will think he only had a hundred.* Carefully removing one twenty from the fold in the wallet, he was startled by the creak in the doorway.

"What in the devil do you think you're doing?" Robert stood with his Bible in hand. "I brought you in this world, and I'm sho 'nuff prepared to take you out!"

6

Sharyn

Sharyn sat idle at her desk. She tried to limit her caffeine intake after the lunch hour, but she desperately needed a cup of coffee. Her laptop displayed the testimony of her drowsiness. A sea of mistyped words plastered on her screen resembled a program code.

Fatigue had taken its toll. Her leg was asleep, her eyes were heavy, and her head ached. She'd hardly slept last night after her argument with Michael. It was hard being so many people. She had multiple roles and even more faces. Singing duo Kindred and the Family Soul had it right on the money—can't she just be a woman first?

Sharyn hopped out of her desk chair, exited her office, and marched onto the central floor of the building. She could still feel the tingling in her leg. Her full lips stretched wide across her face, creating a dramatic smile, but she was careful not to overdo it. Her brown matte lipstick was a perfect complement to her bright white teeth. She could still hear her mother preaching about the importance of good teeth. The asymmetrical bob haircut fit her round face. Red stilettos complemented by a red silk scarf added just enough spice to her gray two-piece suit. The office, quiet as empty cubicles, saluted her along the way.

"Hello, Ms. Brenda," she said as she walked past the silver-haired receptionist perched behind a massive stone desk. Sharyn bowed as she headed toward the breakroom. Sharyn liked Brenda. Brenda was as real as her short-cropped Afro and said exactly what was on her mind. Age had seemed to supply her with wisdom and limited discretion.

"Cute scarf, brown eyes." Brenda winked, a usual acknowledgment between the two women who matched in hue but little else.

"Thanks. It was a gift from my mom." Sharyn playfully fluttered her eyelashes as her cadence slowed in pace and dramatism.

"I knew that fiery red had to come from somewhere. You more of a pink gal." Brenda smiled. "I knew that the first time I saw you. Sweet as cotton candy."

"Thanks, Ms. Brenda." Sharyn winked back. She envied risk-takers like Brenda. It was that special part of her father's personality that she didn't inherit. Sharyn always stood up but never took the leap. Playing the background was a comfortable place. She liked to think of herself as the soul of the canvas. Kevon was the red-and-black ink, and Angela was the yellow and orange. She was the stabilizer, the one who was able to mute the colors or enhance them.

"Hey, Sha. You okay? You looking stressed lately." Brenda raised her eyebrow. "You do know you can take a break or actually leave the office at lunchtime? I haven't seen you get out of here since we went for coffee last week."

"I know. I'll be heading out, I'm moving slow today. Got mountains of work due. Never enough hours in a day." Sharyn could feel her emotions welling up. She blinked away the tears trying to form. Her job was the least of her concerns.

"There will always be work, Sha, but there will not always be hours. Go on and get out of here."

Sharyn tried to remain expressionless. "I will. A quick coffee break and then I'll be heading out to lunch." Sharyn knew she spent too much time at the office, especially lately. She thought no one else had noticed. There was no conflict in the office. No tension. It had become her shelter—a place where she was competent and effective. She smoothed her skirt and tossed her shoulders back.

"I'm glad. A bite to eat might be what you need. Get that blood sugar up and that stress level down. By the way, I heard you've been assigned that university campaign. Congratulations."

"Thank you, I wanted it." Sharyn's eyes ignited. She had desired this campaign since it was introduced. Spending time with young adults was a pure energy boost. She had stopped volunteering at the youth community center more than a year ago. When she'd initially signed up to help with the homework club, she had been surprised to discover that spending time with the kids helped her more than it did them. But they'd eventually triggered her emptiness, and she'd left them as hope left her.

"It'll get you out of these here boring offices and around some of that positive energy on those campuses. Yes, positive energy is what you need. God is blessing you, girl. Keep your faith, and He will continue to work it *all* out."

"So far, so good. I'll see you later, Brenda." Sharyn saluted the silver-haired beauty and turned the corner, passing gray cubicles aligning almost every inch of the office floor as she headed to the breakroom.

After a brief water break, she hurried back to her office. Her left eyelid twitched as she peered through the glass panes of her office from her colleague's corner cubicle. She shook her head in disbelief as she eyed the new reports stacked high atop her desk. The forecast, budget, and strategic planning reports from her main project, the university campaign, were in, and lunch was definitely out.

Kevon

Kevon was glad he found a parking spot on the street instead of the parking garage. Effortlessly he maneuvered his truck between two sedans. He opened his ashtray, grabbed his spare change, and counted several quarters. Disappointed, he realized a slice of pizza was all he could afford. He exited the car and jogged toward campus. His dad thought he'd put him in a bind, but Kevon stuck out his chest like a boxer who'd been victorious at the end of a match. Being caught stealing was the least of his worries.

Making excuses was an art, and Kevon was skilled in using paintbrushes. Telling untruths started when he was in elementary school as he discovered creating visual landscapes could benefit his desires. By high school, he could teach a master class, especially after Big Mama died. The only person who could catch him in a lie was Big Mama. *"Keep your tongue from evil and your lips from speaking deceit."* He'd have to repeat it three times after facing the corner in her large kitchen. One for the Father, one for the Son, and one for the Holy Ghost, she'd exclaim. He remembered the smile he used to plaster on his face when he'd turn around to look at her. White teeth beaming almost all the way back to his throat. A genuine show of the love he had for her. He hadn't smiled like that since she died, and he knew he never would again.

Kevon sighed as he finally stepped onto the university's pathway. Sweat dotted his brow. The top of the sciences building was shielded by the usual blanket of fog that was signature in the Bay Area. The eight-story building stood in the center of the main campus. Hurriedly, he hopped up two steps at a time, but he stumbled on the last step and slammed his knee onto the concrete stair. His book bag skirted across the walkway like a bowling ball careening down the lane.

"Ouch." Kevon's face contorted.

"Hey, you all right?" The tall, leggy redhead grabbed his hand and helped him stand straight up.

"I am now." Kevon's eyes danced. He bent over and dusted off his knee. "How you doing, Nita?"

"I'm all right, and you must be late," she said, grabbing his book bag and tossing it in his direction.

"You right. I hate getting to Dr. Lewin's late too. You wanna walk me? I *am* injured." Kevon swung the book bag back over his chest.

"I'm headed the other way, Kevon."

"I can see that, but any place you're going without me is the wrong direction. Who you playing with these days? Tim?"

"You a trip."

"I'm not a trip, sweetheart, I'm a destination." Kevon cocked his head and stuck out his chest, letting his self-confidence hang in the air.

"No, you're a trip," Nita rebutted. "Tell Niche I said hi." Nita pushed past him and jogged down the steps.

"Niche, who is that?" Kevon yelled after her, watching her curvy silhouette move farther and farther in the distance. "All that fire you got has to keep someone warm."

He limped into the faux-brick building, glad his class was on the first floor. Before entering his classroom, Kevon observed through the small window inset in the door. Spying an empty seat, he slid the heavy door open. Dr. Lewin was commenting on the grading structure from last week's paper. Kevon searched for his graded paper on the side table, grabbed it, and took the seat toward the back of the class.

He sat staring at the top of his paper with the grade circled. The red inked letter at the top looked huge, as if it had been highlighted. *How could I have gotten a C minus again?*

Kevon sat at the desk, looking up at the instructor while his shoes tapped the floor. Academic probation echoed in his mind.

Uncomfortable, Kevon shifted in his seat, knowing that with one more failing class, he would face expulsion.

As Professor Lewin continued reviewing the grading structure, Kevon realized he was at the bottom tier, again. Familiar feelings of inadequacy and disappointment welled to a lump in his throat. His mouth watered as he imagined the burn of alcohol hitting the back of his tongue. He dug into his book bag for a stick of gum. Gum was sure to quell this craving as Kevon tried to remember where he left his other flask.

7

Angela

Angela stood under the hot spray pulsating out of her chrome show-erhead, trying to wash off feelings of uncleanliness. Jonathan had left an hour earlier, but the remnant of him stayed like the aftertaste of a giant gulp of buttermilk.

Angela had retreated to her bathroom, which provided her comfort like no other room in her condo. She loved her warm, welcoming bathroom. The frosty blue-tiled shower stall illuminated by floodlights added the right touch. She had the bathroom remodeled five years ago and never regretted her decision. She removed the old white tub and added a walk-in shower. Sand tile flooring updated the space from the old cracked white linoleum. The round, framed mirrors placed on top of the mosaic glass tile over her dual mahogany vanities still caught her attention.

Angela tried to relax her muscles in the extra-long shower, but as soon as she grabbed her shower gel her heart began beating like a snare drum, her head pounding like the bass in a drum line. She gasped for air. Her hands trembled as she tried not to drop the bottle. *Another panic attack.* Angela rested her body against the side of the tile shower. She could see her closed toilet bowl through the foggy mirrored doors. If she could get to the toilet and sit down she might feel better. She stood panting, afraid to leave the confines of the shower.

"You're not going to die, you're not going to die," she slowly repeated to herself over and over. She didn't know if she would faint this time.

"Breathe!" she yelled, remembering the relaxation techniques she had learned in her group therapy class years ago. Breathing in and out for ten counts finally calmed her. She felt her heartbeat return to normal. Angela grabbed her head in frustration.

"The heart is in the chest, Angela, not on the sleeve." She repeated the mantra her supervisor had trained her on years ago.

Angela stumbled out of the shower and headed toward the elongated toilet seat. She plopped down and sat erect, relaxing her shoulders.

"Don't give in. You're fine. Jonathan will be fine," Angela said, reminding herself. Angela had dismissed tens of men so that she had perfected the art of breaking up. She had established a routine. She didn't let her men down the way some men let women down, never answering or returning their telephone calls. She prided herself on the class her mother had instilled in her.

Angela made her exit from relationships only after a great date. She made it a point never to end things after an argument. Like her mother, she liked conflicts resolved to her own satisfaction. Her mother had drilled in her head from childhood that all loose ends must be tied up. A kiss goodnight after a passionate evening often set the stage. Three days later, she sent a poem and a bouquet of roses. The only problem was she sometimes kept going back.

"Don't give in. You're fine. Jonathan will be fine. The heart is in the chest, not on the sleeve." She repeated her professional mantra. Angela had learned to treat each romance like a case from the office. Detach from emotion and focus on the facts. Each romance had a story, a victim, a perpetrator, and a dance. Her role was to recognize the dance and stay two steps ahead.

Robert

Robert placed the edger back in the shed and looked over his handiwork. His yard was once again clean. The grass looked pristine, and his rose bushes paraded alongside the dog run like peacocks. It had been a long afternoon of hard work.

Sweat dripped down his bare back, and dirt crowned his thinning hairline. His hands ached more than his lower back this afternoon. He fanned his hands out, stretched them toward the sun, and then rubbed them together. He eyed the fine, detailed lines that traced his bronze hands. Hard work measured in each line. His yellowed nail beds, enveloped by rough, jagged skin around the edges, petitioned for lotion. Postal workers often lost their soft skin after the first couple of years on the job. Battered hands and calloused palms were the testament of a valued employee.

Robert smiled, thinking back on the years he had been shuffled to the nail salon for monthly manicures at the request of his then-wife. Rose tried to erase every aspect of his blue-collar labor. He was the only man in his department that had shaped fingernails. He shook his head in disbelief. Rose controlled him back then and still had her thumb on him now.

Robert always felt it was his job to right her wrongs. It started from the first day they met. He'd scooted up next to her, but he hadn't asked her to dance that night at City Lights nightclub. He'd wanted to talk to her, and then their eyes had met. She was the most beautiful woman he'd ever seen. Flawless skin, long lashes, and high cheekbones drew his attention to her face. Man after man had approached her, asking her to dance as he hovered by her side, shorter than most. He'd grown taller each time she declined. One man had accused him of keeping her captive. His heart had skipped when she mentioned that for Robert, she'd go into captivity willingly. Another guy had approached aggressively, trying to pull her out onto the dance floor, to which Robert had responded he didn't fight, but he would for her. Robert and Rose had locked eyes and been inseparable since. Learning each other was the best part of their courtship. They had showed each other the ropes. She had instructed him on how to be a man, and he had helped her become a woman. She showed him how to cut his hair so the bald spots on his scalp, from constant ringworms as a child, didn't show. He hadn't been able to stop laughing when she clipped his underarm hair for the first time. She'd taught him the importance of brushing his teeth, something he'd never learned from his own neglectful mother.

Rose was the first woman he'd ever held, and he was the first man she'd let touch her again. He'd waited three weeks to become one with her after their honeymoon. He still remembered her body recoiling in Barbados that first night. It took another six months after the wedding until she'd let herself be free. Outside of Big Mama, he'd never trusted a woman like that, and he didn't want to. Rose needed him as much as he needed her. Robert didn't ever expect to find another woman that needed him like Rose, except when he encountered her.

Robert pulled up his Ben Davis work pants and headed for his garden swing. It felt relaxing to take a load off. He leaned back into the cushioned swing and rocked his legs gently. He took in a deep breath. The trip to Oakland had done him some good. Walking around Lake Temescal had calmed the outer and inner man. He could still see her so vividly at the picnic bench they'd shared time and time again; he could almost feel her hands in his. He had never imagined he would have to visit their sanctuary alone, but he now knew it was a place where he would find comfort for years to come.

A blue bird landed squarely on his semi-dwarf tangerine tree. Robert smiled as the bird rested and looked directly at him.

"No need to be frightened, it's just me and you, little bird," Robert chuckled, scanning the expansive backyard. "Love don't live here anymore." Robert thought about the last time his family had enjoyed this yard.

"Yards are for families, dogs, and parties, not for a lonely old man and a quiet bird." Tears welled in his eyes. *She'd never been here. She would never be here.* Robert leaned back in the swing. The sidebar wobbled, and a loose screw rolled onto the concrete patio. Robert closed his eyes.

He grabbed his cell phone from his back pocket. It was time. "Sharyn, I've been thinking, and I've come up with an idea."

"What idea, Daddy? What is it?" Sharyn stuttered. Robert could hear the hesitation in her voice.

"I need to get out more. Get more social," Robert declared, stomping his foot.

"What?" Sharyn questioned.

"I think I should get a dog. I heard they're helpful for seniors. They promote walking, socializing, and are good companions. I can't let this house become my hearse. I've never had one before, so I may need help though. Didn't Michael grow up with dogs?"

"A dog? Is this Robert Lovelace or an imposter? Because this cannot be the same father that refused to allow any type of pet in our house," Sharyn's voice squeaked.

"Well, things are different now, and I need to start living. I need some company." Robert eyed the empty lounge chairs.

"Daddy, a dog is not company, it's a pet. And what about Kevon?"

"Kevon ain't no company, he is a dependent." Robert rolled his eyes.

"A pet is not a solution to a bigger problem. I mean companionship, Daddy. There are plenty of golden girls out there, and you are an eligible bachelor. Why not throw your hat back into the ring?" Sharyn's voiced lifted.

"I'm too old for that kind of thing, Sharyn. Plus, your mama was all the woman I could handle. She was enough to last any man a lifetime. I'm still choking on that ham hock of a woman. And you know your mama. High maintenance is what y'all call it, right? Plus, I done already got married once, and it's gonna stay that way until my bed becomes my cooling board."

8

Kevon

"I'm going to pop some more popcorn. You want some?" Niche asked, juggling the large green ceramic bowl filled with kernels as she jumped up from the cream-colored leather sofa in the Lovelace living room.

"Naw, baby. I'm cool. Bring me another beer though." Kevon was on his seventh beer and still hadn't gotten to the high he wanted.

"Okay," Niche said. "But pause the movie for me. I want to see what happens to that girl." Niche bent over and kissed Kevon gently on his lips. He could taste her orange-flavored ChapStick. Kevon eyed his longtime girlfriend as she sauntered toward the kitchen.

"No problem, babe, hurry up though. I'm thirsty," he said, hitting the pause button on the universal remote control. He slid his hand into the pocket of his blue jeans. He hated tremors.

"Hey. What did you get on your essay in Mr. Lewin's class? I was hyped when I saw that I got an A- on my bio paper. It was hard, too, and I was sure I didn't do well. There was a lot of information I forgot to put in. I didn't have the time to do all the research," Niche yelled from the kitchen.

"Cheers for you," Kevon said enthusiastically. "I got a C-, but I scammed Dr. Lewin. He said that I can submit a rewrite by next Friday, and I was like cool. You should've seen my face. I looked like a sad puppy. Professors are so gullible. I told him the divorced parents story, and he fell for it hook, line, and sinker. I was rollin' after I left his class. I definitely put it on thick too."

"You better stop that," Niche chastened him from the kitchen.

"Shoot, I ain't tripping off him. I need a B in his class. I'm gonna start rewriting it tomorrow before I go to the Alpha party. I'll definitely have it done by the social meet and greet Thursday night."

Kevon's stomach churned. He knew he should have eaten something before drinking. Lately his stomach had been aching more than usual. Kevon was afraid to tell his father; the last thing he needed was a lecture from a doctor.

"You should've started working on it tonight, honey. You could've at least had an outline done by tomorrow. You don't want to blow your chance. Do you need any help?" Niche asked.

Kevon rolled his eyes as his irritation began to build. He gathered his breath and attempted to keep his temper under control; he didn't want to spend the evening alone. His body stiffened as he glanced toward the kitchen. Niche entered the living room, maneuvering her popcorn and his requested item.

"Here's your beer. Do you need anything else?" Niche handed Kevon the tall silver can as he shifted his focus to her feet to avoid her gaze.

Kevon surveyed her body from her ballerina flats to her baseball cap. Niche was dressed in black spandex activewear shorts and a tank. The black Delta Alpha Sigma Nu cap almost covered her head completely. Kevon placed his beer on the table and grabbed a handful of popcorn as Niche plopped back down on the leather sofa next to him. He scooted closer to her, his mind no longer on the movie.

"You know, Kevon, I was thinking. We could start work on your paper instead of watching the rest of the movie. What ya think?"

"No. I'm cool," Kevon replied, sucking his teeth. Niche placed the bowl full of popcorn on the table and pulled her knees up to her chest.

"Kev, you never answered me. You know, if you need help with your paper and not just the outline, let me know, okay?" Niche said gently.

"Niche, let it go, all right? I don't need your help. Drop it," Kevon snapped. "Let me watch the movie in peace. I don't feel like studying, no way. You're always trying to be all that. You ain't the only one that can get an A around here. This is not the University of Niche. Or should I say, Ms. Perfect!" Kevon yelled, as he grabbed at the remote control.

Niche scooted to the other side of the couch. "All right, Kevon. I was trying to help you out. And you need to watch your mouth. I'm not one of your trifling friends," she said, her voice cracking.

"You ain't my mama neither. Watch yourself, Niche, before you be up out," Kevon retorted, grabbed the can, and took a large swig of beer.

"What do you mean by that, Kevon? I'm getting so tired of this drama. You better check yourself because you're almost out of luck. Look, ain't nobody trying to be your mama. You the one that act like you don't have one." Niche grabbed a handful of popcorn.

"Shut up, Niche, I'm not playing with you." Kevon threw a loose popcorn kernel at her.

"I hate it when you drink. You act like such a butthole," Niche shot back.

"Keep it up, hear, and I'm walking, cause I don't have to spend my time in this tired, played-out relationship." Kevon clasped the remote so tight it accidently changed the channel.

"I don't deserve this treatment, and you know it. I'm a strong black woman. And in case you forgot, I don't need nobody's man. Especially a too-tired one." Niche's voice quivered as she grabbed the popcorn bowl and headed back to the kitchen.

"Tired! Well if you tired, don't let me keep you. Ain't nobody trying to make you stay here! You can exit my kitchen and walk yourself right on out that door. I think you know the way home. You need to remember whose house you're in. And who the lucky one is in this relationship." Kevon's voice vibrated.

"You know, Kev," Niche said, storming into the living room with her hands stationed on her hips, "I'm starting to think you're the lucky one. Because I stay with you despite your garbage. Despite your tricks and childish games. As a matter of fact, you are simple. A simple boy who needs to grow up! This weekly temper-tantrum thing is played out. I'm not Mr. Lewin. You ain't gonna play me." Niche stood over him like a teacher chastising a pupil.

"Well, if you feel that way about me, then why don't you get out? I'm sure there is somebody else who would like to take your place next to me on this here couch. There's plenty more where you came from. So why don't you run along now? I have other business I can tend to." Kevon took another swig of brew.

Niche backed away from him, but her expression didn't change. "Yeah. You got business. You need to tend to that paper with your stupid drunk self. You want the truth? You know you're messing up one of the best things that could happen to you. You know what? Forget it. Why don't you call one of your gals? They are the only ones who want to be bothered with your old drunken self anyway. And for the record," Niche declared, as she grabbed her purse from the adjacent recliner and headed toward the door, "you aren't my only option for this evening either!"

Kevon jumped up off the couch and blocked the brown double front doors. He grabbed her by the arms, tearing the strap of her purse as he shoved her into the wall.

"What do you mean by that, Niche? Are you headed over to some other dude's house tonight?" Niche shook her head no as her eyes filled with tears. Kevon pushed into her harder. "Who do you think you messing with? You better take your butt straight home. I'm not playing either, Niche. I ain't no joke." He dragged her closer to the door's entry and opened it. Forcefully, he released her arms and pushed her out into the cold, foggy night. "You better stop crying too. Get in the car and go straight home before we say something that we can't fix. And you better call me when your butt gets home too. I mean it. You're mine, and you are gonna stay that way. Like it or not."

Niche stumbled to her car parked in the driveway and tumbled into the driver's seat as Kevon stayed at the front door watching her until he could no longer see her taillights. He walked into the house and shut the doors behind him. "She better watch who she's talking to. I ain't no kid." Kevon plopped down on the couch and took another gulp of beer. He pulled out his cell phone, scrolling through his contacts. "I wonder if Shameka is at home."

Angela

Angela finished jotting down her notes on Trevion's case. Five complete pages of notes on her yellow, legal pad and she still hadn't been able to identify a next of kin. She tossed the pad across her desk to her colleague, hoping to gain some insight. "This is all I have," Angela sighed, leaning back in her chair and locking her fingers. Angela's linen pantsuit fit her snug like a pair of canvas shoes. She had her hair styled last night at the salon the previous night, and green rhinestone clips held the curls sleek and in place. Angela's clips were the perfect pairing with the forest-green pantsuit complemented by black wedge heels. The charcoal-colored matte lipstick filled the fullness of her thick lips and accentuated her smoke-colored eye shadow.

Angela hated to ask for help; although Jeannine was the best in the building and her friend, it still was difficult. Her mother complained she had an independent spirit from birth, always questioning, confronting, and challenging. Angela had spent more hours on punishment than she'd liked, but the end result was all the same. Rose would ask if she'd learned her lesson, and she would reply, "My lesson or yours?" Her mother's eyes would fill with anger, and the instruction would cease.

The buzzing of her cell phone interrupted case consultation. Angela eyed her cell phone as Jonathan's number came up for the third time. He was as relentless as she was. She realized she'd eventually have to talk with him despite her reservations. Anxiety started to pulsate in her chest as his ringtone distracted her again. Unyielding, she smoothed her peplum jacket, closed her eyes, and folded her arms across her lap.

She had been avoiding Jonathan for the past three days and had no intention of addressing him now. She opened her eyes and shifted her vision to the only picture placed on her desk, a picture of her parents and Martin at last year's St. John's Annual Day. His arms draped gently around her parents' shoulders like he was their own son. Her heartbeat slowed as she focused her attention on her three favorite people.

"Are you going to answer that?" Angela's colleague Jeannine asked loudly from across the desk as the phone beckoned once again.

Angela clenched her jaw. "Answer what?"

"That annoying ringtone. I hate that song, Ang. I don't know why you always pick it for your flavor of the month! Aren't you going out with a new guy tonight, anyway?"

"You don't like 'Groove Me' by Guy? Who doesn't like that?" Angela leaned over her desk and looked directly at the petite Filipino woman with the pretty round face who'd interrupted her thoughts. She stuck out her tongue.

"Guy stopped making music decades ago. Move on," Jeannine countered, sticking her tongue out too.

"I loved that group, missy, and I'm not going to change my ringtone because you don't like it," Angela said, grabbing her phone and adjusting the volume. Jeannine and Angela had worked together in the same unit since Angela started working in social services. More friends than colleagues, the two women shared everything from lunch to personal gossip.

"Don't change the ringtone, how about answering the phone? Or how about getting a new ringtone for each new guy like you do with your open cases? You do know that men are not all the same."

"Jeannine, mind your own—" The "Groove Me" lyrics interrupted her teasing. "This is Lovelace," Angela said, grabbing her phone and giving in to Jeannine's demand.

"What is this supposed to be?" Jonathan voice crackled with emotion through the phone. Angela dug her wedges into the office carpet, readying herself for confrontation. "You breaking up with me—now, of all times? Really, Angela. Where is this coming from?" Jonathan exclaimed.

"Jonathan," Angela replied, "calm down, all right? If we are going to talk, we have to talk, not yell. Now, I take it that you received the flowers and poem." Angela swallowed.

"You are right, I received them. Don't get me wrong; both were considerate, but your actions were cheap. Real cheap. What is this supposed to mean?

Nighttime skies are dark, quiet, yet calm.
The mystery of the night lingers on
With every motion waves rise with grave intensity.
Vessels pass on a separate course,
The heat is unbearable, the collision evident.
Meshed intertwined pieces light up the night sky,
If only for a moment, the fireworks fly,
As time moves on, the moment is gone,
Because only memories replay
The explosions of yesterday.

What mess is that? This ain't no poetry slam. I don't roll like that, Angela."

"Roll like what, Jonathan? Exactly how am I rolling?" Angela picked up the picture on her desk, wishing Martin was on the telephone instead.

"It's like what I think doesn't even matter. Like it's all about you. I think this game you're playing is immature and frankly cold," Jonathan huffed.

"First of all, we are both consenting adults. We can make decisions for ourselves without the other's permission. And second, you need to watch your tone. Yes, I made the decision because it suited me. And yes, it is all about Angie, and I was thinking about me. And to be frank with you, I don't need your permission to do that. I need some time."

"Time for what?" Jonathan countered.

"I don't mean to upset you. However, I needed to let you know what's up. My life is too complicated for you right now," Angela snapped as she remembered the sensations of her recent panic attacks. Skin crawling, insides grating, stomach dipping, and head hammering were not feelings she wanted to keep contending with.

"Oh, your life is the only one that is complicated. What about my life and what I want? When did I give you any indication that I was done with us?" Jonathan asked.

"To be honest, I don't know if I'm ready for all that. It's too soon for you to start tugging at my heart," Angela lied, as she gently returned the picture back onto her desk.

"Look, Angie," Jonathan replied. "Don't get me wrong—I don't want to crowd you. I thought that things were good between us. So when I got these flowers, they took me off guard."

"Jonathan, it was easier for me that way. I got a lot of sorting out to do."

"I don't know, Angie. We could meet tonight for dinner or

something. We need to talk face-to-face. I don't believe in that cell phone and texting stuff. I'm a man, and I handle things man-to-man, or in this case, man-to-woman. We need to come to some sort of understanding," Jonathan said calmly.

"Jonathan, I think we need to stay away from each other for a while. If I see you tonight, it'll be hard for me. I know that one thing will lead to another, like it always does. I need to start listening to my head and not my body."

"I'm not an animal, Angela. I do know how to talk. We can talk," Jonathan pleaded.

"I don't know. I don't think that it's wise for me to see you right now. I have to keep to myself," Angela repeated, checking her watch. She looked at Jeannine and mouthed she was sorry. Angela sat, thankful Jeannine was more than a coworker; she was a friend.

"I want to see you. I'm not trying to go down the aisle," Jonathan grumbled.

"Look, I had a lot of fun, but I think we should chill for now. Let things cool down for a minute." Angie spoke softly, like she was addressing a child.

"All right, Angie, if that's what you want. Well, I guess I don't have a choice. Dang, girl, I ain't never been sideswiped. All right, all right. I'll talk to you soon, huh?" Jonathan replied.

"Yes, baby, for sure, and thank you for being so understanding. Well, anyway, I gotta go, I have clients calling." Angela hung up the telephone, scrolled through her contact list, and deleted Jonathan's name. She stumbled to her feet and headed toward the door. "I'm going to grab some water," she said, but she stopped short and turned her head back toward her desk. She glanced one more time at the picture of Martin and was reminded of her own pain. Wanting something that you can't have is torture.

9

Sharyn

Sharyn laughed to keep from crying. The brown paper bag lay crumpled on the tiled floor along with her hope. Even the clerk at the convenience store felt sorry for her. The tiny girl with the crooked smile whom she saw once a month never voiced her feelings, but Sharyn could see it in her eyes as she placed another set of pregnancy tests on the counter. She started to recognize the young girl well over a year ago. The girl must work a seventy-hour week because she always seemed to man the counter. They used to greet each other, but that had stopped several months ago as the reality of the situation became obvious.

Sharyn closed her eyes tight, placed the plastic stick on the vanity, and leaned back against the toilet seat. She rocked back and forth like the crowd at a U2 concert, fighting the urge to say a prayer, but she knew it wouldn't do any good. Her eyes flung open as she focused on her striped pajama bottoms, reminding her that these weren't the lines she wanted to see. She grabbed the plastic stick again, wanting to ensure she read it correctly, one last time. Her heart sank.

"Is it positive?" Tasha mumbled.

"No, it isn't," Sharyn grumbled at her best friend through the safety of the closed bathroom door. She could hear the raindrops plummeting outside as the gloom found its way indoors.

"Oh, Sharyn, I'm so sorry," Tasha responded, shaking the door handle as she tried to gain entrance.

"Hold on a sec, I'm coming out. You know, Tasha, I'll tell you this—when I do get pregnant, I'm going to go 51/50, like Angie would say. People are going to swear I went crazy." Sharyn tossed the stick into the waste basket and washed her hands. The hot water steamed up the vanity mirror, clouding her reflection. She used to love the fog when she was a child, running the faucet until the mirror couldn't be seen. She would spin around constantly to create her own music concert, dreaming she was Diana Ross surrounded by her smoke machine. The fantasy of being someone else had filled her childhood afternoons. Sharyn swallowed hard, still wishing she had the capability of morphing into someone else when things got tough.

"It's gonna happen, Sharyn. Don't worry, keep at it," Tasha encouraged.

"We've been trying for two years. Not to mention the past months Michael and I have over shared each other. I feel like I'm on a treadmill. I've even started to lose weight, which is not a bad thing, I might add. The baby diet, he calls it." Sharyn tightened the drawstring on her pajama pants and blotted her face with a hand towel. "Shoot, it would be a miracle if I can keep up at this rate. I am older and curvier than I used to be." She looked down at her wide hips set atop thick legs, her midsection protruding slightly underneath her pajama top. She stooped down and secured the paper bag and discarded it among the leftover toilet paper rolls and used pregnancy test.

"The baby diet! Mike is the one that should be 51/50." Tasha giggled as she played a hand-bone beat on the bathroom door.

"The thing I tried for years to avoid won't happen now that I'm ready. Not to mention what happened in college." Sharyn slowly opened the bathroom door and sneaked past her friend, avoiding her gaze. "Look, Spinderella, kill the beat," she ordered, pointing her friend toward the lounge chair stationed in the corner of her bedroom.

No other woman knew her better than Tasha. Their friendship went far beyond support, to strength. Like an unbalanced structure, support beams reinforce, but undergirded concrete fortifies from the inside. Tasha was her foundation. They had learned to lean on each other through life and made each other stronger.

"Let the past stay in the past," Tasha lamented, heading to the corner chair.

"I'm starting to think it isn't meant to be for us." Sharyn had highlighted the sections of the Bible that spoke of barren women that eventually became pregnant. She had hoped their stories would become hers, but now she'd begun to lose faith. She wanted to believe in her heart that it wasn't true, that she could have a baby, but she seemed to understand less and less of the God she had learned about growing up in Sunday school. "Maybe God is punishing me for the abortion." Sharyn headed toward her slate, baroque king-sized bed, wiping away fresh tears. She collapsed facedown on the bed and dangled her feet from the bottom, barely touching the patterned carpet. She'd picked patterned carpet throughout the house to create warm learning spaces for floor time with her children.

"Girl, God is not punishing you. You're punishing yourself!"

"Well, I might be getting what I deserve." Sharyn turned around, sat up, and scooted closer toward her best friend's chair.

"When did God start keeping a scorecard? He is not like us. God does not love for what you do, He loves for who you are. You're the one casting stones. *When* you do have a child, are you going to love it because of what it does or because it's your own? Stop speaking negatively like it's never going to happen," Tasha countered, patting her knee. "In His time, not yours!"

"It's not like I'm getting any younger, Tasha. Soon I'm going to be too old," Sharyn said, pulling a loose thread off her throw blanket stationed over the side of her headboard.

"You have to speak life into the situation, you know the tongue has the power of life and death. You're stressing yourself out, which makes it harder to conceive. Plus, you may be missing the lesson God has for you in this, my dear friend." Tasha stood and plopped on the bed next to Sharyn. She wrapped her arms around her and hugged her tight. "Keep your faith. You already know faith is the substance of things hoped for, and as my mama would say, 'Chile, you don't need no evidence.'"

Sharyn shuffled underneath her friend's embrace and rolled her eyes when she met her gaze. "Tasha, I don't need no lesson on faith. You sound like Ms. Brenda at my job." Sharyn shook her head, wishing she could make her friend understand how she felt. Faith was purchasing all the baby clothes she had stuffed in the bottom of her dresser drawer. Faith was the bassinet that had been stored in her garage. Faith had run out of time; she needed evidence. In two months, she'd be the same age her mother was when she'd had all three kids. Sharyn dropped her face in her hands, tiring of hearing about faith; it was becoming like a fly buzzing around her ear. She couldn't catch it, kill it, or even see it, no matter how hard she tried.

"It'll be all right, Sharyn," Tasha said, rubbing her friend's shoulders. "You'll have your baby before you know it. I don't know about wanting children, but that doesn't mean I don't know about wanting. Now come on, let's go downstairs and get something to eat. That'll make both of us feel better, plus you'll need some energy for that diet of yours."

The two ladies marched down the spiral staircase in Sharyn's home to the spacious kitchen. The gourmet kitchen was a work of art. Top-of-the-line appliances, shoulder to shoulder with custom cabinets. Tasha grabbed the whole-grain wheat bread off the stainless steel refrigerator and swung open the refrigerator's double doors, grabbing the ham and Swiss cheese. "Sandwiches okay?" Tasha asked, winking at her friend who had settled on a bar stool in front of the large custom island.

Sharyn cocked her head. "Now you know that's my favorite." She half smiled and leaned forward onto her elbows against the black granite, watching the swift movements of her closest friend.

Sharyn glanced over at the white tiled floors that led through the family room to the patio. She felt like being alone. Tasha had been more than a loyal friend today; she'd served as Sharyn's extra pair of hands. Tasha had washed her hair, taken her car to get detailed, and picked up Sharyn's mail. Her petite, plump frame was also always ready with a bear hug.

Michael had renamed Tasha. He'd dubbed her "Gundy" in college after the teddy bear manufacturer because she was known around campus for hugging total strangers. Hug therapy, she called it. Her fair skin and neatly groomed hair styled in a sleek bob were a throwback to the old television show *The Facts of Life*.

"Dijon or regular?" Tasha asked, holding up the two mustard containers.

Sharyn had decided. She needed to take care of herself. "I want to seek professional help," Sharyn blurted out, like air escaping an untied balloon. "Michael thinks that praying will solve all our problems. If he says to me, 'The prayers of the righteous availeth much' one more time, I'm going to kill him. He fails to realize that all my prayers are leading to no avail."

"Sharyn, he's trying to help. Talking with someone that's objective would be beneficial to improve that communication. I think going to therapy might be a smart idea, girl." Tasha placed the sandwich in front of her friend.

"I'm not talking about a shrink, Tasha. I'm talking about a reproductive endocrinologist," Sharyn corrected.

"You think Mike would go for *that*?" Tasha questioned.

"No. I don't." Sharyn stared at her plate blankly. "We've talked about it a million times. Choosing my career over that pregnancy was the worst mistake of my life. I knew it too. Way back then. I cancelled the appointment three times."

"Sharyn, snap out of it, will you? You got to let it go," Tasha said, snapping her fingers.

"I'm trying, but I want a baby now, and I don't want to seek help behind his back, but what other choice do I have?"

"Sharyn, you better tread lightly, girl."

"I'm not treading, Tash, I'm drowning. Anyway, what are you guys doing for the holidays?" Sharyn nibbled on her sandwich and tried to change the subject.

"Girl, who knows, I hate this time of year. Roy is always looking at me to plan something. Like I'm his own personal activity planner. He says he hates traveling to his mother's, but he has yet to think of something else to do." Tasha threw her hands up. "So this year, I guess we're going to be stuck in the house." Tasha dumped some barbeque chips on Sharyn's plate.

"Well, girl, better your house than hers." Sharyn snickered. "Shoot, I don't even feel like staying in my own house tonight. I hate discussing pregnancy tests. He thinks it's as simple as one, two, and three. A little baby making, take a test, and get a possible pregnancy. His three philosophy in full effect."

"He doesn't mean no harm, Sharyn," Tasha explained.

"He doesn't know how it feels each time I have to throw that stick into the garbage." Sharyn pushed her half-eaten sandwich to the side, oblivious to the sound of the garage door opening.

"Well as Dottie Peoples would say, 'When God is silent, He is giving you more time to pray,'" Tasha said matter-of-factly, as she snuggled up next to her best friend.

"Shut up, Tash, you know I've been praying and praying some more. Anyway, I'm going to set up an appointment without him. Don't even try to talk me into telling him either, because he will hit the roof," Sharyn scoffed.

Michael walked into the kitchen, tossing his leather satchel on the countertop and marching straight over to Tasha.

"What's up, Gundy? Now, tell me exactly why I'm going to hit the roof?"

Angela

Angela slid her fingers across the carved workings etched in the dining room table. She could feel the excitement building in her chest, like watching a winning racehorse take the lead. She had waited long enough for him to jockey to first place, and now it was finally happening.

"Beautiful, huh?" Martin leaned forward in his chair and wiped off some dust from the corner of the ornate tabletop.

"It is, and the cabinet. Nice touch." Angela smiled as she eyed the china cabinet.

"I love the table most. It's *almost* the most beautiful thing in this room." Martin pushed his empty plate to the side and looked at her straight on. His words spread over her like hot butter.

Angela could feel the hair stand up on her bare forearms. The back of her black jersey-knit wrap dress clung tightly as perspiration formed along her spine. She loved when *he* complimented her. She had received flattering remarks and attention from a host of men, but Martin was different. The tone in his voice shot straight to her heart, a place she kept well guarded. "I love the painting," she said, in an effort to change the subject. She avoided his gaze. Her eyes traveled to the main wall in the dining area, which boasted a stunning painting of a farm, hung high, showcased by a small light. It immediately caught Angela's eye due to the unique way the foliage enveloped the farmhouse, almost covering the house entirely. "It reminds me of my great aunt Rosa's home back in Mississippi." Angela grinned as the memory of picking pecans down south invaded her thoughts.

"It's lovely," he agreed.

"What do *you* enjoy most in here?" Angela looked around the room, taking in all its details. The chair in the corner sat alone, covered by the golden runner he removed from the dining table. All the pictures on the wall showcased nature in its glory. A floor vase stood high in the opposite corner, parading dried branches.

"Your company." Martin touched her hand like a lotion salesclerk.

"Thank you." Angela blushed. She could *feel* his testosterone. Her heart raced. Unlike other men she dated, Martin made her feel unsure of herself, like a pupil attending class at a new school. She was nervous about what he thought of her. He made her feel vulnerable, something that was hard for any man to do.

"Would you like some more wine?" Martin grabbed the bottle off the center of the table and tilted it in her direction.

Angela grabbed her glass and gulped her last sip of white wine. "No, thank you. I've had two glasses already, and that's my limit. I like wine, but too much makes my stomach queasy. Why aren't you having any?" Angela's eyelashes fluttered. "Trying to get me drunk?" Unlike her brother, she knew her limit. She'd never liked drinking. College parties and bar hopping had cemented her distaste for alcohol. She'd been witness to stories detailing the collateral damage of being wasted. She pushed her glass toward him.

"I don't drink, sweetheart. I'm an apple cider man, but I do keep wine for my guests. Are you sure you don't want any more?"

Angela knew exactly what she wanted, but she couldn't verbalize it. She imagined if Martin were someone else, they would've been in bed by now. She shuffled in her seat, uncomfortable with her own thoughts. "No, I do have to drive, and 101 is a nightmare, especially around this time. I hate passing by the airport; the traffic is horrendous. I don't know how you deal with it. Don't get me wrong, I love your house, and Burlingame is a great city, but the sheer traffic alone," Angela remarked, as she looked out of the formal dining room toward the front door.

Martin's extensive ranch-style home was the pride of ownership. The layout was spacious, and the backyard was never-ending. Its interior matched the exterior in elegance. The home's central floor looked professionally staged, and the dining room boasted a grand elegance that was unparalleled to anything Angela had seen in a man's residence. "Guests, huh?" Angela imagined how many women had sat at his dining room table. Her heart sank.

Angela still believed in fairy tales and hoped he was her happily ever after. Like Cinderella, she'd dressed the part for countless men, but at her core she was someone else entirely. It wasn't near midnight, but she prayed this night would never lose its magic.

"Yes, ma'am, but not the type of guests you're thinking of." Martin laughed. "I'm stuffed." He grabbed his plate and headed toward the kitchen through the adjoining door. "Do you need anything?" he yelled from the other room.

Angela's mind raced. This was the first time he'd invited her into his private world. It was their second date in two weeks. They spent time together, but at his request, infrequently. Angela suspected he must have missed her this last trip because he'd contacted her as soon as he touched down at SFO. She could hardly wait to see what tonight would bring.

"No, I'm perfect." Angela heard a familiar purr arising in her inflection. She needed to cool the warmth enveloping her heart; she vowed not to get swept away like a teenager on prom night. She scanned the room, trying to find a focal point to calm her down. She grabbed her cell phone from her purse on a nearby chair, being careful not to strike the curved legs of the dining table. No calls. No emails. No rescue.

Angela cradled her cell phone, swiping though pictures. She

stopped short on the one that grounded her. The photograph was taken two years ago at St. John's Annual Scholarship Dinner, the night they met.

Angela remembered that night well. She had navigated the banquet room all evening, smiling broadly like her mother had instructed. She'd immediately noticed him because he looked out of place. Martin didn't remind her of the other men of the cloth that frequented the annual dinner. His personality popped, and his self-assuredness radiated. She would've never approached him, but he'd sought her out, introducing himself as the new associate minister that hailed from Beaumont, Texas.

Martin had towered over her but somehow looked her directly in the eyes. His shoulders had blocked her line of sight. He'd smiled broader when he found out she was the daughter of a deacon, laughed louder when she revealed she was a social worker, and disappeared when he discovered she was single.

"I put an apple pie in the oven, it'll be about an hour." Martin reappeared with a pot of coffee.

"Pie?" Angela questioned.

"I cook, but I don't bake. My mother was the baker. I don't mind store-bought. Do you?" Martin asked.

"Of course not, but I can't eat another bite." Angela pushed her half-eaten plate away from her. She noticed Martin looked more attractive and taller this evening in the dimly lit dining room. His appeal was not understated. His black hair faded into his goatee, which complemented his chiseled caramel face. He looked as if he worked out faithfully, and his tailored suit showed off every muscle. Angela found herself examining what he wore, what he said, and everything he did.

"I can take a hint." Martin casually grabbed her plate and headed back to the kitchen.

"Do you have creamer?" Angela asked, filling her coffee cup in an effort not to get too relaxed. The wine had already set up residence in her extremities.

"Coming right up." Martin entered the dining room with several creamer options before leaning back into his chair. Angela's eyes shifted from the table to him. He did not remind her of the strong, sanctified man that bellowed from the pulpit. Tonight, he was softer.

"I love creamer, it's a thing with me. I have to have my coffee a certain color."

"Like that sorority you belong to?" Martin joked.

"Not funny and not true. Don't you go making fun either, before I get on you about this Martha Stewart home you have," Angela said, sipping her coffee.

"Thanks, but it's my parents' house. They retired to Texas a while ago, so they let me rent it out. They keep it furnished. I was sad to see them go, but I think I was happier to get the house since rent is so expensive these days. Compared to Houston, the Bay Area is Beverly Hills."

"You must miss them," Angela said, adding more creamer to her cup. She was grateful that she resided in the same city as both her parents. They had a small family, and they stuck together. Her father and his brother were adopted by a single woman whom they affectionately called Big Mama. His brother died before Angela was born, and Big Mama died several years back, leaving a legacy of love and togetherness for their family. Her mother was an only child whose father died when she was a teenager, but they kept in touch with his sister down in Mississippi. Her mother was estranged from the rest of her family.

"I do miss them, but the real truth is, as seasoned saints, the maintenance was getting difficult for them. Now they have a cute condo in a retirement village and a big-time social life." His bright smile lit up the dining room. "I took the liberty of starting a fire in the den," Martin said, as he winked at Angela.

"Isn't it too early for a fire? It's barely six o'clock." Angela leaned back in her chair, wanting to cool the fire that was raging in her.

"It's never too early for a fire, sweetheart," Martin rebutted.

"I agree." Angela's voice deepened. She wanted to surrender everything to this man. She pushed her cup toward him. He grabbed it and disappeared into the kitchen. When he returned, he poured apple cider into two glasses and gently pulled her chair out.

"Follow me, beautiful lady," Martin said, walking Angela toward the den. She eyed his stride and enjoyed the way his suit fit. Angela's black wrap dress danced behind him. When they arrived in the den, Angela smiled. The fire was roaring high above the logs, and the coffee table had been pushed back in order to provide a space for a thick cream throw rug for them to sit on. Placed on the center of the rug was a single white long-stemmed rose.

Martin placed the glasses atop the table and helped Angela take a seat on the rug.

"I hope you don't mind sitting on the floor in your lovely dress. I thought that this would be the perfect place for us to talk." Martin smiled.

"It's wonderful," Angela gushed.

"Good. Did you enjoy dinner?"

"Oh, no, mister, not that easy. Let's start with you telling me more about why this is my first invite to your house after all this time."

"We've been friends for a long time, but I'm a private man. I don't invite every woman I'm interested in to my home. The home is dangerous territory. Why do you think we dined so early?" Martin explained.

"I'm not the Unabomber, Martin."

"No, but you're definitely the bomb. I have to be careful not to light a fuse that I can't put out," Martin said, scooting further away from Angela.

"Would it be okay if I kissed you?" Angela smiled sheepishly while gently stroking his hand. She'd never played the waiting game before, and she didn't like it. Angela took a deep breath and decided right then that she was going to jump in; like playing a game of double Dutch, she was waiting for the right time.

"Are you sure you can handle it?" Martin laughed.

"Are you?" Angela slid closer to him and found herself enveloped in his arms.

10

Kevon

Kevon pressed down harder on the gas pedal, honked the horn, and turned the corner like his truck was a Hot Wheel. He drove as fast as he could over to Niche's house and didn't care that his speedometer registered eighty. The speed on the meter matched the racing in his heart. All he could think about was Niche. What was she going to say?

Kevon reached the stoplight near Niche's apartment and barely missed the curb. Manipulating the silver flask between his legs was difficult. Tossing his head back, he took a quick swig of brandy, leaned over, and threw his flask back in his glove compartment. His mind overflowed with the dialogue from their brief exchange. What he should have said taunted him. Thoughts of the worst possible outcome raced through his head.

Kevon slammed on his brakes as he pulled his truck up to the front of her apartment building, almost hitting the car parked in front of him. The string of beads hanging from the rearview mirror hit the windshield hard as the car jerked forward. Kevon popped a butterscotch candy in his mouth to get rid of the smell of brandy. He jumped out while simultaneously rehearsing his excuse. Scurrying up the walkway, he stumbled on one of the cobblestone steps before he reached her apartment intercom. The button caved under the pressure from his finger, again and again. He wiped the sweat off his brow, pulled up his designer blue jeans, and tightened his belt.

"Kevon?" Niche inquired through the intercom. His heart raced.

"Yeah, it's me. Buzz me up," he ordered, straightening his white T-shirt.

"No. I'm going to come down. I'll be there in a second."

"I'm coming up." Kevon's eyes bulged. Left surprised by the dial tone, he lowered his head and wondered what he was going to tell her. The sweat on his brow resurfaced as he walked back toward his truck.

There was no easy excuse for what he'd done, and he'd known the moment he stepped on the dance floor yesterday that he was headed for trouble. His conscience had begged him to stay seated behind the coat-check counter where he'd been for most of the party, but the alcohol had edged him forward.

The apartment's front gate slammed before he saw her, casual in a purple-and-pink hoodie and blue jeans. Niche walked toward his truck, stomping down the walkway. Immediately, he could tell she'd been crying as the light from the car illuminated her face. Niche glided into the passenger seat. Her jeans squeaked across the black leather, breaking the silence that stood between them. Kevon tried to kiss her, but she turned away.

"Kevon, don't. Let me say what I have to say." She raised her hand to keep distance between them. "You know, I'm glad you could come over. I didn't want to ask you to leave the after-party. However, I couldn't hold it any longer."

"What?" Kevon turned his head to avoid seeing the single tear escape onto her cheek. He draped his hands casually about the steering wheel.

Niche wiped her eye. "I heard about last night, Kevon."

Kevon swallowed hard and softened his tone. "What did you hear?" Kevon tensed his body and waited for the storm. He could always tell when it was going to come on. His mother's nostrils flared, his sister Sharyn's lips pursed, and his other sister Angela shook her leg. He'd noticed Niche's body language from the first day they met in the library. She had been sitting straight up like an etiquette instructor, her book opened, several notebooks spread across the study table with a highlighter positioned on each. Her elbows had been off the table, her mouth slightly crooked, and one eyebrow arched. Years later, her facial expression hadn't changed. Whenever she was stuck and trying to figure out her next move, it showed up.

"Meiko called to tell me what went down at the party. She saw you, Kevon! Meiko told me that she watched you, with her own eyes, kissing Shameka while you were dancing. That's right, Kevon, you kissed her in front of everybody, and then y'all left together." Niche twiddled her hands.

"What?" Kevon gripped the steering wheel tighter and tempered his facial expression. He relaxed his mouth and stared straight-faced.

"Please," Niche countered, shaking her head. "You're such a disappointment. Meiko told it all. Drunk again, Kevon!" Niche wiped another tear from her reddened eyes.

"Wait a minute here, you're listening to Meiko now?" Sarcasm dripped from his words.

"At first I doubted Meiko, but I knew in my heart it was true. I was so ready to wring you out like an old dishrag. I know that you can be wild when you're drinking, but this?"

"I *was* drinking." Kevon shook his head, finding his excuse. He tapped his fingers against the wheel, tired of explaining himself. Niche reminded him of his father as she stood in judgment. He could feel the race of his heart as his breath caught. The heaviness of spirit that he constantly fought seemed to start knocking at his door.

"Kevon, listen, this time it's different. This time I'm different. Shameka has been a thorn in my side ever since we were freshmen. I've always made a habit of explaining away you and Shameka's behavior. But no more, I'm not trying to hear it anymore." Niche stomped her foot.

"Look, Niche, I was drinking." Kevon made a second attempt at clarification. "The last three nights have been a blur." He nodded at this truth. He hardly remembered the events of the last few days. He hadn't partied that hard in a while and was still paying the price. Stomach pain he could handle, but he'd lost the jacket Big Mama had given him somewhere along the way, a reality he wasn't ready to deal with yet.

"Even though you were under the influence, *again*, it doesn't even matter. None of it matters anymore. You're always drunk. But there is no excuse for you to disrespect me like that, and with my own sorority sister at that. Do you think I'm stupid? I know about all your other escapades." Niche turned her head and stared out the window.

"What escapades?" Kevon threw up his hands. The last thing he wanted to talk about was more women.

"You know, I figured a man would be a man. I get it, you want to sample the menu first." Niche rolled up the passenger-side window.

"Menu? Girl, you tripping, now here we go."

"I'm tired of the cheating. This time it's over, so don't even try it. Please, I was aware from the first day you went over to Shameka's house. I knew the tricks she was playing. She's a tramp. I knew then that Shameka was no threat to our relationship. And she still isn't, Kevon. You're the threat."

"I'm the threat? What sense does that make? Meiko is the snitch." Kevon's voice raised two octaves. He rolled the passenger-side window back down, needing some air. Confining him was the worst mistake she could ever make.

"I know I don't own you. You have the right to lay your head anywhere you want to, but I've been good to you." Niche bit her bottom lip.

Kevon's voice softened as he tried to sweeten his approach. He'd seen his mother do it a million times. Open her eyes wide, tilt her head slightly, and inflect a melodic tone underneath her words. And it worked. His mother was able to charm almost anyone, and he tried to do the same. "What you saying, baby?" Kevon's forehead crinkled like a cruller donut. He decided it was time to get this situation under control.

"Kevon, I've never cheated on you, and I've had the opportunity, but I'd never hurt you. As much as I hate to admit it, I love you." Tears welled up in her eyes.

"Honey, give me . . ." Kevon interrupted her, gently grabbing her hand. He was tired of fighting; he missed the fun they used to have.

Niche had brought a joy to his life that hadn't been there before. Everyone else in his life was serious and demanding. His parents talked at and not to him. His sisters seemed to only find what was wrong with him. Niche made him happy again. Laughing with each other at the park, at school, or in the movies. He missed the sound of her voice when it used to make him smile. He remembered purchasing five bottles of her favorite cologne, so he'd always smell like a man she wanted to be with. He wished he'd worn that scent tonight.

"No, Kevon." Niche shook her hand away and clutched it to her chest. "Let me say what I have to say, then I want you to go home. I don't want to hear it anymore, Kevon, okay?" Niche squared her shoulders. "I've stood by you for years, time after time, chick after chick, but I think that it's finally time we end it. I've tried so hard to keep you happy, but through all my attempts I realize now that I can't make you happy, Kevon."

"I am happy, so don't speak for me. You don't know how I feel. You make me happy." Kevon rubbed her leg. Love was an emotion he was uncomfortable with, but with Niche he felt at home.

"No, Kevon, you're wrong. Happiness is a responsibility that is on you. I can only add to your happiness. You have to realize what you want for your life, and I know one thing though— I'm not the person for you. I've done the best that I knew how."

"So have I. We got something special. I get up in the morning for you, baby." Kevon gazed directly in her eyes. Niche was the only woman in his life that wanted him to be better for himself and not for his family.

"Granted, we've had some wonderful moments. However, that is all they are, moments. We aren't married. I'm your girl. I don't have to be in this for the long haul."

"This is not about me and you. It's all about Shameka. Before this, we were fine." Kevon gently squeezed her knee like checking a nectarine to see if it was ripe. He wanted to check if she was softening.

"Don't get me wrong. I'm mad about the Shameka thing, but I knew it was over Friday. I've shed too many tears, Kevon. I'm tired of crying." Niche closed her eyes.

"Don't do this. It's me and you, baby, and it always has been." Kevon stroked her face. "Come here."

"That's exactly what I'm talking about. Your touch can't make it better this time. I know what it takes to make me happy, and I'm wise enough to know that this isn't it. I can't keep trying to ride the wave of your emotions."

"Okay, Niche, whatever you want. I'm not gonna sit here and beg." Kevon dropped his head and eyed the gold cap peeking from underneath his seat. He relaxed his shoulders, happy that he still had a stash of vodka. "If you want to go, then go. I have other things that I could be doing."

Angela

Angela glanced over her shoulder. She hated when the light was out in the underground parking garage. Crime was not a problem in her neighborhood, but ever since middle school when she'd watched horror movies for sport, she detested walking to her car alone. She carried pepper spray at the ready, but she'd left it at the office. Social workers were prime targets. Police officers often accompanied them to removals but rarely set up camp at the office. Some of Angela's clients knew how to get to her office and what type of car she drove, and she was sure some had even seen her out in the community. Understandably, some clients were resentful and even downright angry when they lost custody of their children. But others were firecrackers, ready to ignite. Those clients wanted someone to blame for their misfortune, and at times the anger shifted right toward the social worker. Angela had been spit upon, followed, and even threatened. As a result she'd learned to watch her back carefully. So even in the early afternoon, when she could hardly see her car, it became a problem. She'd complained to the homeowners' association the month before, but the overhead lights still hadn't been fixed.

Angela slowed her steps as she eyed a maintenance man in the corner underneath a blackened light bulb. She rolled her eyes, knowing that some things shouldn't take so much time.

"Where are you going?" Sharyn quizzed over the phone, as Angela tried to figure out her game plan. She had to get more information. Her caseload would be open to new clients next month, and Trevion's case would be handed off to a continuing care social worker.

Angela dropped her purse down on the trunk of her car, snatched her hair up, and wiped the back of her neck. She always sweated when she got nervous. "On my way to Dublin," she answered, frantically opening her handbag and digging deep, trying to seize her car keys.

"Dublin, why are you going way out there? That's at least an hour drive," Sharyn replied sympathetically. "And it's your off day at that."

"I know. I hate driving out to the Tri-Valley, but it has its high points." Angela sighed when she felt the car remote within her grasp. Trevion managed to make his way back to the forefront of her mind. She had already pieced together that Trevion and his mother,

Samantha, had lived in San Francisco for the past two years. Neighbors knew both the boy and his mother. They also knew that the woman was a methamphetamine addict. It was clear that she'd made several enemies in the building because most residents were willing to talk.

"Like what high points?" Sharyn asked skeptically.

"Well, I love going to that mall out there. It's way better than Serramonte or San Francisco Centre, and it has parking. And there is this mom-and-pop shop out there that I enjoy. They sell the best burger in the Bay Area. I do have my favorites." Angela unlocked the door, slid in, and turned on the ignition.

"I hear you. I love Millie Bagels in Brentwood. I'd drive an hour for their turkey sandwich. What else is out there? I know you ain't driving no hour for a burger," Sharyn stated matter-of-factly.

"Hold on, let me get this Bluetooth working." Angela threw her black duffel bag into the back seat and almost dropped her cell phone. She tossed her cell phone to the passenger seat of her black sedan, removed the Bluetooth from her ear, and rubbed it on her skirt, careful to avoid ruining her nylons. "There we go," she said, fiddling with the small device dangling from her ear. "I'm headed out to Dublin to check on this kid I removed weeks back," she explained, as she accelerated out of the parking structure.

"How does that fall on you? Isn't that the smoothie kid you took out last week? Angela, you're emergency response, not a continuing case worker."

"I know, but we have started a new pilot program, so it falls on me now," Angela stated, pushing harder onto the gas pedal.

"What do you mean? What new pilot?" Sharyn asked.

"Well, a select number of cases I follow all the way though the six-month hearing. It's called the Cultural Continuity of Care Advantage." Angela adjusted her rearview mirror.

"That's a mouthful," Sharyn replied.

"I know. Kevon could've thought of a better name." Angela

laughed. "The CCCA program allows me to pick two cases a month that I follow based on some guidelines like client interaction, cultural matching, and level of traumatic exposure," Angela explained. "You know the county is always thinking of something new to try to improve services."

"Hmm, sounds pretty interesting. But weren't you doing that anyway? And why does that take you to Dublin?" Sharyn quizzed.

"Yes, I was doing that anyway. But now I get paid for it. I'd always watch a couple of clients, but only when the continuing worker was a quack that I didn't trust with the case. This way I get a case reduction, paid, and I can choose who I follow. And I want to follow this one," Angela said, heading across the San Francisco Bay Bridge.

"What's so special about this one?" Sharyn asked.

"It's hard to say, Sharyn," Angela remarked, thinking back to Trevion's sad eyes. "I removed a boy who was in a bad place. He doesn't have anyone. No family. No friends who care. He's all alone, and he shouldn't be." Angela sighed.

Trevion's mother had left him with hardly anything of value that Angela could identify. She couldn't find anything consistent in his life except school. Trevion's neighbor across the hall informed Angela that the boy was taken to school daily. No matter what condition the mother was in, she had him at school. Her neighbor also explained that his mother wasn't a prostitute but had men frequenting her apartment. Angela's stomach lunged when she considered her father could be one of those men.

"How sad." Sharyn sighed. "But what can you do about it except buy him some more smoothies?" she asked.

"For starters, I can go to Dublin." Angela laughed. "I found him a placement out there, and I'm going to check on him. I didn't want him placed in the city. He needed a change. More quiet. Hopefully he'll find some peace." Angela changed lanes. She knew the fast lane would get her there sooner.

"Why today though? Mom said she needed you to come over tonight and help her organize the canned-food drive," Sharyn interrogated.

"I know. I also heard that Martin is back in town and is going to be helping out. That is part of the reason Mom wants me down there. I don't want to see him right now, and this kid is a lot more important. This boy needs someone," Angela said. She'd taken the day off to investigate on her own time.

"Well, that leaves me to take your place on the canned-food drive. Enjoy that burger," Sharyn scoffed.

Angela hung up her Bluetooth and headed off the bridge, mulling over the details of his case while she made her way through Castro Valley. Trevion's mother had made enemies. Not one person had something nice to report. Her cell phone had left Angela even more puzzled. Trevion's mother had hardly any contacts in her phone—only three: Trevion's school, someone named Ray, and another man named Studebaker. Studebaker hung up as soon as Angela spoke. Ray never answered his phone. Angela figured Studebaker must have been her dealer. The only info that could be helpful had to come from Trevion. Her thoughts were interrupted by the buzz in her ear.

"Hey, Angela," Niche sang.

"Hey, girl. I haven't heard from you in a while. Where you been?" Angela said, lifting her foot off the gas pedal as she eyed the police officer to her left. The last thing she wanted to do was get caught speeding. She didn't want a ticket or a pink slip. She had been investigating Trevion's case and neglecting her others. If she didn't get a break in this case soon, she would have to do what she feared most, confront her father.

"In these books. It's almost final time, so I'm putting my grind in. I've been trying to get your brother to do the same, but you know how he loses focus," Niche detailed.

"Who you telling? I thought you guys were on the outs anyway. He told me that you were not taking his calls. He wanted me to call you, but I told him that it's none of my business. Y'all grown folks." Angela laughed.

"No, he didn't try to pull you in, that boy is crazy. I love him and don't wanna let him go, but this last time I was done. I didn't even want to hear him out. If it wasn't for his frat, he would've been out," Niche declared.

"What you mean his frat?" Angela asked inquisitively. She wondered what Kevon had done this time.

"He had a gift delivered by his frat brother, and he told me all about why your brother was making out with another woman," Niche answered.

"He did what?" Angela shrieked.

"Yes, he did. I was hot. Kevon better be grateful to his frat for clearing it all up," Niche responded.

"How on earth did he clear that up?" Angela asked.

"Well, the truth was the old-school frat had challenged the new-school guys to step their dating game up. They were trying to show them about what they call 'mack attacks.'"

"Mack attacks? Girl, that sounds like something out of a fast-food restaurant." Angela giggled.

"Stupid, right? All the brothers bet that when a certain song came on, all the dudes would kiss their dance partners. All they were trying to do was impress."

"That's crazy. Men and their egos." Angela shook her head.

"Well, you know I called to check it out and was told a lot of kissing going on. Girlfriends all over the campus was fuming. My friend neglected to tell me that," Niche said.

"They never do." Angela eyed the movie theater that signaled her freeway exit. "Martin was telling me about some rumors he heard. I get so tired of women talking. What was that Run-DMC song? People talk way too much and they never shut up." Angela slowed her car as she turned off Interstate 580.

"I was so mad, girl. People never tell the whole story."

"Sometimes they don't, but it's our job to keep them honest," Angela said, turning the corner that led to Trevion's foster home.

"I been thinking it's time for me to do some housecleaning," Niche bellowed.

"I heard that, and you're not the only one. I'm on my way to clean up some mess right this minute," Angela countered.

11

Sharyn

Sharyn relocated papers from pile to pile. The cadence of shuffling sheets sounded like a musical score created by a photocopier. She hated reorganizing her desk, but her new project had her drowning in paperwork, and she vowed not to start another week in disarray. The reports had constructed several skyscrapers lined up along the edges of her desk, and she was moving slower than she liked.

Sharyn prided herself on keeping things in order. Her sister, Angela, always teased her that she would've been the perfect event planner. She smiled, knowing that her sister was accurate. She'd become the master at organizing family and church functions. She'd chaired so many committees that her name was now printed on programs that she had little to do with.

The growling in her stomach commanded her attention. She rolled her chair back, grabbed the paper bag on the floor, dug her hand inside, and grabbed her breakfast. The smell of burnt toast met her nose before the carbohydrate. She chomped off a bite of bagel as soon as the telephone rang out. Chewing fast and swallowing hard, she grabbed the receiver before her voicemail picked up. "This is Sharyn," she said forcefully.

"Hi, sweetie, it's Mom. How are you?" Rose asked.

"Hi, Mom. I'm good." Sharyn wiped cream cheese off her chin and stuffed the bagel back in the bag.

"I'm sorry to bother you at work, especially so early," Rose apologized.

"As a matter of fact, I'm so glad you called." Sharyn looked down, noticed cream cheese on her blazer, and lifted it off with her fingernail. The black pinstripe suit was not clothing for her today—it was a statement of purpose. She alone would achieve her goals. She felt as determined as ever; like the poem "Invictus" by William Ernest Henley, she was the master of her fate, the captain of her soul. Sharyn decided she was going to master this project and parenthood in the same season. She no longer required her husband's or her colleagues' approval.

"Well, I'm glad I finally reached you. I wanted to tell you thanks for helping with the canned goods and setting up my computer for me. I was able to pull things together so quick. I don't know if Angela could've gotten me up and running that fast." Sharyn smiled at the comparison. Angela was the definition of confusion, and her mother knew it.

Sharyn had everything figured out by the time she was ten years old. She'd discovered that keeping things orderly kept chaos down. If she woke up early and cleaned her room, her mother gave her more allowance. If she handed in her homework before it was due, she got better grades, and if she was her mother's sous-chef, her parents wouldn't argue before dinner.

"No problem, Mom. Helping each other out is what families are for—that's what Big Mama always said, anyway. I think this may be the biggest canned food drive in her honor yet."

"I hope so," Rose professed.

"Speaking of help, I wanted to ask your opinion about something, and be honest with me," she commanded. The alarm in Sharyn's voice was palpable.

"Sure, baby. Ask me. You know I'll tell you exactly what I think," Rose reassured her. Sharyn turned her swivel chair around toward the window so no one in the office could see her face. The loud squeak of her chair echoed as she rose and headed toward the window. Downtown looked spectacular at this time of morning. The skyline was illuminated by the rising sun's natural light. Sharyn took in a breath to inhale the promise of a new day.

"I want to ask you about marriage," she divulged. It had taken weeks for Sharyn to decide to discuss marriage with her mother. Worrying her parents was for critical matters only. She kept complaints for her best friend Tasha's ears, but she couldn't ignore how Michael had treated her, again. He who had quoted Ephesians 4:32 to her countless times. Where were his kindness and compassion? This time she didn't think she could forgive.

"Okay," Rose acquiesced.

"Mom, Michael and I have been arguing. We haven't spoken any more than fifty words to each other in the past two weeks, and he doesn't seem to understand how I'm feeling, you know?" Sharyn's lips trembled. She wished she could wrap herself up in one of Big Mama's crocheted blankets. Big Mama named them "better blankets," professing whenever her coverings touched anyone, they were bound to recover. Her grandmother created a special one for each grandchild, but Sharyn packed hers away after Big Mama died.

"Well, he's a man." Her mother offered advice but no understanding.

"That's not it, Mom. He doesn't even seem to care." Sharyn plopped back into her swivel chair and turned it away from the door to ensure no one was listening.

"Care about what?" Rose questioned.

"The argument was about a baby. He was so inconsiderate you wouldn't believe it was Michael. I'm so tired of fighting in my own house. As much as it pains me to say, I'm going to do it without him."

"Do what without him, honey?" Rose asked.

"I'm going to get pregnant on my own." Sharyn could feel the tears welling up in her eyes. She moved to face toward the window again and bit down hard on her lip. She inhaled deeply, afraid to let the tears fall.

"Sharyn, what are you talking about?"

"I've been looking on the Internet, weighing my options. I'm going to see a specialist right away. I figure the sooner I get started, the better off Michael and I will be," Sharyn confessed.

"I don't think I understand. Are you talking about divorce?" Rose probed.

"I'm going to see a doctor, Mom, and let the chips fall where they may. Am I wrong?" Sharyn asked.

"Well, baby. This ain't Vegas. I think you need to talk to your husband. I hope you're not jumping the gun here."

"I'm not, Mom." Sharyn rocked back and forth, reminded that her mother was often the cause of the conflicts in their family home. Rose didn't talk to anyone; she talked at them.

"Talk to Michael again, Sharyn. First, you need to find out if both of you are infertile. I mean, that's the first step, right? Once you find out, then decide what to do."

"He won't, Mom. He won't."

"Sharyn, you know I support you, and we've talked about this. You know what I think. Matter of fact, let's meet up and discuss this further before you make any plans. There are some major implications here."

"I know," Sharyn said, regretting bringing it up. Like a pastor addressing tithing, her observations seemed to be falling onto deaf ears.

"Let's have lunch or something so we can talk about this. But pray before you go do anything—anything at all," Rose said gently.

"Okay, Mom. I'll talk to you later. I love you." Sharyn laid the telephone on her desk. She lowered her head, feeling defeated. Praying had left her stranded in the middle of nowhere—like following a navigation system while traveling through rough terrain, she could not find the signal.

Sharyn reached for her breakfast bag and eyed the charred edges of the bagel. She tossed the bag to the side, reminded that sometimes scraping the surface helps uncover what is salvageable. Immediately, she disregarded what her mother said, grabbed the telephone, and dialed the infertility clinic.

Angela

The residence was expansive. The rustic stone garden at the entryway towered over her. Angela rang the doorbell, stepped back, and straightened her navy pencil skirt. She looked down at her black pumps and sheer black nylons. Angela grinned. She looked like a lawyer but felt more like an investigator. Wanting to make a good impression on Trevion's foster mother was important, so she'd put on her Sunday best. She eyed the flowerpots on each side of the wooden doors that matched the flowers outlined on the welcome mat. The wrought-iron bistro set was placed off to the side underneath a small stone arch, creating a perfect place to sit and watch neighborhood goings-on.

"Morning, Ms. Lovelace," the slender blonde said as she opened the stately double doors. "So sweet of you to come all this way."

"Thanks for seeing me, Donna. It's important to see the child out of the office and in the actual foster family environment." Angela shook her hand, relaxed her shoulders, and followed her into the well-appointed home. Her heels clanked on the hardwood floors as she eyed the marble fireplace in the front office. Vaulted ceilings were lined with recessed lighting, and classical music played softly throughout the house. "I hope all is still going well." Angela trailed the foster mother into the large living room adjoined with a formal dining area. She looked around, impressed with the surroundings. The home was beautifully outfitted but still warm and inviting, like its owner.

"Trevion is adjusting well. Please have a seat." Donna pointed to a white upholstered chair.

"I was so glad you had room for him. I try to place my kids with Bethel Foster Families, but they are often booked." Angela remembered calling around all afternoon trying to find a place for Trevion to live. She knew Bethel had an intensive screening process and wonderful families, plus therapeutic support services for their removals. "How long have you been with them?" Angela asked, trying to focus. Her mind overflowed with potential questions for Trevion, but first she had to get through the gatekeeper. She didn't mind the interview part of her job, but today was different. She needed to assemble the pieces for herself before time ran out.

"I've been with Bethel for years, but we've only fostered four other children. I only take one child at a time and for however long they need a placement. Three of my previous kids were adopted. I'm hoping that will also be true with Trevion." Donna smiled.

"I'm glad to hear that. I hope so, too. He's a special boy who has been through a lot. I also appreciate your time today. I'm looking forward to getting to know you and Trevion a lot better. Collaboration is so important for our children." Angela placed her satchel on the floor and leaned back in her chair. She had hoped she'd selected a foster placement that fit well for Trevion, and she was certain she'd succeeded. Finding a foster family was like picking a watermelon. It may have the right color, stripes, and sound, but the quality inside was the only thing that mattered.

"Well, I appreciate all the calls and the time you've spent so far. You have been more attentive than any other social worker we've had. You've gone above and beyond."

Angela avoided her eyes, reached into her tote, and grabbed a notepad. "If I could inquire more formally about Trevion's adjustment."

"Sure, anything you want to know. He's outside with my husband in the backyard swimming, of all things. My husband is working from home today, and Trevion loves the pool. Thank God it's heated. My husband hates swimming in the fall and winter months, but he loves the kids. If Trevion wants to swim, my husband does too. Don't worry though, Trevion is out of earshot. If the patio door opens, an alert sounds. What's on your mind?" Donna asked.

Angela stirred in her seat. She wished she could tell her or anyone else what was on her mind. She'd ruled out confronting her father until she could ascertain if he had any connection to this boy. Her father was born and raised in the city, and Samantha could've gotten his picture anywhere. Talking to her mother was out of the question, especially if she did not want her father to know. Besides, her mother would make a big deal, something Angela wanted to avoid at all costs. "I didn't know Trevion could swim. That's great, Donna. How is he doing in other areas? Is he sleeping and eating?" Angela inquired.

"Well. He is eating fine. At first it was a challenge. He seems to have an affinity for fast food. He hates anything green, but he can't get enough of carrots."

"Well, at least you've found something." Angela made a mental note. The kids at her school used to call her Bugs because she toted carrots and ranch salad dressing daily in her lunch.

"He's doing well at school. His teacher says he's quiet but listens well. He takes pride in his homework. We have to call him several times when he is working on it. It is like he is lost in another world, and he laughs a lot."

"He does?" Angela asked, surprised.

"Yes. He has a sense of humor and seems to enjoy church. Oh, and he has an angelic voice." Donna smiled.

"Really?" Angela was shocked.

"Yes. I overheard him singing in the shower, and I could hardly believe it myself. His pitch is perfect. He reminds me of a young Wonder. Stevie, that is," Donna clarified.

"I'm familiar with Stevie Wonder." Angela smiled.

"I guess the world is. What a talent." Donna's face reddened.

"And inspiration," Angela added, remembering the time her brother, Kevon, sang "Isn't She Lovely" to their mother at Christmas. She made another mental note.

"Trevion has had three meetings with a therapist through Bethel. She says he is adjusting well, but he still isn't sleeping," Donna said, disheartened.

"Is it night waking? Or is he having difficulty getting to sleep? It may even be both." Angela jotted down notes.

"It's both. He takes forever to go to sleep. We have created a bedtime routine at the recommendation of his therapist, but it has yet to yield success. He sits in his room staring at the wall. After a couple of hours he finally sleeps, but he wakes several times throughout the night," Donna shook her head.

"I bet that's disheartening," Angela empathized.

"It's not. It's to be expected, but the reason is unusual. He says it's too quiet in our house. We have tried music and nature sounds, but nothing seems to soothe him. It's sad."

"Trevion has been through a lot. Thank you for working with him," Angela said, patting her hand.

"Well, it's our pleasure. He's a delightful boy. We've been around the block and so we know how challenging it can be, but God gave us a calling, and it's our intent to fulfill it."

"What about socially? How's he getting along?" Angela inquired, wondering if he was stoic like her father.

"Great. He is kind to other children. He's the caretaker. Thoughtful, you know. Always willing to lend a hand. He has only had one incident."

"Incident?"

"Another boy at church was being aggressive with him, and he retreated to the corner and started crying. It took us an hour to calm him down. The other boy later apologized," Donna explained.

"I see. Can I speak with him?" Angela requested. She scoured her memory, trying to find any incidents of cowering in her family history.

"Sure. Let me get him. Would you like some refreshments?" Donna asked.

"No, thank you." Angela watched the beautiful blonde walk toward the back of the house. Angela scanned the adjoining dining room. Not a plate was out of place; it was as if Emily Post had set the table herself. Anne Geddes's pictures adorned the walls. Angela viewed some toys peeking out from the corner on the floor of the living room.

It reminded her of the innocent boy at the center of her angst. Why was her father's picture in their apartment? How was she going to get to the bottom of this? She was sure of one thing: Trevion was her first step. Angela's thoughts were interrupted by the small handsome boy who entered the room encased in a Power Rangers beach towel.

"Hi, Ms. Angela. Thanks for coming to see me." Trevion plopped into a chair, leaned back, and wiped droplets from his forehead.

"Hey, Trevion. Good to see you again." Angela extended her hand. "I haven't seen you since our trip to Juicy Freeze. I see you like cold things. Donna was telling me how you like swimming in the fall." Angela smiled.

"I do, and their pool is awesome. Wanna see it?" Trevion invited, and looked toward the back of the house.

"Maybe another time. I came to spend time talking with you. Plus, I heard about a yummy hamburger place near here. You interested?" Angela enticed. Big Mama had taught her well. Tea, toast, and a talk would announce Big Mama's investigation. Angela discovered early on that by the time she'd engaged in all three, she had spilled her guts. Food was truth serum for kids, and she planned to capitalize.

"No, thanks, Ms. Angela, I ate lunch already. I like Juicy Freeze." Trevion laughed.

"Juicy Freeze it is. But let's talk for a while if that is okay with you, then we can have some fun," Angela said, turning the page on her yellow pad. "Well, Mr. Trevion, how do you like it here? I know it's different from home, but are there some things you like about it?" Angela tried to loosen him up.

"I like the pool. It's warm and has a slide. I like Ms. Donna and Mr. Paul. They're nice," Trevion said, wiping his face with the beach towel.

"I see. Anything you don't like? What sucks?" Angela quizzed.

"Oh, yes, Ms. Angela, I don't like nighttime. It's scary here. I go to the bathroom a lot. It's not like my house."

"It's different from your house. I know you must miss your mommy." Angela watched his body language.

"I miss my ball and my video game. Oh, and I miss my snake. I wish I had my snake. Do you know where it is?" Trevion's eyes widened with hope.

"Snake? I didn't know you had a snake. What did it look like?" Angela's voice filled with concern. She'd come across one other neglect case that involved a snake, and she'd dreamed about it for weeks.

"It was long and green. I used to sleep with him at night. It was my favorite. My mommy sewed it back together when it got torn." Trevion's eyes saddened.

"Sounds like it was special. I wish we could find it. It sounds like you lost special things when you came here," Angela acknowledged.

"Ya." Trevion's eyes filled with tears.

Angela's heart dropped. There was no way she could show him the picture now. Her answers would have to wait. Trevion's pain had entered stage left, and she was sitting in the front row.

12

Kevon

Kevon squinted as he made his way along the route, the sun blocking his view of the familiar pathway. All he could see through his dry eyes was the backdrop of a powder-blue sky. The bird-filled sky accentuated the frames of the soaring apartment buildings on both sides of the street. He rested his hand on his forehead in an effort to shade his sight. The dampened armpit of his blue-and-white dress shirt felt warm.

The beautiful San Francisco fall day reminded Kevon of the luck that had surrounded him all weekend. Self-confidence oozed from his pores as he walked from the BART transit station. The nickel-plated pocket chain rattled from his blue jeans. He'd finished his biology project yesterday afternoon, and his chest was stuck out like a bodybuilder in the championship round of a competition. He had finally gotten something accomplished. He felt great despite misplacing his car keys last night after he left the bar. Kevon's eyes widened as the smell of skunk appeared out of nowhere. He shifted his hand to plug his nose, remembering his mythology section in class—he might not be lucky after all.

Niche's street was quiet. Midafternoon found most people at work in this crowded Glen Park neighborhood. Today the wide brick walkway to her apartment seemed remote and endless.

Kevon pressed the buzzer, trying not to think about the last time he was there. He missed their long telephone conversations and yearned for the time they spent together. He felt like flashing fireflies over a pond when she called him; they needed to connect. His heart raced as he moved closer to the apartment door.

"Kevon?" Niche said softly.

"Yeah, it's me." Kevon missed the sound of her voice. He had hooked up with Shameka once, but being with her wasn't the same. It was like putting on a new pair of shoes when the old favorites were still perched on the shoe rack. He needed her.

The door buzzed, and he pulled it open, gliding up the carpeted stairs two at a time until he reached her apartment's floor. Quietly rehearsing his apology one more time, he knocked intently at her front door. He wasn't sure how she would receive him. His heart lunged underneath his dress shirt that complemented his dark blue jeans. He heard the clacks of the deadbolt lock.

Niche slowly opened the door. Always beautiful, her face didn't require makeup. Kevon smiled; he could smell the lavender aromatherapy oil penetrating the air. The floor-length purple robe he'd bought her last year covered her body, and fuzzy red slipper socks concealed her feet. Her long side ponytail danced on the top of her shoulder as she turned her back to him.

Kevon tentatively entered the darkened two-bedroom apartment and immediately noticed the sun from outside was shaded, as all the blinds in her apartment were closed. All the lights in the apartment were off. No noise from the television or the stereo echoed. He was familiar with this dark energy. It colored his heart, his environment, and his world. It was a haunting shadow living on the inside that seeped its way out. It had emanated from him too many times to count. His sneakers squeaked loudly against the hardwood floor as the black leather sofa against the wall bid him to sit down.

"Hi, thanks for letting me up." Kevon sat down, looked down at his shoes, and waited for her response. When Niche became overwhelmed she shut him out. She locked herself away, submerged in aromatherapy and self-help books. He remembered the time he had to bribe her roommate, Therie, to sneak him into their apartment. Kevon fiddled with his fingers, trying to ward off the shaking. He hadn't had a drink since last night.

"Hi, Kevon. Thanks for coming through," Niche finally spoke, as she sat down on the matching leather love seat.

"No problem. I've been wanting to see you for days." He wasn't sure where that confession came from. He hated to be vulnerable. Kevon sat up straighter.

"Is that right?" Niche raised her eyebrows.

"Are you going somewhere? You just got out the shower."

"Yeah, I did. I needed to unwind before you got here."

"I smell the lavender." Kevon tensed his shoulders, bracing for the worst. "Niche, what's up? After all the silence, what am I doing here? You haven't answered any of my calls, and then you summon me over here. What's going on?" Kevon blurted out. He breathed hard, remembering the promise he'd made to himself not to lose his temper. Like a wick standing at the ready waiting for a flame, all he needed was the right conductor to ignite him. His lips pursed.

Niche removed the elastic band from her hair, shaking her hair loose until it cascaded onto the top of her robe.

"You don't get it, do you? You got something I want," she said, flashing a mischievous grin.

"Huh?" Kevon stared at her, confused. Niche sauntered over to him and squared off, pushing him deeper into the couch.

"Quiet now, don't say a word," Niche whispered. She grabbed his chin and pushed her lips onto his, kissing him forcefully. Kevon was surprised yet delighted. There was no way he could resist this woman. He pushed her shoulders back off of him and looked at her. Her face flushed as she arched her body backward, confirming that she wanted to be with him. His chest rose and fell as she touched him. His muscles rippled down his arm as he grabbed her hand. The smell of cologne intensified as his body heat rose to meet hers. Kevon kissed the soft, delicate skin that encapsulated the palm of her hand and remembered how much he loved this woman.

Kevon pretended he was asleep, a skill that he had mastered by the time he was six. He didn't want to move, talk, or play. He wanted to stay in this moment. No demands or expectations. The peace and quiet that had settled about the room was soothing, like a hot shower after a workout. He fought past the headache and the longing that had formed in his mind over an hour ago. He wanted a drink but didn't need one. The craving was a whisper this time; he was still in control.

"Kevon, move over!" Niche grabbed her brown flannel sheet off the floor and pulled it back onto her bed. The hunter-green comforter still lay tossed on the floor. "I'm getting tired of you hogging my room."

Kevon and Niche lay comfortably in her full-size sleigh bed. Both glistened in the darkened bedroom. The wooden rocking chair her grandmother had left her sat near the small closet with sliding glass doors. The chair was piled with clothes. Kevon swallowed hard, still desiring silence. "You know you like this lovey-dovey stuff, girl. Don't try to front. You was missing me," Kevon said confidently, as he rubbed his foot against Niche's leg. "How about a round of applause?"

"Stop, Kevon. I'm trying to rest, plus I've got a lot on my mind," Niche rebutted.

"I had things on mine, too, but not anymore." Kevon grinned playfully.

"Seriously, Kevon. You don't understand. Not only have I been dealing with our stuff, but my family's stuff too," Niche said.

"What you mean?" Kevon grabbed the comforter off the floor.

"It's nothing you could relate to. It's the struggle," Niche replied.

"So I can't relate to struggle now?" Kevon resented Niche's implication. Kevon knew Niche was an only child raised by a single mother in East Oakland. Her dad was murdered before she could even walk, and her mother, Nancy, was a billing clerk at a small dental office. The only way Niche afforded college was on the sale of her deceased grandmother's home, but she had no right to insinuate that he didn't struggle too. He may not know the struggle of poverty, but he knew the feeling of discontent that came with it. Discontent was nothing new to him. It was an emotion that had followed him since before he could remember. Standing in the shadows, a heaviness loomed over him daily, sometimes overtaking him to the point of suffocation.

"Let's say your struggle is different from mine. You know nothing about The Town," Niche retorted.

"What's that supposed to mean?" Kevon sat up and rested his back against the bed.

"Well, for starters you were raised by both your parents. And I don't understand why finances are such a big problem for you. You work part-time for the parcel service, and your daddy pays every cent of your tuition and books. Your mama works for the government and is always dressed to kill. Your family is the most financially stable family I've ever met in my life," Niche grumbled.

"If I got it that good, then why I have to borrow from you?" Kevon tried to quell his anger.

"All I know is while your family is preparing for Black Friday, my mama is still trying to keep the lights on. While your mama is dining at all those fancy restaurants in Union Square, I'm trying to pull together another installment of my tuition."

"So my mom likes to shop. What about it? Money doesn't solve problems," Kevon fussed, wishing she could understand the bigger picture. Problems came in all sorts of packages, and she refused to see that, which is why he refused to talk to her about his real feelings. She made her problems always trump his.

"Look at Sharyn. She bought that house in San Carlos. San Carlos is crazy loot, Kevon. It is one of the most expensive neighborhoods to live in the Bay Area. The entire Peninsula is crazy high," Niche replied.

"San Carlos is not Palo Alto, Niche, but okay, you have a point. Sharyn and Mike do have some loot, but that has nothing to do with me." Kevon grabbed the side of the bed and shook his head. "I know struggle, Niche. I struggle all the time," Kevon confessed, wishing he had his flask as the whisper of a craving now had started a small roar. His struggle had nothing to do with money. All he wanted was a tenth of the love she received from her mother. His mother barely even called him anymore.

Kevon remembered the year his mother changed. He was fifteen and flirtatious and had shown up to his high school dance wearing his best khaki shorts and strategically ripped T-shirt. Balloons cascaded all over the gymnasium, and flashing lights filled the room. The disc jockey played all his favorite songs, and he'd danced with almost every girl in the sophomore class. His buddy Tony had supplied the alcohol, and a popular senior, Deon, had supplied the marijuana. They'd sneak to the bathroom to get high because the smoke machine made it difficult for administrators to detect who left the dance floor.

Kevon had never liked the smell of marijuana so he never indulged, but he loved Hennessy. By the time the dance was over and all the students flooded out into the parking lot like bees leaving the hive, Deon was too intoxicated to drive. Kevon called his mother instead of his father to solicit a ride. The last thing he wanted was to get into trouble with his dad, but his mother arrived at the school sooner than he'd expected.

Kevon sat up startled and half-naked when Rose flashed a light into the back seat of Deon's car and caught him with a girl. He'd tried to cover himself, but he was too late. He saw a look on his mother's face that he'd remember for the rest of his life, but he hadn't known that when her face distorted, her heart did too.

Niche grabbed a pen from her headboard and stuck it underneath Kevon's chin, simulating a microphone. "Please, enlighten me. What do you struggle with, Kev?"

"I struggle with us." Kevon changed the subject. "Why am I here? Is this for the afternoon, or are we together?" Kevon grabbed her shoulders and looked intently in her eyes.

"You know, I don't know what's going to happen. All I know is that I love you, and your apology is accepted."

"I figured that." Kevon chuckled.

"Next time though, I swear, I won't take you back. This last time was the last time." Niche kicked his leg.

"There won't be a next time. I was drunk that night, and I apologized a million times in a thousand ways." Kevon gestured to the dozen roses on her student desk. "And I promise I'm gonna stop drinking."

"I love the flowers you sent and the balloon bouquet your frat brought to my class. But this is my last time, Kevon. I mean that." Niche pushed his bare cocoa shoulder playfully.

"Did you call me over here to make love or war?" Kevon grabbed her tightly around the waist.

"Both," she confessed.

Sharyn

"Hello, I was calling to gather some information on infertility." As soon as she said it, her eye began to twitch. The eyelid earthquakes hadn't happened to her in years. "I saw your website, and I decided to contact you for more information." The voice on the other end of the telephone explained their services and inquired briefly about her medical history.

Sharyn rubbed her eye. She didn't care if her eyeliner smudged, she had to stop the involuntary spasms. She closed her eyes tightly and then opened them several times until the twitching stopped. Now she could concentrate.

The pain resonating from the reality that she was doing this alone stung, but she was determined to move forward. "I would like to begin the process of exploring some of the avenues your clinic offers in infertility treatment," Sharyn cemented. She looked out of the window of her office, noticing the shape of the building across the street: a large brown rectangular box. Glass windows outlined each side of the building, but it still had no character. It reminded her of what her life had become, predictable. She was tired of succumbing to others' needs; this time, she was stepping outside the box.

"No, I haven't had any testing done. Thursday would be great. Thank you for your assistance. I'll see you then." Sharyn hung up the receiver.

"Tsk, tsk, tsk," Ms. Brenda said. Sharyn jerked in her office chair, startled at Ms. Brenda's voice behind her. She glanced over her shoulder and smiled at her aged coworker. "My friend, you are treading into some dangerous territory." Sharyn glanced at the ageless beauty outfitted in a green turtleneck sweater and black formfitting skirt, her makeup bold and flawless.

"Ms. Brenda, I didn't know anyone was standing there." Sharyn changed the subject, wondering how much her colleague had heard.

"I'm on mandatory overtime." She winked. "I put some gumbo on last night. I knew you'd be working late, too, so let's go dig in." Ms. Brenda lifted a weighted grocery satchel and gestured for Sharyn to join her.

"My pleasure." Sharyn stumbled to her feet. Her mood lifted as both women headed in search of an empty conference room. She could feel the knots in her shoulder loosening like after a massage, and Sharyn was sure that sixty minutes with Ms. Brenda would leave her feeling just as refreshed. The woman supplied a wisdom that Sharyn couldn't deny. "Let's eat in here." Sharyn motioned her head toward the wooden door. Both women hurried in and closed the door behind them. Sharyn closed the blinds on the floor-to-ceiling windows, giving them more privacy. The grand conference table stood in contrast to the three portable dry-erase boards propped against the only solid wall. The trash can overflowed with discarded coffee cups left over from meetings held in the midday. Sharyn checked the speaker on the table used for conference calls. "I love this conference room. It's the perfect shade of cognac."

"Chile, don't mention no cognac." The silver-haired woman laughed as she gently laid down a white tablecloth and unpacked two empty bowls.

"Is that your poison, Ms. Brenda?" Sharyn plopped into a rolling leather chair. She couldn't imagine her sipping on a drink. A latte maybe, but alcohol didn't seem like it would be her thing. Sharyn smiled at her own naivete. She reminded herself that addiction had no preference for color, gender, or social status.

"No, chile, not *my* poison. My poison didn't come in no bottle."

"It didn't, huh. Mine doesn't either. It comes in those containers you pouring that gumbo out of." Sharyn squeezed her ample stomach as she smelled the aroma of boiled crab. She'd always carried some extra pounds, which her husband teased were stationed in all the right places.

"Food ain't no poison, baby, it's an elixir. Excess is the toxin . . . not being satisfied with enough."

"I can never get enough gumbo." Sharyn plunged her spoon into her bowl, now chock-full.

"I hear ya. Sometimes what's right in front of you is not good enough." Ms. Brenda returned the emptied containers to her satchel.

"I agree." Sharyn licked her finger, wondering if they were still talking about food. She wiped her lips with the back of her hand.

"Did I tell you about the first time I made gumbo?" Ms. Brenda passed Sharyn a napkin.

"No, Ms. Brenda. How'd you learn?" Sharyn could taste experience layered in the juices. The right amount of seasoning frolicked in her mouth. She'd never fit back into her size seven jeans again if Ms. Brenda kept feeding her like this.

"The hard way." Ms. Brenda shook her head. "I had recently married, we were about five years together, and the mister and I had our first child. My baby was about two 'round then, and I wanted me a house of my own so bad. Cook in my own kitchen. We were staying with my in-laws back then."

"I can understand that. My best friend Tasha lived with her in-laws when she first married, and she was going nuts." Sharyn pulled a crab leg from out of her bowl and bit down hard as juice escaped from the sides of her mouth.

"It was hard. Seemed like we were the only ones in our community of friends that didn't have no land. Each time I opened the doors to that tiny old house it was like walking into a cell. I forgot all about my daily bread. No gratitude, honey, I had an attitude. I begged my husband to get another job and get me that house, and he begged me to cook him some old-fashioned New Orleans–style gumbo."

"Did he now?" Sharyn giggled.

"Sure did, but I refused. Told him, 'Get me that house, and I'll get you that gumbo.' Well, he sure did want that gumbo because he done went out and got him a second job."

"How sweet," Sharyn said, as she popped a shrimp in her mouth.

"Good job too. So good, I eventually wanted him to quit the first, imagine that. He refused, too. He said to me, 'Baby girl'—that's what he called me now, baby girl—'I'm gonna get me that gumbo.' Used to tease me all the time about getting my recipe together." Ms. Brenda smiled, looking off into the distance.

"Well, you sure got that recipe together," Sharyn said, looking down into her near-empty bowl.

"Got me that house, too. Beautiful house, what I always wanted. Cost a lot though."

"Back in them days? Probably cost you forty thousand." Sharyn laughed.

"Much more than that, baby. Cost me a price I didn't want to pay, my husband." Ms. Brenda chuckled like a card shark who'd lost his ace of spades.

"What do you mean, Ms. Brenda? You've been married a lifetime."

"Sure have, but my first husband got me that house. About a year after we moved in. Got all settled and even had me another baby on the way, and I lost him. On his way home from that second job, he done went and fell asleep. Ran straight into a tree. My second child never even met his papa. Hmm, that's when I learned to make that gumbo. Grieving gumbo is what I call it. Shoot, even my kids call it that too. Served it right after his funeral service. He never had it but made the greatest sacrifice for it."

"That is so tragic, Ms. Brenda. I had no idea you were married before."

"Sure was, and to the love of my life, but what was meant for evil, God done turned it around for my good. Like Hannah in the good book, God done up and went and gave me another opportunity."

"How so?" Sharyn asked.

"He gave me my Tate." Ms. Brenda nodded. "You know, chile, I never sold that old house. Still sitting pretty up there in Louisiana. I thought my in-laws' home was the jail, but I was wrong. My greatest desire eventually became my prison. That house, humph, was a daily reminder of my sacrifice. Always reminded me that a place to

lay my head and a devoted husband was not enough to fill me up."
Ms. Brenda laid her soft hand on top of Sharyn's and gave it a gentle
squeeze.

"Sharyn, are you full?" Ms. Brenda asked. Sharyn eyed the fine
lines that covered her hands and was thankful for the wisdom they
carried.

13

Niche

Niche tugged at the zipper on her white windbreaker, anxious to get it over with. She paced the confined space like a woman unaccompanied at a bus stop, nervous and wanting to get home. Her brown leather boots echoed after each step, reminding her this wasn't a dream. Her eyes scanned the room. She'd imagined herself in this space hundreds of times but not in this capacity.

She was tired of thinking and wondering; like logging in waiting for grades to post, she wanted to know right now. Niche hardly noticed the door open.

"Well, congratulations. How are you feeling?" The medical assistant outfitted in teddy-bear scrubs floated into the exam room all smiles.

Niche leaned against the exam table, overwhelmed. This *was* happening. The paper sanitation liner crinkled underneath her fingertips like her hope. "I'm glad you guys could fit me in on such short notice. I wanted to make sure the test was accurate." Niche accidently kicked the side chair. "Oops, sorry."

"Happens all the time," the medical assistant reassured her, typing furiously into the computer.

"Not to me," Niche said, reflecting more on the positive pregnancy test than the table. She had dressed in all white, jeans and an ivory mock turtleneck, hoping that the home test was inaccurate. It seemed when she wore white, she started menstruating, so Niche had cast off the Labor Day rule and dressed for success. She knew the chances of starting her menses were slim, but she hoped.

She didn't want a baby, and her relationship with Kevon was still uncertain. She'd planned to take a break from him after the holidays, but her trip to the dollar store had changed everything. She wasn't one hundred percent sure the test was accurate, but if the results were correct, she'd need Kevon in her life more than ever.

"I'm glad you came in. The sooner a pregnancy is verified, the better." The slim assistant rose from the silver, rolling stool, gave her a wink, and headed toward the door. "The doctor will be right in."

"Thank you." Niche eyed the closing door. She was never claustrophobic, but this room felt like it was growing smaller by the minute. The exam room resembled a tiny classroom, filled with parenting books, handouts, and posters. Each wall displayed a teaching tool. Niche couldn't help but focus on the birth control poster that hung high on the wall. She read all the outlined options. The pill, ring, sponge, IUD, and the shot were all viable options that she never used.

Niche felt her eyes welling with tears. She took a deep breath, traveled to the small sink stationed in the corner of the room, grabbed a paper towel, and blotted her eyes. Niche glanced at her reflection. The round face, almond eyes, and thick lips looked familiar. The brown skin and crooked bottom tooth resembled that of someone she knew, but she was unacquainted with the girl who found herself in this situation. She'd played his game and lost herself. Kevon had been present each moment that had led her to this office, but now she stood here all alone, wondering how she was going to carry the load. Her heart dropped when she heard the knock outside the door.

"Hi, Niche! Pleasure to see you again." Dr. Bateman glided into the room.

"Hello, Dr. Bateman. How are you?" Niche mumbled, walking

back to the examination table and lifting herself up. She tensed her muscles, trying to sit still.

"How are you?" Dr. Bateman asked, looking Niche directly into her eyes. Niche sat up straight and dangled her legs off the edge of the table.

"Depends on the results," she admitted. "I suspected that I could be pregnant from my missed period. I'd been feeling nauseated for the past couple of weeks, but I thought it was stress. Schoolwork and the other girls at school keep me in a state of confusion, but..." Niche sighed.

"So, how are you now?" Dr. Bateman quizzed.

"The two pink lines are sorta weighing me down," she confessed, leaning in closer to the physician who had provided her medical care since she was a teenager.

"I understand, Niche. The thought of a pregnancy can be overwhelming. Those tests are pretty accurate, and coupled with your other symptoms, a pregnancy may be likely. If pregnant, do you have any thoughts about how you'd like to proceed?" Dr. Bateman asked.

"I have mixed feelings. My initial reaction was to get an abortion, but I changed my mind."

"You did?" Dr. Bateman looked confused.

"Could I abort it without regretting it for the rest of my life? I don't know. There's so much to debate, is it killing a baby or killing a fetus? After a while, it didn't matter to me anymore. I knew what I had to do for me."

"Which is?" Dr. Bateman asked.

"Carry on. I know that my life and career plans may be ruined, and it won't be easy, but I'm gonna have it."

"A child would definitely change your life," Dr. Bateman confirmed.

"I had plans, my family, but what can I do?" Niche's eyes filled with tears. She had worked hard to be the first person in her family to go to college, and the thought of letting her mother down was devastating. Niche wiped her tears as she stared at Dr. Bateman straight on, hoping that her doctor would have some answers.

"First, get confirmation. I know your graduation is close and you had plans, but first let's see what you're dealing with." Dr. Bateman grabbed the tissue box near the sink and handed it to Niche.

"I'm not so sure that I could support a child." Niche wiped her nose. "Or that I even want to."

"What about Kevon's support?" Dr. Bateman asked. Niche shrugged her shoulders.

"Truth is, I don't know what he'll do. I did know the first thing I had to do was come see you. I had to make sure this was for real. I would hate to alarm Kevon for no reason."

"I agree, Niche. Let's get another test on board," Dr. Bateman instructed.

"Okay. Let's do it." Niche nodded. Telling Kevon before she knew for sure was out of the question. She knew Kevon wouldn't want her to get an abortion, but her choice would be between her and God—no one else.

"Niche, I'm going to have one of my medical assistants come in. They'll provide you with a urine cup so we can take a sample. If pregnancy is confirmed with the urine, we'll do some blood work." Dr. Bateman stood up and squeezed her shoulder.

Niche smiled, trying to hide the fear that crept up her spine. She knew taking another test was risky; like pulling a hangnail, either the outcome would be good or it would be bad. If the test was positive, she knew that her future demanded answers. She'd be forced to answer the questions that bounced around in her mind. If negative, God had given her a second chance, and she would be sure to take birth control pills from now on—religiously.

The same assistant entered the room and smiled. "Here you are," she said, handing Niche a plastic cup.

"Thank you," Niche replied, following her to the bathroom. Handing the cup and its contents back to the assistant standing guard in the hallway was the hardest thing Niche had ever had to do. She dragged herself back into the examination room and awaited her fate. Fifteen minutes later, Dr. Bateman knocked at the door.

"Come in," Niche said, as Dr. Bateman took a seat on the silver stool in front of her. Niche tried to read her face, but it only registered kindness.

"Are you ready for the results, Niche?" Dr. Bateman looked at Niche with concern in her eyes.

"No, but I have to be ready, Dr. Bateman." Niche bit her lip, clutched her purse tightly, and swallowed hard.

"The home pregnancy test was accurate. You are pregnant, but I want to reassure you that you have options, Niche. At this time you can decide what course of action you wish to take, but I don't advise it. I want you to think about it more. At minimum, I want to set up another appointment with you to talk. Okay?" Dr. Bateman patted her leg.

"Okay," Niche whispered, holding back tears.

"I would also like to administer a blood test now, and once you've made a final decision, I urge you to contact me as soon as possible. We have a small window for termination," Dr. Bateman reassured her. Niche stared off in the distance, wondering what Kevon was doing right now.

Robert

Robert pulled into the first available parking stall. His heart raced as he looked at the familiar building. Gray paint, concrete steps, and blurred windows. It was remodeled, but it was the same old, dark, and desperate place. He turned up the radio to drown out the memories of the last time he was here. Similar circumstances, different decade. He'd lost another woman he loved, tragically. Robert had been a child then, holding his younger brother's hand while they both sobbed. He'd vowed never to return to this police station, but this time he wasn't forced; he wanted to be here. For her, he had to find out what happened. This time, he could do the interrogating.

When his mother died, he hadn't wanted answers. He'd wanted to move on with his life, to go back to Big Mama's house or any other foster home and start over. Big Mama had hugged him all night, and sang "We Shall Overcome" when he woke with terror. She'd informed him it was going to be all right and assured him that God had a way of making all things beautiful in His own time. This time he struggled with that belief.

The rap on the window startled him. Saved from the tears that he could feel welling in his eyes, he pulled his brown polo shirt down and plastered a smile on his face. Robert turned off the car, rolled his window down, and nodded to the brawny officer.

"Hey, Deac. How are you?" Eric asked, hardly recognizable in his starched blue uniform. Robert tilted his head.

"Fair to middlin'. How about you, Eric?"

"I'm great. Pulled a double though, so a tad bit tired. Almost headed home now." Eric beamed.

"I'm sure that's *always* a blessing." Robert smiled.

"Yes, sir, always. What are you doing here, Deac? You need help with something?"

"No, sir, I was taking a break around here," Robert stammered. "My body is not as limber as it used to be. Driving too long hurts my back sometimes, so I decided to stop and park. What better place than here?" Robert watched as Eric folded his arms and shot him a glance he knew well. Rose had produced that expression when she knew Robert was lying.

"I can think of a few." Eric's eyebrows crinkled. "Well, if I can help with anything, you let me know."

"Will do, sir, will do." Robert extended his hand through the window feeling self-conscious. The last thing he needed was someone poking around, especially a cop. "Now, I'll see you on Sunday morning, right?"

"God willing." Eric squeezed his hand before letting it go.

"All right now." Robert rolled up his window and watched Eric disappear in the sea of cars. The air thickened as Robert thought about where he'd sit on Sunday to avoid all interaction with Eric. Frustrated, he rubbed behind his neck, squeezing the tender spot above his shoulder blades. Questions hung in the air. Now unsure if he should enter the station, Robert grabbed his cell phone and dialed Martin. He wanted perspective, and he needed a Word.

"Hi, Mr. Lovelace," Martin answered, after the first ring. Robert breathed a sigh of relief. He wasn't the type of man to seek advice, but this time was different—lives were at stake.

"Hello, Reverend Broussard. How are you?" Robert tapped his foot against the brake pedal like a musician trying to keep a beat.

"I'm well, sir. How are you?" Robert could hear the concern in his voice.

"Well, truthfully, son, I'm in a pickle, and I'm calling for some feedback."

"Yes, sir." Martin sounded off like military recruit. "Angie okay?"

"Angela is fine. Thank you. *I* am in this situation, you see. And as much as I want to throw my hat into the ring, I know it won't turn out well if I get involved." Robert rested his hand over his heart, where she'd also felt comfortable placing her hand. It had been her way of letting him know she cared. "If I jump in and do what I feel is the right thing, someone will get hurt. So, you see, there is no clear right thing. You understand?" Robert scanned the parking lot, looking for familiar faces.

"I do, sir. You might get your hand chopped off for reaching in," Martin replied.

Robert shook his head, grateful for Martin's counsel. "Yes, exactly." He knew Martin would keep his confidence and provide him with valuable insight.

"It's always hard when there's no clear right thing, or one easy way. Reminds me of the parable about the two mothers," he affirmed.

"At least you don't have to cut a baby in half."

"True, but this *is* a difficult situation." Robert shuffled in his seat, wondering if he should move his car.

"Have you gone to the Lord in prayer?"

Robert eyed his golden key chain that displayed *Prayer changes things* in big block letters. It had been a present from his ex-wife a year before she walked out on him. "Of course, but no answer." Robert's foot tapping amplified.

"Been there." Martin chuckled. "You know, sir, when this occurs in my life and I don't feel led by the spirit or the Lord hasn't answered, I take it as a reminder for me to be still."

"I've been still. I been a statue for years." Robert clenched his jaw, remembering all the times he held his tongue and sacrificed his needs for his family, something he'd learned to do as a child.

"Deacon Lovelace, you cannot force the Lord's hand, and neither would I recommend it. I'm always reminded that He is sovereign, not me. When God says go, you must go, and when he says stay you must stay."

"I know He is sovereign, but waiting is difficult, especially when something has recently come up that could change everything," Robert explained.

"For who, you or the Kingdom? Mr. Lovelace, it's not His job to keep us comfortable. During difficult times, we must find ourselves trusting Him all the more. It's like when you're blindfolded and you can't see where you're going; you have to reach out for objects that are stable. Find the things in the environment that are truly there and can hold the weight."

"Well, I'm tired of holding the weight." Robert wiped his sweaty palms on his khaki pants.

"I understand, sir, but right now you can't see your way, and to move can cause more harm than good. Mr. Lovelace, you must consider yourself blind, and even the blind usually walk a half step behind the person leading them. You walk a step behind the Master, and things will work out fine," Martin declared.

"But things are so cloudy right now. How do I know what God is saying? Maybe He is leading my heart to get involved," Robert explained.

"Yes, I understand, but like when traveling on a foggy day, remember that sometimes the higher you elevate, the clearer things become."

Robert's shoulders relaxed. "Amen, Doc. Amen."

14

Kevon

The tiny room was hot and muggy. The stillness of the air made Kevon even more uncomfortable. He gazed at the ceiling fan, spinning leisurely. The small breeze couldn't cool the heat that was coming from the hiked-up thermostat. He threw the covers off his muscular body, turned over, and looked at Shameka. She was sleeping peacefully. Her hair was messy and her makeup smeared, but she looked passive, not at all like the animated girl that had stumbled into his car last night.

Shameka bore no resemblance to the woman he loved. She was free and lively. Niche was proper and well taught. He smiled as his mind retold Niche's account of her grandmother's drilling, "Manners matter, and lipstick does too." His mother never said anything like that. She was too modern. He wished his mother had kept some of old Mississippi in her blood—the part of Mississippi that was enriching, like the soil that nurtured the crops.

The loud vibration of Kevon's cell phone interrupted his thoughts as it echoed in Shameka's modest room, equipped with a bed, a white chair, and a small television. Her bloodshot eyes flew open.

"Go on and get it. You know you want to," Shameka instructed, as she closed her lids.

"How do you know what I want?" Kevon asked, stroking her hair back into place. His cocoa hand rested on her cheek. A crooked smile graced his lips as he glided his hand down her cheekbone.

"Stop flirting with me, Kevon. You always get what you want. You're spoiled." Shameka covered her torso.

"It's like that now. Oh, how the tables turn," Kevon grumbled. They must have spent her entire paycheck last night in Lakeview at Jabari's Bar. He'd lost count of his tab after the twelfth tequila shot. How they'd made it to her apartment was still a blur. He remembered pulling into San Francisco State University for a quick romp in the back seat and heading back onto the interstate but hardly anything that followed. Kevon sat up, stretched out his arms, and laid them across the metal headboard. "Don't forget you got into *my* car."

"True," Shameka agreed. "No worries, I don't have papers on you."

"Turn around, let me rub your back," Kevon instructed, moving the bedspread that separated them as the vibration of his cell phone beckoned him once more.

"Again? Hmm, somebody is determined. Where did you tell her you were today?" Shameka giggled.

"Somebody got jokes. I didn't come over here to talk about Niche. I came over here to spend some time with you," Kevon declared. He hated discussing Niche when he was with Shameka, but she always found a way to bring her up. Kevon scooted up next to her, trying to put an end to the small talk. He already was in a relationship; he didn't need another one.

"Remember, I let you in *my* apartment, and believe me, Niche is the last name that I want to hear in my bedroom." The phone vibration again interrupted them.

Kevon jumped out of the bed and grabbed his jeans off the floor. Shameka attempted to grab him, but he was too fast.

"No, baby, don't check it. What about my back rub?" Shameka rolled her eyes. Kevon pulled the phone from the pocket of his blue jeans, looked at the display, and groaned. The display read *911 Niche.*

"Let me guess. Hmm, tell Niche I said hi." Shameka laughed, rolled over, and turned her back toward him.

Kevon sat down on the foot of her bed. His stomach was sour from the aftermath of too much tequila and beer. "Shut up, Shameka. This must be important, you see she called three times." Kevon dialed Niche's telephone number. "I wonder what she wants. I told her I'd be busy doing some volunteer hours at the food bank with the frat. She never bothers me when I'm doing community service." Kevon hunched over and rested his elbows on his knees. He wanted to keep their conversation private. "Hey, Niche. What's up? Is everything okay?" Kevon probed, waiting for her response.

"No, baby, it isn't. It's an urgent situation, and I need to see you. I'd rather not go into it over the phone," Niche uttered.

Kevon's heart raced. "What's wrong? Is it your moms? What's going on, Niche? Bump that, I wanna know now," Kevon declared, scooting further toward the edge of the full-size bed. He could feel the edge of the mattress pressing hard against his thigh. He wished he could go to another room for privacy, but Shameka shared a two-bedroom apartment, and her roommate was always too interested in what was going on behind Shameka's door.

"I don't want to tell you over the phone," Niche resisted.

"Now, Niche," Kevon ordered.

"I need to see you first," Niche explained.

"Now, Niche. I'm starting to get frustrated," Kevon barked. Sweat dotted his forehead as his body heat began to outpace the temperature in the room.

"You're going to be a daddy, Kevon," Niche blurted out.

"What are you talking about? Has my dad been calling there again?" Kevon grumbled, as a familiar pounding in his head returned.

"Kevon, you're forcing it out of me. Where are you, anyway? It's quiet."

He stood up to walk over to the closet in the corner of the bedroom, but in one swift motion Shameka twisted around and secured her long legs around his waist, pulling him back toward the bed. "I'm at Tony's crib, everybody else went to go get something to eat. Now quit beating around the bush and tell me," Kevon said, trying to wiggle out of Shameka's grasp.

"Well, I did, Kevon. I'm pregnant!" Niche exclaimed. Kevon's eyes widened as he held the phone quietly. He was stuck like an old piece of chewing gum lodged in the pocket of a pair of freshly washed jeans. "Kev, I didn't want to tell you this way, but you couldn't wait."

Kevon struggled to calm down. He unclenched his fist and took a deep breath. "Are you serious right now? Yeah, we definitely need to talk. I'll be over there in a minute. Don't you go anywhere either!" Kevon hung up the phone and slumped down at the edge of the bed.

"What's wrong, baby?" Shameka scooted in closer behind him, feathering his back with her fingernails. Kevon turned, glanced at her, and shook his head.

"I have to go. I stepped into a nightmare. Where you hiding the brandy? I need a drink."

Angela

Angela dug her heel into the hole on the floor mat. She hated when people kept her waiting. She glanced at her watch, regretting that she'd answered the call. Blue skies and temperate weather were incentives for outdoor activities, and the miniature golf park was filled with patrons. Angela took in a deep breath as she eyed the parking lot becoming more crowded by the second. Sitting in her car was the last place she wanted to be.

Jonathan had been gracious as she walked off the course in her gray wedge boots, cradling her phone. Grabbing her professional cell was a mistake, but she didn't want to miss any potential information regarding Trevion's case. She had fielded calls from Trevion's mom's so-called friends and neighbors, but she'd still come up with nothing except that Trevion's mother, Samantha, wasn't going to have a funeral. There were no family members to notify. Angela discovered his mother had been adopted, and both adoptive parents died when she was eight years old. Sadly, she'd been placed back into foster care. With no family, Angela didn't have much to go on.

"Thanks, Ms. Ang, for holding," Tyra whined, like a toddler scared to sleep alone. "I'm so sorry to call you again, but you're the only person I thought of. Shaun got arrested again, and I'm terrified we gonna get reported." Angela had a feeling she knew why Tyra was reaching out. Tyra had stopped checking in with Angela about her progress over a year ago.

"Tyra, I thought you guys had separated for good. As you are well aware, separation was part of your case plan." Angela pulled down her visor and checked her lipstick. She smiled, double-checking her teeth. She had given this case too much of her time and energy already. Unlike Martin, Jonathan was happy to allow her to take another call, but she didn't want to keep him waiting too long.

"I know, Ms. Ang. I was doing well, but about six months after our case closed, Shaun and I started talking again. You know it was that visitation. We should have kept exchanging the kids at the visitation center," Tyra explained.

"Is that right, Tyra?" Angela asked distractedly, fighting the urge to tell Tyra to take responsibility for her own choices. Angela leaned her head back on the headrest, readying herself for a barrage of excuses.

"Ms. Ang, we've been together forever. It's hard to be out here on my own," Tyra confessed.

"I understand. You two have been through so much. You've been through good times and difficult times. I remember when I first received your case, it was a hard time for you. Do you remember?" Angela easily recalled the week she'd received Tyra's case. It was also when she'd gotten her first bouquet of flowers from Martin. He'd surprised her at the office with an armful of white tulips and eyes bursting with adoration.

"Yeah, I remember. That's why I called you. You know how hard I worked to get my kids back," Tyra reminisced.

"You sure did. That's exactly how I remember it. You went through it, and you did it all by yourself too."

"You helped me, Ms. Ang." Tyra's voice softened.

"No, Tyra, you finally decided to help yourself. At first, it was forced, but then you took it and ran with it." Angela ignored the other call coming in on her phone.

"I sure did, didn't I?" Angela could tell Tyra was smiling.

"Yes, you did, and although you didn't get there alone, you got out of there alone," Angela reminded her old client.

"I know. I don't want to go back to that," Tyra replied.

"Is that true?"

"What do you mean, Ms. Ang? Of course it's true."

"Well, what was it that got you into CPS in the first place?" Angela closed her eyes, praying her client would remember.

"When Shaun got arrested before, he was drunk, remember? He was getting into it with everybody."

"Who?" Angela asked, even though she already knew the answer.

"Mainly Connie from downstairs, then her cousin Charles got involved. It was a mess." Angela could hear the irritation welling in Tyra's voice.

"So that's what Shaun was doing, but what does that have to do with you?" Angela pushed.

"With all that drama I had to go and get Shaun before things got heated. He had threw something at Charles, and then the fool turned on me for trying to help."

"Oh yeah, that's right. He turned on you."

"Yeah, he started to swell up and get all up in my face, and by that time the police came. I was the one trying to help the situation."

"That's what happened the other times too. You're the peacekeeper. But that's what happens though, right? Shaun loses it, and then you end up losing the most." Angela again ignored another incoming call.

"Yeah, but now things are different. That's how it was, but not anymore. He's much better now."

"I'm glad, Tyra. Now why are you calling?"

"Well, I thought you could help." Tyra's voice relaxed.

"Help with what? I thought things were going good," Angela countered, crossing her fingers.

"Well, this one time he got out of control again." Tyra's voice stammered.

"This one time, Tyra?" Angela shook her head.

"Yeah, one time," Tyra declared.

"Or do you mean one time, this time? Look, Tyra, you know I've always had my office open to you and the kids, but my door is closed to Shaun. If *you* choose to reunite, that's your choice. Life is all about choices, which result in outcomes. You know that if you touch a hot stove for whatever reason, you have a chance of getting burned. My hope will always be that you decide and don't let the circumstances decide for you." Angela sat up straight. Thanks to Tyra, she had made a decision. She knew what she had to do; she was going to go directly to her father and let him tell her why a junkie had his picture.

"You'll see, Ms. Ang. You will."

"I hope so, Tyra. You take care now, and in the meantime, keep me posted on how you're doing. Talk to you. Bye." Angela hung up and eyed her cell phone display. Two missed calls from Jonathan registered. Her heart dropped.

The lines in the golf course were so long that Angela could hardly find Jonathan. His green sweater blended in with the backdrop of artificial grass. She was able to spot him back by the sixth hole after walking almost entirely through the intricate course. Angela began to perspire in her tight gray sweater and black jeans as she climbed up the hill to where he stood. Wisps of her hair danced out of her neatly coiffed French roll.

"Sorry, Jonathan, I had to take that call." Angela fanned herself as she carefully stepped over the artificial turf, happy to have finally found him. She took a step back and surveyed his strapping frame, glad that she'd remembered his number. Lonely nights were always difficult.

"No problem, beautiful. I also answered phone calls while you were gone. Water?" Jonathan pulled a water bottle from the back of his blue trousers.

"No, I'm fine. I'm glad you were able to get some things done too." Angela looked around at the growing crowd and hoped she wouldn't run into any familiar faces. She grabbed her club off a nearby bench. "I love this place. I haven't been to the Prix since I was right out of college. It brings back some memories of the times I spent here." Angela smiled as she glanced out over the landscape. Fake statues and buildings were strategically placed all around the course. Water stations stood near each hole. Small solar lights were positioned next to the cement pathway that traveled the length of the course.

"Did you come here a lot?" Jonathan tried to maneuver his golf ball closer to the dated castle.

"I used to cut class and come here to hang with my friends back in high school. We used to spend all day in the batting cages," Angela said, as they waited to retrieve his golf ball.

"Aren't you the daughter of a deacon *and* a deaconess? Cutting class is against the rules, right?" Jonathan picked up the tiny golf ball and tossed it toward the castle.

Angela rolled her eyes. "Don't you know by now, I hate abiding by rules. I like to do things my way, and that is why spontaneity is my middle name." Angela smiled, remembering the first time she visited the Prix. Her mother, Rose, and her friend had taken the family for a day of leisure while her father was working. Her mother had fawned over Kevon and cheered every time Sharyn made an attempt, but when it was Angela's turn, she'd barely looked on. Angela had realized then that if she played for anyone else other than herself, she'd lose.

"I know 'by the book' doesn't exist for you nowadays, but I thought as a kid things were different." Jonathan winked.

Angela picked up her golf ball and placed it carefully on the marker. "Watch this." She swung and hit the ball far left, missing the seventh hole.

"Ooh, the way you play golf is an embarrassment. Try following the rules to this game." Jonathan laughed.

"I'm unconventional, Jonathan. I color outside the lines. By the way, your score isn't that much better than mine." Angela grabbed her ball.

Jonathan walked over to Angela and pulled her close from behind, whispering in her ear.

"Don't worry, I have a comeback planned. Building excitement is the name of my game."

Angela pushed him off and sashayed toward the next hole. She turned around when she was sure she had his attention and shot him a coy glance. Jonathan picked up his ball and followed her, and as he approached the front of the huge faux elephant, he wrapped his arms around her waist again. He looked into her eyes.

"You know, you're starting to get under my skin." Jonathan licked his lips, slowly leaned in, and pressed his against hers. The long, passionate kiss took Angela by surprise. She pulled away and looked around the course, making sure Martin or anyone else from St. John's wasn't around. She exhaled. She was in the clear.

Angela wrapped her arms around his neck and pulled him closer, communicating her feelings with the warmth of her lips. She pulled away. "Oh my goodness, you see them looking at us?" Angela stood shamefaced as she noticed an elderly couple looking on.

"Let them look, I want the whole world to know that you got my nose wide open. Come on, babe, let's sit down for a minute." Jonathan gestured toward a nearby park bench. "I want to share something that's been on my mind for the past couple of weeks." Jonathan grabbed Angela's hand and guided her toward the seat.

"Jonathan, I'm enjoying the game." Angela blushed, pulling him back toward the course.

"It's more than the game, I'm enjoying you. I care about you. I think I'm falling for you, girl." Jonathan linked arms with her and walked them off the course and onto the shaded cement walkway.

"Jonathan." Angela could feel her throat drying. She hoped he wasn't getting too serious.

"When you tossed me to the side, I sweated it. I didn't want to seem like a sucker though, but I knew then that you had me open. You intoxicate me. You're a special woman, Angela Lovelace, and I'm glad that we made a new connection and are back on." Jonathan rubbed her hand.

"Me too, last week was special." Angela winked.

"Ang, this isn't about hooking up," Jonathan replied sternly. "I don't want you to think that I'm telling you this to get you in bed, because I want to hold off on that too."

"Hold off?" Angela looked puzzled, hoping he hadn't caught the piece of piety that Martin carried around. Angela had decided long ago that this was a relationship of convenience. Her love was already held in reserve.

"Well, maybe I was getting ahead of myself," Jonathan laughed. "You know if you want to take it to the next level again, I'm okay with that too. But I think we got off to a fast start—too fast. I don't know,

I'm trying to say that I'm glad that you're here with me." Jonathan kissed her hand. Angela fought the urge to run away. *The heart is in the chest, not on the sleeve,* she murmured to herself. She wasn't going to allow him to pull her in too.

"I'm also glad, Jonathan, and you can expect a spanking on *and* off the course." Angela hopped up and sashayed back toward the putting greens.

15

Kevon

Kevon entered the pub's sliding doors and immediately surveyed the scene. His eyes darted left to right as he stuck his chest out and pulled his shoulders back. The pub was filled to capacity with college students lined up, sitting down, and standing in large and small groups. Loud conversations echoed in corners. Laughter ricocheted from tables to booths.

O'Malley's during lunch was like a nightclub: colorful, hot, and pulsating. The stench of mildew and sweat permeated the air. With each step Kevon's blue-and-white sneakers stuck slightly to the barely mopped cement floor. Kevon's gait slowed as he nodded at familiar faces. He'd agreed to meet Niche for lunch to discuss the pregnancy, and this time she insisted it must be in public. O'Malley's was his suggestion. The pub was the only logical choice; he could get some beer and tune her out at the same time.

Kevon removed his blue aviator sunglasses, which matched his blue tracksuit. He spotted some friends at a nearby table and headed in their direction. He glanced at his reflection in the tinted windows of the pub, wishing he had his blue baseball cap. He needed a haircut bad.

"Hey, frat, what's up?" Kevon glided up to his friends' table, hoping they still had some food and drink left. He didn't have any more money in his bank account, and Shameka wasn't returning his calls. He hadn't had a drink all day, and he could feel the agitation crawling throughout his body.

"What's up with you is the question, homey." Andre nodded in his direction.

Kevon instinctively eyeballed the nearly empty pitcher positioned in the middle of the small, round wooden table. There was only a mouthful of beer remaining. Kevon snatched the pitcher out of the center and buried his nose inside. "Dog, y'all didn't save a player none." Kevon frowned.

Andre laughed and threw up his hands. "A player didn't give us no change either," he corrected.

"Here, frat, help yourself." Tyrell handed Kevon his mug. Kevon took a gigantic swig, leaned down, and placed the mug back in front of Tyrell, wishing he had a jug of his own. He needed a jolt after staying in bed all day yesterday after his mood had taken a dive like his bank account. Blowing his last fifty dollars at the bar was a mistake.

"Yo, don't be looking over here at mine, we all know you be acting like them chickadees," Andre said.

"Hello, gentlemen." Niche strolled up to the table and secured her hand on Kevon's waistband.

"Speaking of chickadees." Andre winked.

"I hope y'all don't mind if I take your boy away," Niche said as she grabbed Kevon's arm and pulled him toward an empty table.

"Naw, Niche, please take him, because he's leeching again," Andre jabbed. Kevon nodded his head in an effort to say "see ya" to his friends.

Once settled at a small, round table near the corner of the room, Kevon reached into his pocket and placed a playing card in the center. The ace of spades glimmered under a small lamp stationed next to the napkins.

"Okay, Niche, we need to make a decision. My card is on the

table. Bottom line is, I ain't ready to be no daddy. I mean, I can't be nobody's daddy. I love you, baby, but right now is not the time. Think about it. There isn't anything wrong with abortion. We don't want it." As soon as the word *abortion* escaped his mouth Kevon sensed a familiar sting and swallowed hard. He knew what it felt like to be unwanted.

At seven years old, he'd first overheard his parents arguing about if they should keep a child. His mother had been adamant that she didn't want any more children, but his father wouldn't let it go. His mother had argued that Kevon was enough and she didn't want more kids in the house. His father had countered that Kevon was not enough and that what was done, was done. His mother, unyielding in her refusal to add another, had declared she was going the next day to get it taken care of.

"There's nothing wrong with abortion? Kevon! One of the biggest debates in U.S. history, and you make it seem like it's going to get groceries."

"Women get abortions all the time. If I was pregnant, I would get one. We'll have plenty of time to have kids," Kevon whispered, glancing around the pub, not wanting to be overheard.

Niche shrugged her shoulders. "The problem is, Kevon, we are having one right now."

"True. But I'm thinking about you too. What about you, baby? What about applying to medical school? Niche, what about your mother? She'll kill you."

"The last thing I'm worried about is my mother. She has nothing to do with this," Niche rebutted.

"This is insane, this is not only your choice. It's not only your life." Kevon snatched a dirty napkin out of the holder, crumpled it, and began playing hockey.

"I'm getting angrier the more you speak. I can hardly believe you're *my* Kevon. It's as if someone has taken over your mind."

"My mind? My mind is clear. I told you to get rid of the thing, but you won't." Kevon shoved the napkin onto the floor.

"Here you go again, acting like a jerk. Last week, busting into my apartment, half-drunk, raging, like this is all my fault. Not to mention, throwing my phone against the wall. Forget this, forget that, was all you could say. You've never even asked me once what I was thinking." Niche's shoulders slumped as she stared down at the table.

Kevon leaned forward and raised his eyebrows. "Oh, blame me again. I'm not the only one that was off the hook that day. Let's not forget how you acted. Locking yourself in the bathroom was stupid. We were both acting childish. Which happens to further illustrate my point, we're not ready."

"I hate when you act like this. You could be so insensitive sometimes, and I'm tired of making excuses for you. Yes, I locked myself in the bathroom."

"Yes, you did," Kevon reiterated.

"So what! I refused to come out and talk to you, but did you have to leave? I feel guilty enough." Tears welled in her eyes as she grabbed a napkin from the dispenser. "I'd hoped that you would come around because I definitely don't want to do this by myself, but I will if I have to."

"So that's it? You're deciding this thing whether I like it or not." He pushed back from the table and stood up, ready to take off.

"Sit down!" Niche growled, her face reddening. "Kevon, this is not about you, this is about us. We have to work together on this. Why can't you understand that?"

"You better lower your voice," Kevon spat, looking toward his friends' table.

"I'm sorry, but try to understand, there's a child growing inside me, inside *me*, Kevon, not you. I don't want to vacuum it away and pretend it never happened. Kevon, this baby could be a gift from God."

Kevon stood up again, pulled a chair from the nearby table, and slammed it down next to her. He sat down, pulled her chair close to him, and whispered in her ear. "Gift from God. I don't know if you know this, Niche, but God doesn't conjure up nightmares. Leave God out of it, because He didn't get us in this situation. We did." Kevon rolled his eyes and shoved her chair away from him.

Niche steadied her legs underneath the wobbling chair. "I'm getting real tired of trying to convince the man I love to love me back."

Kevon picked up the playing card from the table and stuffed it in his back pocket. "If you have this baby, you do it alone!"

"If that is how you want it, fine!" Niche glared at Kevon straight in the eyes. "I'll schedule it, but I want you to know I'll never forget this." Niche rose and stormed out of the pub.

Robert

Robert rubbed his temples. He'd taken ibuprofen and acetaminophen but couldn't get rid of his headache. The throbbing behind his eye was nearly unbearable; he hadn't experienced a headache like this since Big Mama died. He secured the pill container and eyed the back of the medicine bottle. Every four to six hours had turned into two and still no relief. He slipped the bottle back into his shirt pocket and watched other patrons enjoying their meals.

Robert hadn't slept the entire night in days. He'd cleaned the garage, the storage shed, and the attic, and he still couldn't stop thinking about her, but when Angela had called him that morning insisting on breakfast, he had another reason to get out of bed. At first, he'd wanted to decline, but he hadn't spent time with his daughter in weeks. He hoped her smile could finally release him from his funk.

He glanced at his watch. It used to be his favorite. The black leather strap looked nice against his cinnamon skin, and the watch never pulled too tight or gave him a rash at the clasp. It had been a gift from Big Mama on the day he had his first child. She'd smiled at him, her teeth yellowed with time, declaring how proud she was of the man he'd become. Her laughter had roared, while he'd blushed. She'd repeated several times that he was no longer the foster child she'd raised but the son she'd always wanted. She'd squeezed his elbow and reminded him, like always, she was "just a phone call away." He wished he could call her now. Smell the hint of cigar that stayed on her breath. She'd help him through this. Depart a wisdom that only time and faith could supply.

"More water, sir?" The waiter stopped right in front of his table.

"No, thanks, my daughter is late, but she's on her way," he assured him. The small diner off Alemany Street was hardly noticeable from the freeway. He had run into it years ago on his postal route. He'd ordered a BLT when he came in to deliver their mail and picked it up on his way over to his next street. He'd been a regular customer here ever since. The walls were freshly painted, the menu updated, and the chairs repaired, but the delightful food was still the same.

Robert loosened the button constraining his neck on his starched white shirt and scrunched down in the booth. He was sure no one would notice if he shut his eyes.

He closed his eyes, and as soon as the light settled underneath the lids, he saw her. Her large brown eyes filled with laughter. She twirled around his mind's eye in the turquoise sundress he'd given her for her birthday. His eyelids flew open, he shook his head, and he swallowed the lump that had formed in his throat. He couldn't handle seeing her image so beautiful, lively, and alive.

Robert sat up, grabbed his glass, and gulped water to try and drown the memory. He picked up the menu and scoured the breakfast selections, gazing at the picture of a short stack doused in maple syrup. The saliva in his mouth pooled with anticipation. He'd stopped eating carbohydrates two months ago in preparation for the holidays, refusing to gain another ten pounds. His postal route had kept his body in shape and his hands in the community, but since retirement Robert had picked up a spare tire. Walking the streets was still a part of his morning routine, but he hadn't walked more than two miles in months.

"Hi, Daddy." Angela startled him as she slid into the opposite side of the booth. "Why are you scrunched down so low? I could hardly see you."

"I'm relaxing, I haven't had breakfast cooked for me in a while. How you doing, sweetheart?" Robert inquired. Angela grabbed the other menu that lay flat on the center of the table.

"I'm okay. Sorry I was late, but I got caught up with a client being reunited with her mother, and I said, for this, Daddy can wait." She smiled.

"Always. You hungry?" he asked, admiring his daughter's forthrightness. She didn't hold back, which made him proud. He was the same way as a young man, direct. Robert winked at his middle child who resembled his birth mother today. Before the drugs had blown the winds of ruin. Beautiful brown eyes set atop high cheekbones. Her complexion flawless like she'd been airbrushed. He was thankful she was gentle and kind, not at all like his mother who'd yelled at him for sport.

"Starving. I hardly ate dinner last night," Angela pouted, burying her head back in her menu. "I've been working on a tough case that I stumbled into. The case is consuming my days *and* nights. The mom . . ." She trailed off as Robert pulled her menu down toward the table and made direct eye contact.

"Angela, I didn't leave my morning coffee and drive all the way down here to talk about some case. I came to talk to my daughter." He could see the disappointment register in her eyes. "I haven't spent time with you in weeks, sweetheart. I want to catch up," Robert said, in an attempt to soften the blow. "Now, what's been going on in your life besides work?"

Angela reached for his hand. "That's exactly what I'm trying to figure out. I don't know what's going on for me. What have you been up to, Dad?"

Robert squeezed her hand. "Well, I been reminiscing. I was cleaning out the garage and found tons of old stuff." Robert couldn't help scouring through the garage for memorabilia from happier times. He needed to be reminded of what it felt like to be a father, a family, a lover.

"Daddy, you still cleaning that garage every fall? You're divorced, remember? Mom is not there to nag you anymore."

"Who says I cleaned the garage for her?" He threw up his hands. "I cleaned it for us." His eyes lifted. When he was a teenager all he'd thought about was starting his own household. A normal family that didn't have to move each year, live in cars, or beg for food. A family that only had one man with a key to the front door.

"Daddy, lying is a sin," Angela declared. Robert rolled his eyes playfully. He was grateful to look past his birth mother's reflection and hear his adoptive mom's imprint.

"Well, you got me there," he confessed. "But I got you here." He reached into his back pocket and pulled out a high school picture of her riding on her favorite bike. "Look what I ran across the other day. I was sifting through family photos, and I found this. This was the only picture that made my belly ache. I bet you don't even remember that bike." He slid the snapshot across the table.

"Oh, yes I do." Angela ran her finger over the image. "You bought it for my sixteenth birthday." Angela laughed. "All my friends wanted cars, but I wanted a new bike."

"You could've gotten a car, too, for as much as that bike cost." Robert shook his head.

"Well, I was a cyclist, Dad. I had to have the latest and greatest. I can't even count the amount of marathons I entered."

"Too many, I'd say. Weekends out biking, coming in dirty, sun-burned, and ashy in that stinking jersey shirt and shorts." Robert pinched his nose like he was trying to stop a nosebleed.

"You know it. Sixteen was a great year. When I buried that beater bike and started styling on my new wheels, no one could stop me." Angela simulated her hands like she was shifting gears.

"I couldn't figure it out, why you spent so much time on the open road, until about your senior year."

"What did you discover?" Angela leaned forward and whispered like a private investigator in a spy film.

"I finally discovered it was your passion. That bike was the only place I think you felt free from expectation. Honey, people are dedicated to things like work, school, relationships, music, but only some things bring joy. Remember when you used to harass me about taking the bike in for maintenance? You swore it prolonged the life of the bike. Well, that is also true for us. We have to clean our chains, grease our seat post, and use those gears. I, too, had something that brought me joy once, but I let it go and now I wish I had it back. Don't let joy slip out of your hands. Work is only a facet of you, don't neglect the other parts." Robert waved his menu at the waiter. "Now, let's get some of those pancakes."

16

Sharyn

The San Francisco Fillmore District had changed from when she was a girl. Gone were the large single-family homes. Those dwellings had been expertly transformed into duplexes and multiplexes. Trees had been planted, restaurants had sprung up, and streets had been cleaned. The people had changed also. Once rich with diversity, the Fillmore seemed reduced to a few cultures. Yet one thing remained, the jostling of people scurrying about to various destinations.

The waiting room of New Horizons Infertility Clinic was chilly, but her body temperature was almost feverish. Sharyn pulled the handkerchief from her purse and wiped sweat from her brow, again. She'd been overheating all day. Changing her shirt twice, blasting her air-conditioning, and stepping outside three times hadn't helped at all. Big Mama would've said the devil was at her heels.

Sharyn tried to distract herself by staring out of the huge bay windows. She'd seen men—from businessmen to skateboarders—pass, but it seemed like every woman looked inside to catch a glimpse of the barren. Sharyn dropped her head low when she thought she recognized the head usher from St. John's. The television mounted on the wall played several advertisements for the clinic, but the pounding in her head made it difficult to concentrate.

The waiting room was plush and modern. Chairs made of

imitation black leather were so comfortable that if Sharyn could relax, she knew she would be tempted to fall asleep, especially since she'd only slept three hours the night before.

"Here, try a magazine." The miniature brunette passed Sharyn a periodical. She'd hardly even noticed the center table filled with publications. "Hormones can be rough."

"Thank you." Sharyn smiled, surprised someone had noticed her. The waiting room was crowded, and the clientele mirrored the diversity of the San Francisco Bay Area. Some women appeared upper middle class without the burden of deprivation, and others looked like relics plucked straight out of Woodstock and everything in between. The women reflected a rainbow of cultures, and no dominant age was apparent.

Sharyn fanned herself with the *Parent Buzz* magazine. Her face crinkled as she noticed the front cover. She hated seeing images of babies, and today it felt like a shot in her arm. No matter if she looked away, the aftermath still ached. She sat quietly in her chair, biting her lip and tapping her foot as she waited for her name to be called. Her pulse quickened as she scanned the room and noticed one commonality that screamed in silence yet spoke volumes. The elephant that commanded the room . . . each woman had a flat abdomen. Sharyn took in a deep breath. She couldn't let her surroundings cloud the list of questions that played in her head; she had to try and keep her mind straight.

Sharyn's navy pantsuit bore a coffee stain that was a result of the jitters. Her snug Jones of New York ensemble emphasized her curvaceous figure, and her short hair framed her frightened face. She'd curled her hair around her face this morning in an attempt to go unnoticed, but it had frizzed uncontrollably from the fog that blanketed San Francisco today. She dug in her purse, searching for a stick of gum to help with the ball that was forming in her throat.

Frizzy hair, perspiration, and trembling hands kept Sharyn from inquiring of the receptionist about wait times. Her office and her husband thought she was out on a research assignment. She'd never lied like this before.

"Ms. Lovelace, you can come in now." The tall Peruvian nurse startled her. Her serious face and heavy accent stood in contrast to the lighthearted polka-dot scrubs and white baby-doll sweater she wore. Sharyn paused for a moment; she hadn't been referred to as Ms. Lovelace in years. Hearing her maiden name made her stomach lunge. *"Are you full?"* echoed in her head.

Sharyn had been careful to pay for the visit out of her personal checking account, and she'd even hid the appointment confirmation in her glove box. Her deception was concealed, but she still couldn't settle her nerves. Sharyn placed the magazine carefully back on the table like it was marked fragile. As she followed the nurse, she was stunned by the wobbling of her knees as she finally walked toward her future.

Once alone in the examination room, Sharyn waited in silence for the physician. Confidentiality was paramount, so she checked her telephone twice and made sure her ringer was off and the safety lock was on. The echoing of doors opening and closing from the hallway made her more anxious. Her heart fluttered when she heard the bang of a clipboard outside her door.

"Hello, Sharyn. I'm Dr. Shankar. Sorry for the delay. We are busy today." Dr. Shankar shook her hand enthusiastically.

"I understand. It's a pleasure to finally meet you." Sharyn avoided his eyes.

"Likewise. I look forward to assisting you throughout this discovery process. Now, let's get down to business, as it were." Dr. Shankar started fast and never slowed down. His sterility caught her off guard. She was expecting someone less scientific. Sharyn felt sweat gathering again on her forehead as her lips chapped from constant licking. She wanted a doctor who was sensitive and caring like her personal practitioner. The handsome specialist didn't even look up as he pointed out fallopian tubes on a poster hung high on the wall and explained the reproductive system.

"Initially, I'll run you through some of our standard testing procedures. These are routine tests to help us complete our assessment process, and remember, Ms. Lovelace, my staff and I are here to help you in any way we can," Dr. Shankar explained robotically. "We are your partners in fertility." Sharyn cleared her throat and looked down at her spiral notebook full of notes she could hardly understand. She wondered if she had done the right thing. He didn't look like the man on the television commercial, but he sure sounded like him.

"Thank you. I look forward to finally getting some answers." Sharyn lowered her eyes, missing her life partner. Michael always accompanied her to doctor appointments. Ever since her abortion she'd developed white-coat syndrome, her blood pressure skyrocketing at the start of each office visit, later only to return to normal once the appointment was complete.

"My staff took your medical history, and from the self-administered questionnaires you completed, we gathered some necessary information." Sharyn reviewed her forms along with the emotionless physician while she carefully watched the clock hung over the sink. She'd been at the clinic almost two hours, she realized, as he continued to explain the various barriers to conception. "Statistically, most couples who have intercourse without contraception conceive within the first year, but a whole host of factors can affect fertility, from age to tubal status. Some fertility issues can be corrected with minimal intervention or medications, but some require more invasive strategies, as I have already outlined," Dr. Shankar said.

"I would like to start the process as soon as possible. I could set something up for next week." Sharyn glanced at her telephone stationed next to her and thought about checking for missed calls.

Timeliness was important to her, and she didn't want to arouse Michael's suspicion.

"From the information I've obtained from you, it appears we can move right along into the second step of the process, Ms. Lovelace. I've examined your history, and I believe we can proceed to the next phase." Dr. Shankar smiled.

"The next phase? Today?" Sharyn questioned, unsure if she wanted to move forward.

"Don't worry, the first tests are simple. It's a standard pregnancy test and some blood work. We can do that right here in the office. After administering the pregnancy test, then we will set up a time for an ultrasound and send you down to the lab for a draw," Dr. Shankar said, handing her a brochure.

"Dr. Shankar, negative pregnancy tests are what brought me here. I've taken about a hundred pregnancy tests, and they all have the same result." Sharyn worked to maintain her composure as she tried to remember the time she told Michael she'd be home. She must have spent over a thousand dollars on pregnancy tests already, and like the lottery, she came up short each time.

"Pregnancy testing will become common throughout this process. Most of our clients are used to frequent testing. I also need to forewarn you that infertility is complex and results aren't immediate. No patient will see results overnight. However, finding out if there are roadblocks and what kind that exist is a very important step."

"That's exactly why I'm here," Sharyn lamented.

"Well, my staff and I will also determine what, if any, treatment options could benefit you. We also have mental health professionals on staff who are available for ongoing support throughout this arduous process," Dr. Shankar reassured her.

"Treatment options?" Sharyn questioned, readying her notepad.

"A couple of options occur at our clinic and others at our contract facilities. It depends on the type of testing required. Remember, a third of infertility issues stem from the female, but another third can stem from the male."

"My husband will not be a part of this process," Sharyn said, feeling the weight of her aloneness.

"Semen analysis is generally the other central part of our testing, but we can definitely proceed without your partner." Dr. Shankar smiled reassuringly. "I know this is an abundance of information and it can be confusing and overwhelming, but we want you to have a clear understanding prior to undertaking the initial testing process."

Sharyn ran her fingers through her hair, anxiety building in her chest. "So do I, but this is overwhelming," she exclaimed, thinking more about deceiving her husband instead of the physician's revelations. She placed her hand over her belly button to try and reassure herself that the end justified the means.

"As I stated before, there is no need to worry. The first test administered is a pregnancy test."

"Yes. And if at any time I have questions, can I give you a call?" Sharyn was on overload, and she needed to get out of there.

Dr. Shankar stood up and headed toward the door. "Certainly. Nice meeting you, Sharyn. I look forward to working with you."

Sharyn smiled at Dr. Shankar as he closed the door. She began to examine her notes when a lofty African-American nurse entered the room.

"Ms. Lovelace, here is your sample container. Good luck." The nurse smiled and winked simultaneously at Sharyn, and she couldn't help but smile back.

The adjoining restroom was clean and smelled of citrus. Filling the sample cup was easy, but looking in the mirror was more difficult. Sharyn reminded herself that she didn't lie to her husband habitually, then exited the restroom, handed the urine sample to the nurse, and waited for further instructions. Sharyn cautiously hopped up on the exam table and further studied her notes. Dr. Shankar opened the door minutes later and took a seat on the silver stool.

"Sharyn, you've improved our success rate." He laughed. "Congratulations—our test indicates that you are already pregnant."

Kevon

Kevon slammed the front door, threw his leather bomber jacket onto the living room couch, and headed for the kitchen. The dark quiet greeted him like the stillness of an empty movie theater.

"Daddy, you home?" Kevon grabbed a bottle of cranberry juice from the refrigerator, took a swig, and sat the half-empty bottle on the granite countertop. He glanced to the back of the refrigerator, wishing he could grab one of the beers his father kept in the vegetable cooler for company. "I can't even have a beer in my own house," Kevon murmured, closing the stainless steel door. A familiar resentment cemented in his stomach. "One day Robert Lovelace will recognize the man that I am," Kevon professed, picking up the landline to dial Niche. "I make my own decisions." He leaned against the counter and eyed the framed artwork that he'd created in elementary school. The rickety house stood next to a beautiful stick figure family, all holding hands. Kevon chuckled at the fairy tale he'd once created. His family was nothing like he'd imagined.

Niche's voicemail message responded after the first ring. "Hey, baby, I wanted to tell you that I appreciate what you're doing for me," Kevon said. "When you get the date and time for the abortion, let me know. I plan to be there with you every step of the way. It's going to be fine, you'll see. Holla back." Kevon hung up the telephone, snatched his cranberry juice off the counter, and grabbed a granola bar from the cabinet. Stuffing the granola bar in his back pocket, he turned on his heels and headed toward his bedroom.

Startled, Kevon felt tingling register in his extremities, and he almost dropped the bottle. He stood eye to eye with his father and couldn't avoid his menacing glare.

"Hey, Daddy." Kevon's voice skipped like a deeply embedded scratch on a vinyl album. Kevon knew from the look on his father's face that his message to Niche hadn't been private. Anxiously his mind raced, looking for a way to escape the impending confrontation. He nodded and attempted to walk past his dad, but Robert grabbed his arm and shoved him back toward the refrigerator. Kevon stared him down, like a Wild West gunslinger about to shoot.

"Boy, you might want to sit down, now!" Robert's nostrils flared. Kevon retraced his steps and slowly sat down at the kitchen table. Robert yanked out an adjacent chair.

"What's up, Dad?" Kevon asked, trying to sound lighthearted as he took another swig of juice. Acting was not his craft, but playing dumb was.

"What's up, Dad? *What's up, Dad?* I'll tell you what's up. We need to talk." Robert eyeballed his son.

"About what?" Kevon took a sip of cranberry juice, avoiding eye contact. Like the juice, his father was bitter to the taste but had some benefits.

"Listen here, boy, I don't want to hear another word out of you until I ask you to say something. I heard your telephone conversation, and I take it from what you said Niche is pregnant and you want her to have an abortion."

"But Dad—" Kevon interrupted, wishing he'd never come home.

"Kevon, I'm going to be straight up here. I've had to put up with your irresponsibility and bull ever since you turned eighteen. I can't even begin to tell you how I feel about the man sitting here before me."

"Dad, let me explain," Kevon pleaded, boxing himself into his usual routine of sad eyes and remorseful banter.

"It's taking everything in me not to jump over this table right now. Don't push me. You've disappointed me time and time again." Robert wiped his brow. "And you know what, truthfully on several occasions I've even blamed myself for not raising you right. Did I spoil you too much? Was I too hard on you or not hard enough? I tell you what though, I couldn't come up with any answers. You are who you are, and there is nothing else I can do about it." Robert shook his head.

"You're right, Dad, I am." Kevon sat straight up in his chair.

"I'm not playing. Be quiet, boy. You act like a wayward child. I say a child because you're not a man, and that's what disappoints me the most—you don't even try. You're turning into someone I don't even know or even care to know. You're lazy, disrespectful, and you drink too damn much. Do you hear me, boy?" Robert slammed his fist down on the table.

"Yes, sir, I hear you," Kevon mumbled, wanting to break free of his father's tirade. He wondered if Shameka was still going to the club tonight. After a fight with his dad he always required some shots.

"You better hear me and hear me clearly. I'm not going to stand by and watch you force this woman into getting an abortion. I'm not, Kevon. You're a Lovelace, like it or not. Your father is one, your uncle, and we tried hard to set examples. If you do this, you aren't a Lovelace in my eyes. Life is not a party, and at some point you are going to have to stand up and take responsibility for what you do."

"I don't think it's your—" Kevon started.

"Who told you that I want to know what you think? Not only will this family hold you accountable for your actions, but the Almighty will as well. Psalms 53, boy: *God looks down from heaven on all mankind to see if there are any who understand, any who seek God.* Until you're willing to be accountable, and seek God, I don't want you in my house. And I'm sure that your mama will feel the same way when I tell her."

"Daddy, don't." Kevon shook his head.

"Kevon, you've become someone else, something else. I'm getting tired of your highs and lows, and now you gonna go ahead and mess up this girl's life."

"But Daddy!" Kevon yelled. Robert placed one extended finger in the air as to silence him.

"I told you, don't speak until you're told, unless you want to go and pack your clothes right now. This is your last and final warning, and I mean it. Thirty days, you got thirty days."

"Daddy, can I speak?" Kevon's eyes lowered.

"What?" Robert barked.

"I didn't do anything." Kevon rubbed his forehead, flabbergasted by the irony. His father preaching how irresponsible he was but thinking it was a good idea for him and Niche to have a child.

"You never do. Now, if you're not going to take responsibility for that baby, I'll have to. And I'll tell you this, too, all that I give that child will be taken away from you, because you don't deserve it."

Kevon lowered his head and slumped in the chair, unsure of what to say to make him understand. He could hardly even take care of himself.

"I will not enable you to turn into the type of man I despise, not in my house right under my nose. I release you." Robert raised his hands and looked up to the ceiling. "I release him, Lord." He stood up and headed toward the family room.

"But Daddy, it's a fetus." His eyes widened as he noticed his dad stop short at the entrance of the kitchen.

"As sure as I drink coffee in the morning, I'll kick you out for good. Thirty days, then we'll see what type of friends you got. One day we will all have to choose, son, whom we will serve, and as for me and my house, we will serve the Lord."

17

Angela

The Sanctuary was bursting with energy this morning. Joy pulsed from clapping hands and shaking tambourines. Church members celebrated the goodness of the Lord on this Thanksgiving Day. The building was crowded, and the ushers diligently manned the floor. The doorkeeper outfitted in black and white shifted her white glove–covered hand toward the front of the church. Angela and Sharyn followed her direction down the middle aisle. Angela elbowed her sister as she spotted another white glove perched in the air directing her to move forward. Both ladies smiled as they squished into the tenth pew near the front. Angela leaned down and placed her handbag on the floor, accidently bumping the parishioner next to her.

"Excuse me," Angela apologized, and leaned forward, attempting to adjust to the sardine-can arrangements. She could hardly see the pulpit from behind the display of hands raised in worship.

Members of St. John's were standing as they finished the morning hymn, and Angela still couldn't find her voice. "I got Jesus on the inside, and He is working on the outside," Angela mouthed in unison. She couldn't help but notice the watchful eye of Reverend Martin Broussard looking on from the pulpit. Angela dodged his glance and darted her eyes toward her mother,

Rose, perched in the third row of the choir stands. She sat down hard next to Sharyn and crossed her legs, trying not to crowd the woman next to her.

"Look at Mama." Angela leaned into her sister's ear. "I haven't seen her in two weeks."

"I hope she sings my song today. She killed it last week, the whole church caught the fire." Sharyn took a paper fan from the usher walking down the aisle.

"I bet she did," Angela agreed. Rose sang tenor and was a featured soloist in the harmonious mass choir. Angela and Sharyn's voices, high and squeaky, were the exact opposite of their mother's deep and soothing voice. "What did she sing?" Angela grabbed her sister's fan to cool herself off from the oversized camel sweater she'd picked out at the last minute.

"'How Great Thou Art.' Where were you, anyway?" Sharyn elbowed her sister.

"Now, you know I wasn't gonna come to the revival last week, *even if* the mass choir was on the program. Martin was the keynote speaker for the entire week, and I need to shut down the rumor mill. I'm not trying to deal with that," Angela whispered.

"I think you're avoiding him altogether." Sharyn patted her sister's leg. Angela knew Sharyn was right. Ever since their date, she'd been feeling more uncomfortable around him. She couldn't look Martin in the eye anymore, convinced he could see the darkness bubbling within her, like an oil spill tainting the ocean. Fornication had taken residence in her flesh. She used to feel bad, but last year the guilt had subsided. Recently it had resurfaced, complete with panic attacks.

"He has no right to inquire about who else I'm dating. Who does he think he is? I'm not Potiphar's wife. I'm having fun and not with him, mind you." Angela rolled her eyes.

"However you want to justify it, Ang."

"I'm working on it, but I'm human," Angela lied, knowing she needed a change but was unsure how to make one.

"Excuse me," Sister Jackson said quietly as she tapped Angela on the shoulder. "Can you pass me that hymnal?"

Angela's thoughts were interrupted as Sister Jackson forced her into the present, and she caught her mother winking from the choir stand. Angela loved her mother, and that simple gesture filled her heart with joy. She disagreed with her sister; her mother wasn't selfish. Rose was a driven woman who looked beautiful, standing with confidence in a navy-blue-and-gold dress with gold-tone buttons down the middle, her navy-blue-and-gold hat parading above the other choir members. Her mother didn't try to be the center of attention, but she often was. Angela decided she was exactly like her mother, misunderstood. Only God knew what her father had put her through.

Angela nudged her sister. "It might be helpful to spend some alone time with Mama. It's been a while since we had a mother and daughter bonding day." Angela smiled. "I'm going to try and see what her schedule is like next week. Maybe we can take her out for some of that Texas barbeque off of Market Street."

"I haven't been to that restaurant in a long time. Those ribs are the real deal." Sharyn's eyes widened.

"Are you and Mike headed over to Mom's right after church? Where is he today, anyway?"

Sharyn grinned. "Michael had to work a half-day today. I haven't heard from Kevon. I think Thanksgiving will be Mike, me, you, and ole Reverend Broussard." Sharyn nudged Angela's arm.

"You think so, huh?" Angela shook her head emphatically.

"He's not on the menu today, huh?" Sharyn teased.

"He is definitely on the table, but I got me a new side dish. He might not be the one for life, but he just might be the one for tonight."

Sharyn raised her eyebrow and stared directly at her sister. "I thought Jonathan was no longer a side."

Angela's shoulders raised. "Who's talking about Jonathan?" Angela smacked her lips thinking about the man she met yesterday.

"I thought you were trying." Sharyn rolled her eyes.

"I am, but a sister's got to eat," Angela said, fanning herself.

"Shhhh," Sister Brown whispered behind them. Angie and Sharyn giggled like they were still kids.

"Save room for the turkey." Sharyn sighed. Angela smiled at her sister and vowed to keep silent for the rest of the service. She had to communicate old school, so lowering her head, she slipped Sharyn a note and prayed that Sister Brown didn't see her.

Angela loved preparing for the Thanksgiving family feast. She couldn't wait to get to her mother's house. Thanksgiving was almost in full swing, and Rose was a stickler for promptness. The church service was excellent, and now it was time to celebrate with her family.

Angela shuffled to the bathroom once more to survey her reflection. She'd changed clothes as soon as she got home, wanting to be picture-perfect before he arrived. Strategically placing three bobby pins in her hair ought to do it. The smell of citrus and gladiolas danced in her nostrils as she lifted her arms. Angela smiled. She loved her new fragrance.

Her sage-green cashmere sweater complemented her charcoal-gray slacks. She plopped her gray bowler hat onto her head and adjusted it slightly. She smiled at her reflection and snuck a quick peek out of her bathroom window at the overcast sky overhead. It had rained most of the night, and her apartment temperature testified. She grabbed the gray cashmere scarf draped on the door handle and headed back to the living room.

Angela headed straight to her blue tooth speaker and turned on the music. Martin loved Richard Smallwood, and Angela owned each album. Her body swayed to the rhythm of the gospel music.

She hadn't danced since receiving Trevion's case, and it felt good. She could feel her stress melting away.

Angela twirled around the room, singing loud and off-key. Hearing a horn honk, she skirted to the window again, in time to view his red Honda maneuvering into the empty parking space in front of her condo. Martin jumped out of his car and galloped up the walkway steps to her building entrance. Angela fanned her face. He looked handsome, dressed in a gray pullover sweater that matched the dark, gloomy sky. His tailored black slacks accentuated his confident stride.

Angie opened her door and greeted him with a strong, tight embrace. They stood in the doorway holding each other like a riveter saying farewell at a train depot. She glanced into his dark brown eyes, adorned with thick, long, black lashes. He tilted her face upward and touched his lips softly against hers.

"Good afternoon," he said, licking his lips. "You look beautiful as usual. Now, I know I'm late, but I ran into traffic after church. Forgive me?" He loosened his embrace, walked past her into the living room, and headed toward the kitchen. "Where are the groceries?"

Angela looked him up and down. Who was this man? He was unfamiliar in her experience, a truly rare breed. Martin seemed to always put her needs first, and she loved how he always was sensitive to her feelings. He was gentle, thoughtful, and caring. She didn't care if he was late or not. All she cared about was that he was here with her now.

"They're packed and ready right here. If it was a dog, it would've bit you. Now come on, we'd better get out of here, Mom is going to kill us. Well not me, you, Reverend Broussard." Angela grabbed his arm and tugged him toward the door.

Angela snatched her purse off the couch as the telephone rang. She swayed her hips as she skirted back toward the kitchen. Martin waved frantically from the door, signaling her not to answer. He smiled and hunched his shoulders as Angela picked up the cordless receiver.

"Hello?" Angela answered, smiling shamefaced.

"Happy Thanksgiving, baby," Jonathan responded from the receiver.

"Happy Thanksgiving to you too. How are you?" Angela queried, her voice light and airy.

"Missing you," Jonathan chuckled. "What are you up to today?"

"I'm going to my mother's for dinner. And you?" Angela held one finger in the air and smiled at Martin as his eyes danced with curiosity. He placed the bags on the floor, crossed his arms, and leaned against the door.

"I'm headed over to my parents'. Check this out, lovely, I have a question for you. Would it be cool to stop by your mom's? I have something for you," Jonathan said enthusiastically.

Angela turned her back to Martin and whispered into the receiver. "Oh, you're too kind; however, that isn't such a great idea. We could arrange something later, okay?" Angela said.

"Okay, cool. I'll definitely get with you later. You have a wonderful Thanksgiving Day, sweetness." Jonathan hung up the receiver before Angela could say goodbye.

Angela turned back around and slowly placed the telephone on the base. Martin's jaw tightened.

"Sorry about that, Martin. Now, let's get going." Angela followed him to his car. The passenger-side chair was stiff as she slipped into her seat. The cold black leather matched the mood that was rapidly growing between them. Martin placed the groceries in the trunk and plopped down hard in the driver's seat. He turned on the ignition and drove hurriedly down the empty street.

Angela flipped on the radio, reclined her seat backward, and closed her eyes as the music soothed her. She could feel Martin shifting in his seat as the tension thickened. His hand patted her thigh.

"Angela, who was on the phone?" Martin squeezed her leg softly as he hopped onto the freeway.

"That was Jonathan. He's a friend I see from time to time. It's nothing too serious," Angela reassured him. Martin's eyebrows furrowed as his calm vanished.

"I should hope not! You know, I've been meaning to have a discussion about this. After two years, you should know how I feel about you, right? But this thing here, I have to tell you—something has been bothering me."

"What's that, Martin?" Angela opened her eyes, tiring of his insecurities. She turned her head, refusing to look at him, instead focusing her attention out of the window, watching cars jockey on the freeway.

"Every time your telephone rings, it's someone new."

"What's that supposed to mean?" She could feel her heart palpitating.

"Well, it's like some new brotha is always hanging on the line. What's up with that?" Martin asked, rubbing her leg.

"What's up with what? I'm a single woman." Angela pushed his hand away.

"Now, hold up, I try to give you all the space you need. Believe me, I don't want to crowd you. But it bothers me when someone calls you while I'm at your house. It bothers me when someone from church sees you out to dinner with someone else. I'm being honest."

"Oh, not the church gossip again," Angela said, adjusting her car seat upright. She wanted to sit up for this challenge.

"This isn't about people at church. This is about me. It troubles me that you keep seeing different men. Not to mention, you don't even tell me about these guys."

"That's not true, Martin. I told you. You don't listen. Last year, I even brought Curtis to church so you could see him *and* to shut down the rumor mill. I didn't have to do that. You're the one who keeps telling me we're just friends. What else do you want from me?" Angela smacked her lips as she tasted his condescension. Martin was like a piece of sour candy, so sweet at times, but his aftertaste could be off-putting. She gathered her breath.

"I knew Curtis was nothing. He wasn't even your type, but at least while I was sitting at your house watching a movie, I knew the guy who was on the phone. It was okay with me for you to see him on and off. But who is this Jonathan cat?"

"Look, Martin, I cannot and will not parade my friends in front of you. I don't need your approval. That is too much to ask, King Xerxes."

He shot her a strange look. "Angela, ain't nobody trying to rule over you. I only want you to govern yourself."

Angela felt the sting of this truth burn in her chest. She gathered her thoughts. This situation was his fault, not hers. "We had an agreement, Martin, and now you're flip-flopping. At first, it was important for the church to see me with someone else, so folks wouldn't be aware of the woman you were interested in. Now, things have up and changed. Seriously, Martin? When you're ready, really ready, I'll be all yours. Until then, I'm not going to put my life on hold. You're the one choosing your good thing. Not me." Angela crossed her arms, grateful that the freeway exit to her mother's was next.

"Flip-flopping is one thing, but I feel like you got me on an assembly line. Truthfully, I'm having the hardest time keeping up with you. Do these men even know about me, Angela?"

"What?" Angela threw her head back. The temperature in her body was rising faster than a teakettle set on high.

"Do these guys know who *you're* choosing? I have all these unanswered questions in my head. How do you feel about me? Goodness, I only hope you're not sleeping with them. Are you, Angie? Are you sleeping with them? I know what goes on."

"Now you want details about my sex life." Angela threw up her hands.

"You don't even know what goes on in my head at night. All the questions. Believe me, I don't want any details, and I hope there aren't any. Am I not enough for you?" Martin asked with disgust.

"Enough? Enough what? We've been friends, Martin. When I try to get close to you, you pull away. For goodness' sake. We *just* started kissing. Did you hear me, kissing, Martin, after two years? The real question is, am I enough for you? Good enough, that is!" Angela yelled.

18

Sharyn

Sharyn glanced down at her watch and wondered where her sister was, fighting the urge to get up and call her. She was tiring of taking care of everyone and needed to focus on herself. Now more than ever, her priorities had to change. She snuck her hand under her sweetheart crimson blouse and rubbed her stomach.

"Where the heck is Angie?" Kevon snapped. "I'm hungry, and personally, I don't think we should have to wait for her. If I got my butt out of bed and made it to the house, she could too." Kevon raised from his mother's rocking chair and peered out the window.

"Shut up, Kevon." Sharyn grabbed the tail of his white dress shirt and pulled him back toward his seat. "As many times as we've waited for you and you didn't even make it out of bed, you need to shut your fat mouth. Besides, we all were at church this morning except you." Sharyn had been keeping Kevon in line for years, and she planned on continuing this family tradition.

Rose cleared her throat. "Both of you need to be quiet and watch your mouths. Kevon, sit down, Angela will be here shortly. I already called her apartment and she wasn't there, so relax."

Kevon sat back down, and Niche snuggled comfortably between his legs. Rose leaned back on her cream couch and robotically wiped dust off the hand-carved wooden leg. Michael sat motionless on the cream love seat next to Sharyn.

"Mother, what are we having, anyway? I'm starving." Michael dramatically grabbed his stomach. Sharyn rubbed his leg, grateful for the redirection. Her cinnamon hands blended in with his russet slacks. She was thankful he didn't move his leg and embarrass her in front of the family, and she slipped him a knowing glance. Their eyes met, and a tenderness came over him. She wondered if she was reading into things or if it was the spirit of Thanksgiving that made him more welcoming.

"The usual, honey." Rose smoothed the black apron tied about her waist.

"You sure must've put it together fast, Mom. There's not a speck of flour on that apron." Sharyn shifted her gaze and admired her mother's ensemble. After church, her mother had changed into an eggshell angora sweater and matching pleated skirt that blended in with the couch. Rose's hair cascaded over her shoulders, creating a dramatic appearance that resembled a 1960s movie star.

"Honey, I can make salmon croquettes in my sleep." Rose tossed her hair over her shoulder, garnering the attention Sharyn knew she always craved. Robert appeared at the entryway of the living room. His black mock turtleneck and black slacks made him look as if he'd committed a burglary.

"The game over, Daddy?" Sharyn asked.

"No. Finally, that gal is here. Let's eat." Robert pointed toward the window. One by one they all filed toward the dining room, leaving Sharyn and Michael behind.

"I'll get the door," Michael said, as he motioned to the others. Sharyn wondered if he hung back to keep distance between them.

Martin opened the door before her husband could get to it. He walked in the house and headed toward the dining room, barely glancing in their direction. "Happy Turkey Day."

Angela staggered in behind him, balancing shopping bags in both hands, and walked straight toward the kitchen, nearly knocking Sharyn over. "Sorry I'm late, you guys, but traffic was a nightmare!" Angela called.

"And hello to you too. Everyone's in the dining room." Sharyn grabbed a bag, linked arms with her sister, and pulled her toward the rest of the family.

"There is no one here. We starved to death." Kevon stuck out his tongue as his sisters appeared in the entryway. Almost every chair in the dining room was occupied. The formal decor set the stage for their annual holiday brunch. The red tablecloth matched the red drapes her mother hung only during the holidays. The china serving dishes and polished silverware were handled with care, and fresh poinsettias occupied the room's corners. Sharyn spotted two empty seats near Michael. She hurried past Angela and sat down next to her husband.

"Shut up, I didn't hear nobody asking you." Angela set her bag on the floor and popped him over the back of his head as she scooted by his chair. "You too good to go to church now?" she teased. Angela circled the table, kissing her family. "Kevon, grab those bags and put them in the refrigerator. Where's Mom? Still in the kitchen?" Angela asked.

"You know it." Sharyn pulled out the chair next to her, wondering why her sister was so late. Angela sat down near Sharyn and shot her a knowing glance as Martin and Rose entered the dining room, hands full of white serving dishes.

"All right, let's eat some brunch. Reverend Broussard, you wouldn't mind saying grace, would you?" Robert winked.

"No. Not at all, Deac. All heads bowed and minds clear. Father God, we praise Your Holy and Righteous Name. We thank You today for providing us with wonderful families, friends, laughter, food, and love. We pray that the food will provide nourishment for our bodies, as Your Word is to our hearts and souls. We pray for blessings on those who are without food, a home, and a family, Lord, provide and encourage. These things, we ask in Jesus's name. Amen."

"That was a short prayer, Martin," Sharyn said, used to his prayer sermonettes when they broke bread with him. She placed some bacon on her plate and wondered what had occurred this morning between him and her sister. The last thing she wanted was conflict on the day set aside for gratefulness.

"To be honest, Martin, I was thinking the same thing," Rose agreed.

"Well, I apologize, Lovelace family, but this here minister is hungry," Martin said, as he dug the serving fork into the scrambled eggs. "To make up for lost time, I'll be sure and pray for about thirty minutes on Sunday."

"Sorry I brought it up!" Sharyn elbowed Angela in the side and then grabbed some eggs. Her appetite had grown ever since she found out she was pregnant. She'd heard about morning sickness and cravings, but her ravenous appetite had taken her by surprise. "Kevon, pass me a piece of that salmon before things get any fishier."

The marble island in the kitchen was full of various ingredients piled high. Onions, bell peppers, and garlic commanded their own corner while seasonings owned the other. After brunch, each woman worked dutifully at her own station, preparing something essential for that evening's feast. The rattling of spice bottles, the rhythm of movement, and the sound of laughter synthesized like a drumline.

"Hand me the brown sugar and orange juice, please, Mom." Sharyn doused the ham with lemon-lime soda. She'd learned Big Mama's recipe by heart and planned to carry it out to perfection. The sweet smell of brown sugar made her mouth water as she dumped it over the ham. Sharyn grinned as memory of her grandmother in the kitchen warmed her heart.

"Did someone say brown sugar? Angie, Reverend Broussard is sure looking like some brown sugar *today*." Niche chuckled.

"Yes, he does. However, he is more like salt than sugar," Angela confessed.

"Really?" Sharyn glanced at her sister, knowing that look on her face spelled trouble. Pursed lips, crinkled eyebrows, and the left-sided jaw clench were always indicators that something was amiss. Sharyn wondered what her sister had done this time. Frequent fighting on the elementary school playground had become the norm for both girls because of what Angela had said. "I was wondering why you came in carrying the bags?"

"Yeah, we aren't on the best of terms right now. He happens to be mad at me," Angela disclosed, as the rhythm in the kitchen slowed to a halt.

"What happened, girl?" Niche asked.

"Well, let's see. He has the audacity to be angry because I didn't tell Jonathan about him. My position is, why should I? Martin and I are *just* friends." Angela grabbed a handful of string beans.

"Friends?" Sharyn poked out her lips and reached for an orange. She sniffed the peel and squeezed hard, knowing sometimes pressure helped to release all the juice.

"C'mon, Sharyn, you know I'm still getting a peck on the lips and a date here or there."

"No, you come on, Angela," Sharyn prodded, squeezing the citrus and her sister harder. She knew her sister had the lion's share of male friends, but no other man had captured her heart like Martin Broussard.

"At the rate we are going, by the time we get to fondling, I'll be forty-five. Needless to say, I don't think this stage in our relationship warrants full disclosure." Angela shook her head.

"Fondling? Did you say that in my house?" Rose looked up from the simmering stockpot on the stove and raised her eyebrows.

"Sorry, Mom. Martin pissed me off, that's all." Angela resumed snapping string beans with renewed intensity.

Sharyn agreed with her sister. She was gradually learning to submit to her husband, but a boyfriend was different altogether. Her mother had instructed them long ago that when it came to men, no papers meant no permission. "You're right on this one, Ang. That's bold. I mean, unless he makes some sort of permanent move, he can't tell you what to do." Sharyn laughed as she pictured Martin trying to instruct her sister.

Angela threw her hands up in the air. "I know, it's funny, huh. Like I'm supposed to announce to men I'm dating, 'I'm also seeing this reverend, periodically, but he takes priority over everyone else in my life.' Please!"

"But he does," Niche said.

"Whatever, Niche. If I meet Mr. Right, then I meet him. I refuse to scare away any man with the drama Martin brings to my life. I'm not anybody's Sister Teresa."

"Isn't that Mother?" Niche wagged her finger at Angela. "Anyway, Kevon gives me his opinion all the time, and I don't mind. I like it when he gets bossy."

"I bet you do." Angela laughed.

"Okay, ladies, that's enough." Rose stomped her foot. "Look, I try to stay out of you women's lives. However, this time, listen to your mother. Martin is an honorable man."

Sharyn smiled, knowing her mother would take Martin's side. He was a man of status, and that's all that mattered to her. When Sharyn had told her mother about her first boyfriend, all she'd asked about was where he lived and his parents' occupation. "Girl, Martin is . . ." Sharyn intercepted her mother's advice as she stepped back from the island, beheld the ham, and admired her handiwork.

Angela interrupted, "I know what y'all about to say. Martin is a believer who works in ministry. He has a good job. He cares for me.

He's smart. He's all that, but I tell you what he isn't . . . committed. I would marry him tomorrow if he'd ask me. There is one problem, he hasn't." Angela could feel her face heating up.

"Maybe he's working up to it, honey," Rose said, stirring a can of broth into the stockpot.

"As a strong black woman, I'm prepared to deal with whatever. I love him and I know that, but my heart is in my chest, not on my sleeve. I'm not willing to sacrifice myself, and I'm not the type of woman to wait around," Angela proclaimed.

"I think we *all* know that," Sharyn confirmed.

Sharyn hated to leave the warmth of the family household and return to the icy domicile that she and Michael had created. She left her mom's home with arms filled with leftovers, a mind echoing with merriment, and a tender heart.

The ride home was quiet as she dozed off once Michael pulled onto the 280 freeway. She was awakened by the thump of their car pulling up into the driveway. Sharyn stumbled out of the car, still half asleep, almost hitting the green recycling container in the garage that led to the adjoining hallway.

The white tiled walkway was clear, but she couldn't help but notice that Michael had left the clean laundry stuffed in the hamper off to the side. Sharyn could feel dryness surface in her throat as her frustration built. She swallowed hard as she entered the living room and plopped down on the couch, exhausted. Michael juggled foil-covered plates as he trailed behind her.

Sharyn's eyes fluttered as Michael unexpectedly plopped down on the couch next to her. He set the plates on the coffee table and rested into the couch. She closed her eyes but could feel him watching her. Replaying the evening in her mind made her smile.

"What are you thinking about?" Michael squinted his eyes like a private investigator searching for a small clue. "Hmm, let me guess—dinner. It was fun, huh? It was a good Thanksgiving this year."

"Yes, it was." Sharyn stretched out her arms and slipped them behind her neck. The oversized throw pillow caved like a marshmallow underneath her lower back. She was not pregnant enough to feel back pain, but the cushion seemed to hit the right spot.

"I had a good time. Did you?" Michael asked, mimicking her position. Sharyn turned her head and gazed into Michael's eyes. "Yes, I did, but I'm tired." Sharyn rested her head on the back of the couch, feeling more exhausted today than she'd been in weeks. Pregnancy was certainly taking its toll on her.

"You looked beautiful tonight. I couldn't help but notice that red blouse. I felt like I was looking at *my* wife for the first time in months." Michael slid off the couch and knelt before Sharyn. He slowly removed her black pumps and massaged her feet.

"It's crimson." Sharyn sat up startled, then leaned back, enjoying her husband's touch. She wanted to apologize, but her resentment wouldn't allow her to move forward. Fear flickered like a flashing stop sign, and she vowed not to make the first move.

Michael kissed each toe and slowly massaged her legs. He stopped abruptly and met Sharyn face to face.

"Let me see it," he ordered.

"See what?" Sharyn giggled as he tickled behind her knee.

"C'mon, just once. Let me see it," Michael pleaded.

"See what, Michael?" Sharyn questioned playfully.

"Let me see what I love, that Whitney smile."

Sharyn smiled brightly as the joy in her heart erupted throughout her entire body. To Sharyn's surprise, Michael swept her up in his arms and carried her upstairs. The skylight in their guest room enhanced the atmosphere of love.

Michael lay sound asleep as Sharyn watched her favorite late-night talk show. She held her stomach and pursed her lips together, swallowing her laughter. Sharyn wished she could carry this feeling with her always. Closeness to her husband, love toward her family, and life growing within her belly were blessings she'd never thought she'd receive. She eyed Michael resting peacefully as his chest gently rose and fell. Reaching out and touching him softly, Sharyn finally felt at ease. No haunting thoughts of a baby. No arguing. Only love. "Thank you, Lord," she whispered.

Afraid her laughter would erupt, she reached for the television remote perched on her night table next to her cell phone. She was surprised to notice she had a missed call. Angela had tried to reach her. Sharyn eyed the clock stationed on Michael's side of the bed. Eleven o'clock was not too late to return her call.

Sharyn slipped out of bed, opened the door quietly, and headed back to her guest room. The bed still lay unmade as a witness to the time spent with her husband. She slid into the dismantled bed and dialed her sister. "Hi, Angie, you called?" Sharyn pulled the covers up over her legs.

"Girl, I was waiting for your call, but it was starting to get late."

"Sorry about that. What's up?" Sharyn could hear the quiver in her voice.

"It was awful. I can't believe it. He yelled. I yelled. I think this is it."

"What was awful?" Sharyn quizzed, hoping her sister would pull herself together.

"Martin and I. We've never got into such a heated argument. When we got back to my place, he came in to help me put my things away, and as soon as I took my coat off, the telephone was ringing. I answered it, of course, and it was Jonathan again. He had called earlier," Angela recounted.

"He called earlier, while Martin was there?" Sharyn asked.

"Yes, and that's what started the whole thing in the first place. I mean, before there was tension, but nothing like this. I told Jonathan I would call him back, and that is what set Martin off. He starts in on this 'other men' thing again. I'm so sick of that, I can't tell you," Angela declared.

"Well, why did you answer? You should've known better," Sharyn countered.

"You think I should alter my behavior to pacify him," Angela accused.

"No, I didn't say that, but you guys were already fighting. Why pour alcohol in the wound?" Sharyn professed.

"My sentiments exactly! Why put alcohol in the wound? I'm not going to cower to anybody, Sharyn. Jonathan has the right to call me anytime, and I have the right to answer. I'm not going to change who I am for nobody. I respected Martin and told Jonathan I was going to call him back."

"Ang, I agree, it's your right to answer the call, but is this the hill you wanna die on?"

"What's that supposed to mean?" Angela smacked her lips.

"I mean, is this the thing you want to lose him over? A phone call should not make or break any relationship."

"You're right, Sharyn. This isn't the hill we should die on, but it looks like it's gonna be. If he's going to storm off and say it's a done deal over a phone call, boy, bye. My heart can't take it, I can't keep dealing with this."

"You've been spinning your wheels for a long time, Angela. You need to decide what you want and then go for that. If you want Martin, then devote yourself to that relationship, and if you don't, then don't." Sharyn tried to reason with her sister.

"I'm already doing that. As a matter of fact, Martin is on his way out of town, as well as my life. I don't care, either. Besides, Jonathan is on his way over here right now. I've decided what I want, and I'm going to go for it—tonight anyway." Angela laughed.

"Too much info, Ang. Too much info. Sometimes you have to remove the plank from your own eye, and that's part of the problem." Sharyn sighed.

19

Niche

Niche rubbed her eyes, turned off the alarm on the clock radio, and turned over. Pregnancy had zapped her stamina, so she allowed herself extra time to sleep in. But even after the alarm went off, her drive wavered.

Niche had mustered up enough energy this morning to sneak to the lab to complete some tests Dr. Bateman had ordered, but she'd failed to keep the office visit. On the way home she'd vomited twice and nearly gotten sideswiped pulling over to the side of the freeway to dry heave. She'd rushed home, dove back into her unmade bed, and fallen fast asleep.

Evening arrived faster than she'd realized. The shadows from the blinds danced along the wall of her bedroom as the dusk cascaded. Niche yawned, stretched out her arms, and tried to sit up. She still felt exhausted. The assignment for biology was due tomorrow, and her laptop sat at the corner of her desk, waiting to be opened. The creak of the opening door startled her.

She jumped.

"Niche, why do I have to hear through the grapevine that you're pregnant?"

"You don't knock anymore, Therie?" Niche relaxed her muscles. It was the first moment since Thanksgiving that she'd had time to rest. She barely made it out of the house most days, and the nausea and vomiting made it difficult to travel. Prenatal vitamins seemed to make things worse. Wiping drool constantly had even diminished her toilet paper supply. Pregnancy had taken its toll, but she constantly reminded herself she was reaping what she'd sown.

The ceiling fan circulated cool air around the room, but her body temperature started to rise. "I was going to tell you, but Kev and I wanted to keep it private." Niche rested against her pillow, uncomfortable in her own skin. Her stomach ached.

"Private. Please. It's all over campus. I even heard that you guys was squabbling about it in the pub. What the heck is going on with you?" Therie propped herself against the wall. "I heard you slapped Kevon, he slapped you back, and you ran out crying."

Niche sat up and threw her small orange decorative pillow behind her neck. The taste of bile suspended in her mouth. "What? That is not true!" She and Kevon were the focus of campus gossip constantly. Her mother had encouraged her to leave him a year ago when she found out Niche was seeing the campus counselor, but Niche refused. Knee-jerk reactions were her mother's staple approach, and she refused to be like her mother.

"I'm hurt that you didn't trust me enough to tell me about this. I thought we were girls." Therie shook her head.

Niche sucked her teeth. She didn't have the energy to contend with someone else's feelings while she was still learning to manage her own. She understood that Therie was concerned, but Niche wanted to be alone. Her eyes softened. "I'm sorry I didn't tell you, girl, but I was going through it. Kevon and I was trying to figure it out. It wasn't in my plan, nor his." Niche was glad they had finally gotten on the same page. Kevon had changed and was beginning to like the idea of having a baby.

"What are you guys going to do?" Therie questioned.

Those same words hung in her mind like a gymnast ready for

dismount. Either she was going to land on her feet or fail miserably. "I'm going to do what I feel is right. I'm having a baby. It's going to change my plans, but with God's help and family support, I hope it'll be all right." Niche smiled, reminded of the support she'd already received.

Kevon's mom had left two messages on her machine expressing support, and his father was also reaching out to her. They had talked several times over the phone. It was apparent that they both loved their son, and anything that was connected to him was a part of them.

"I heard that, but what about school?"

Niche looked down at the tattered carpet that now stood reflecting her life. A fresh black spot had appeared out of nowhere last week. No matter how many times the building superintendent cleaned it, the imperfections would still appear. "Well, that I haven't figured out yet. I'm still putting all the pieces together. That's why I wasn't sharing all this. I don't have the answers to any questions yet. I only know my next step."

"What's your next step?" Therie threw her arms up in the air.

"I plan to take good care of myself, and part of that is getting enough rest." Niche eyed the door.

"Oh, I get the hint, but we're not through with this yet." Therie headed toward the door. "Your mama is going to kill you. Have you thought about that?" Therie peeked back over her shoulder.

"I have, but right now I got to get some homework done and rest." Niche leaned her head back against the upholstered headboard. She had assignments to complete and a visit to her mother scheduled tomorrow. "Out." Niche pointed her finger toward the door as her telephone rang. She reluctantly grabbed the phone off the nightstand.

"Hello, Dr. Bateman." Niche smiled. "Nice to hear from you. Sorry I missed my appointment."

"You better be glad that ain't Moms!" Therie rolled her eyes as she surveyed Niche from the doorway.

"Yes, I feel fine. Come by tomorrow morning? I left your office today because I was too sick, but I have an appointment in two weeks. Is there a problem?" Niche's heart raced. "What type of situation arose?"

Therie backtracked and headed to her friend's bedside.

"No, I'd rather you told me now, Dr. Bateman. I've been coming to you for years now, and if there is a problem with this baby, I want to know immediately. I can handle it, and I think you know that." Niche's eyes began to water as she clutched her stomach. "No, I won't come in! Please, Dr. Bateman, I have class tomorrow, and I work too. Dr. Bateman, it's my body and my child, and I have a right to know immediately!" Niche shouted into the telephone receiver.

"Calm down, Niche." Therie rubbed her friend's arm.

"HCG levels? Hold on, Dr. Bateman." Niche jerked away from her friend and pointed toward the door again. Therie marched off and shut the door gently as Niche's high-pitched scream echoed well into the hallway. "Miscarriage!"

Angela

Angela smiled broadly as she exited the freeway. The city lights sparkled in her line of sight. Friday nights in San Francisco were effervescent. Women in stilettos and guys outfitted in blazers atop of blue jeans swarmed the sidewalk. Bistro tables were full as lines started to form outside of restaurants.

Angela turned the corner onto her block and relaxed her shoulders. Finally she was close to home. Her drive had felt longer than usual as she played stop-and-go all the way down Interstate 101. The balls of her feet had started to ache from the frequency of accelerating and braking, and her gas indicator light had illuminated miles back.

Refilling her tank would have to wait until tomorrow because she couldn't wait to get home to show off her new hairstyle to Martin. Adjusting the rearview mirror toward her direction, she breathed a sigh of relief; her lipstick was still intact.

Angela loved reconciling. She could never stay angry with anyone for too long. A forgiving heart, Big Mama called it, and her grandmother announced to all that Angela was a carbon copy of her. When Angela would complain about her siblings, Big Mama would grab her by the hands and ask, "Where's my Joseph?" If Angela complained about her teachers, Big Mama would ask, "Where's my Joseph?" By the age of eight, Angela had begun to ponder if Joseph was her middle name. It wasn't until Angela was in middle school that Big Mama shared the Bible story about Joseph and his ability to forgive.

Angela grabbed a butterscotch candy from her purse. She wanted to look sweet and taste it too. Martin had her heart, and she knew it. Her skinny jeans and her fitted coral sweater were directly purchased off a store mannequin. She'd gone to Sandy's Beauty on San Bruno Avenue on her lunch hour and had her hair coiffed special. Her long hair was neatly tucked into a French twist adorned with rhinestone clips. She'd even decided to splurge on a French manicure. She was in the mood for love, and although she'd spent the night with Jonathan, she couldn't get Martin off her mind.

Her heart leaped when she spotted Martin's black truck parked in front of her condo. She knew he must be restless because his hazard lights were blinking and their reservation would be cancelled in less than thirty minutes. She spied him standing idly behind his truck. Angela readied her excuse, pulled up behind him, opened her car door, and flew into his arms.

"Hello, stranger," she greeted him, exuberance dancing in her eyes.

"Hello to you! Babe, you look amazing, and you smell even better. Is that the perfume your mom gave you for your birthday?"

"Thank you. Yes, it is. I love it. It smells better than the one you gave me," she said, waving her wrist in front of his face.

"We'd better get going." Martin walked over to the passenger side of his truck, opened the door, grabbed her hand, and helped her into the large cabin. She placed her purse near her feet and noticed red rose petals adorning the floor mats.

"Martin, what's this?" she asked, her eyebrows raised.

"At your service, madam," he said, and immediately walked closer to her with two red roses dangling from his left hand. "One rose to honor you tonight, and the other is another apology for our spat." He winked and headed to the driver's side. "I've been thinking about you, Angela," Martin said, once secure in the cabin. He grabbed her hand as they headed toward Fisherman's Wharf.

"What have you been thinking?" Angela rubbed his hand.

"Well, you've been *more* than patient with me, and I want you to know that I appreciate you. It's challenging managing a business and a ministry, and you know that I try to practice what I preach, which has resulted in this unconventional relationship. I know that it's been hard on you, baby. I've been hard on you, and I'm sorry."

"I accepted your apology already when you got back to the city. No need to apologize again, it was an argument, that's all. You are different from any other man that I've known. I like that. I like you." Angela squeezed his hand.

"You're a special woman, Angela Lovelace, and I want you to know that I recognize purpose in you. You have the gift of caring and a heart for people. I'm glad I'm one of them." Martin glided off the freeway.

"Me too." She blushed. "I do care about you, not as much as my dad does, but I do care." Angela threw her head back and let the laughter bubble up inside her.

"I know you don't like to deal with your feelings head-on. You joke or start a fire, but I'm serious, sweetheart. You're special, and I hope you know that." Martin glanced in her direction.

Angela turned her head and looked out of the window, unsure of what to say. The sudden onset of emotion welling inside her took her by surprise. Her leg trembled as she fought back tears. The silence between them loomed loud. Angela stared at the empty intersection. The homeless man pushing a cart into the street snapped her back to the present. Angela soon realized they were not headed toward Sydney's Mexican Grille at Pier 39. "Martin, where are we going? I was looking forward to some nachos."

"I changed our reservation. I had something different in mind for tonight."

Angela's thoughts raced as she hoped this was *the* night. "Where are we going, Reverend?" She tapped her foot as her nervousness began to rise.

"We're already here." Martin turned a sharp right and pulled into a dark, empty parking lot. He navigated the lot until they were positioned in front of an old warehouse. Two lampposts illuminated the front door. "Come on, let's go," Martin directed.

Angela could see the dancing red balloons from the car. The balloons shimmied frantically from the steel door. She jumped out of the car and headed for her surprise. Her head swooned.

Martin followed, pulling keys from his pocket. He made his way in front of her and opened the door. Angela eyed the sign posted above the door. *In Flight.* She peeked inside. All she could make out was a red cloth swaying from a table near the door.

"Your evening awaits." Martin curtsied and turned on the lights. Angela sneaked past him into the building, trying to catch her breath.

"Is all this for me?" Angela spied a picnic table filled with covered baskets and, behind them, vibrant purple, air-filled jump houses that looked as if they could almost touch the ceiling. "I'm blown away," Angela said, fighting back tears.

"This is all for you, my special lady. I missed you so much when I was traveling."

"I missed you, too." Angela wiped a tear from her eye. "But this?" Angela could hardly keep her composure. No man had ever made her feel this special. She nibbled the inside of her lip to try to gain control of her emotions.

"When we were fighting, it bothered me. I don't want to fight anymore." Martin gently grasped her elbow and guided her to the picnic table.

"I have a confession too. I know it's inappropriate for a single woman to accompany a minister while traveling, but sometimes I wish I was with you." Angela sat down on the opposite side of the table.

"It would've been a joy to see you sitting out there in the congregation, you know, offering up an amen now and then." Martin pulled two red plates out of a basket.

"How do you know I would've done that? Confident, huh? I could've been in that congregation dousing you with the evil eye." Angela giggled, trying to shift the intensity of the moment. She grabbed a small turkey sandwich from the other basket.

"What exactly is an evil eye?" Martin laughed.

"How did you do, anyway?" Angela wondered how his messages were received when he was outside of California.

"The Holy Spirit was with me. I preached on Nehemiah. You want to hear something funny? I always find a message in that book when I'm missing you. You would think a poetry book would remind me of you, but it doesn't, it's Nehemiah."

"Why Nehemiah? I'm not a leader or anything like that."

"Not yet anyway, but you do have a knack at rebuilding things, restoring and rebuilding relationships. In a way, you've built something new in me." Martin looked down at the table. "Want some chips?"

"I'm not going to let you off the hook that easy. What do you mean something new?" Angela wiped her mouth, reached across the table, and lifted his chin.

Martin grabbed her hand, locking his fingers in hers. "Well, before you, Angela, I thought I knew what I was looking for. The landscape was clear to me, but then you came along and changed everything for me. My perspective, for one. My heart, for another."

"Your heart?" Angela longed to hear the three words she had already pressed upon her mind.

"Yes, my heart. Before I met you, I would've never had the courage to get up and do this!" Martin leaped up and ran toward a jump house shaped like a castle. In a flash, he disappeared beyond the air-filled entry door. Angela hopped up and headed after him.

It was difficult for Angela to gain her footing as she climbed inside the enormous castle. She fell to her knees and crawled after Martin. He sabotaged her by jumping up and down and making her topple over. Angela gave him a dose of his own medicine, jumping as high as she could, leaving him flat on his back.

"You aren't going to get away that easy," she said, throwing her arm over him.

"Who says I'm trying to get away?" Martin replied coyly.

"Is that right?" Angela jumped on top of him and straddled his lap. "I got you now," she said, grabbing his arms and pinning them above his head. She leaned in and kissed him passionately.

"Angela," Martin panted, as their lips parted. Angela could not stop herself, kissing him again with the fervor of her passion. Martin joined her in the crescendo of desire. Angela released his hands and found hers exploring his face, longing for him. She moved her hands to his chest and tugged at the button on his shirt, but Martin snatched her hands away.

"Angela, stop!" His harsh tone startled her. She'd forgotten his rules.

"Why? Why do we have to stop?" she asked, her voice rising. "Don't you want me?" Her face flushed and she shook her hands free. "No one will know."

"You know that's not the issue here, Angela," he said, gently guiding her off of him. "It was a mistake to come here alone. It was my mistake."

"You regret being with me?" Angela barked.

"I don't regret being with you, I regret being here alone with you and arousing our temptations." Martin scooted further away from her until he exited the castle.

"What's wrong with a little temptation?" Angela snarled, following him.

"Temptation leads to fornication, Angela, and I respect you, myself, and my God enough to make my way of escape. Now let's get out of here." Martin placed the plates back into the picnic basket.

Angela shoved the other basket toward him. "Forget it then. My heart is in *my* chest, not on my sleeve. I don't need this."

Martin shook his head. "I'm well aware you don't need this, and I don't know where your heart is right now. Why do you always say that to me?"

Angela crossed her arms defiantly. "It's a reminder for me. I'm not going to fall in love with those who don't love me."

"What on earth?" Martin scratched his head.

"Yes, Martin, my supervisor taught me that a long time ago, and it helps me get through times like these."

"Angela." Martin glared at her square on. "We're called to love those who don't love us, and we're called to love those who do. I don't know what your supervisor or any of these other guys are teaching you, but you first have to open your heart before you open your legs."

20

Sharyn

Sharyn exited her leisurely shower after taking extra time to apply her favorite vanilla sugar scrub followed by her lavender-scented baby oil. The bathroom was still as fragrant as an aromatherapy specialty shop, even though the walls had begun to perspire and the windows looked like she'd sprayed them with a frosted glass paint. She slunk into her green terrycloth robe and memory-foam slippers.

The master bathroom was her sanctuary and Sharyn's favorite room in the house. She'd placed special decorative embellishments around the room that offered her the quiet calm that she loved. A marble elephant figurine took center stage, a gift from Big Mama when she'd made her first dean's list. The bathroom was adorned in Sharyn's favorite colors: burgundy and slate gray.

The large master bath, complete with two large double sinks, was twice the size of her other bathrooms. The shower and oversized bathtub didn't have curtains, but each was designed with etched glass doors. Her decorator had laughed when she'd insisted that both the bath and the shower be equipped with encasings.

Sharyn had fallen in love with the bathroom as soon as she'd laid eyes on it, and she'd decided to purchase the house soon after leaving the bath's expanse. The bathroom was where she found her calm and tranquility, her panic room.

She wiped her hand across her steam-filled mirror, finding her reflection waiting. How was she going to tell Michael that she was pregnant? She looked at the wet walls and lifted up her shower cap to check if her hair was frizzed. Her hand glided up underneath her shower cap but shifted and rested on her abdomen.

Sharyn pulled at the belt on her robe, letting it fall open. She caressed her stomach as her nails tenderly embraced her dampened skin. She wondered if the baby's heart was beating. Had its genitalia formed yet? Boy or girl, it didn't matter to her. She delighted in the truth that she was now a mother.

Sharyn knew she didn't look different, but she felt different. She knew this emotion well. It was a feeling she had identified long ago. She'd acknowledged its whisper when she moved out of her parents' home. She'd shouted it loud when she danced across the stage at her college graduation, adorned in cap and gown. Freedom had arisen again, and it had never felt so good.

She floated out of the bathroom without even noticing Michael sitting on the bed, playing on his laptop.

"What's wrong, honey?" Michael's face crumpled. "Are you okay?"

Sharyn jumped. "Michael, you scared me," she remarked, as she walked toward him, entering the space that belonged to her husband. Their bedroom was large enough to house two king-size beds, but it wasn't where she found her peace; it was where he found his. "What are you downloading now?" Sharyn chuckled, as she knew he was engaged in his favorite pastime: tinkering with apps, playing video games, or downloading old films.

Michael looked handsome, comfortable in his green fleece jogging suit that matched Sharyn's robe. His newly grown beard enticed her. Sharyn walked toward him and kissed him gently on the forehead.

"I'm checking out some things," he said matter-of-factly, barely looking in her direction.

"Well, I'm fine," Sharyn said, taking his empty hand in hers. "How are you?" She played with his fingers.

"I'm good, baby. I'm good. I found this game yesterday, and it's crazy." Michael gestured toward his computer. "I don't know how people come up with this stuff."

"I have a game we can play." Sharyn's voice deepened as she pulled his hand around her waist.

"What game is it?' Michael looked up, giving her his undivided attention. "Lonely neighbor, traveling salesman, cable guy?"

"No, honey, this is a different game. I made it up today, but we're going to need a prop or two." Sharyn grinned.

"Props?" Michael laughed. "I like the sound of this already."

"You wait here. I'll be right back," Sharyn declared, as she skirted out of the room and headed for the garage. Sharyn returned with two red satin blindfolds and a gift bag.

"What took you so long?" Michael stood eagerly.

"Hold on, Tonto. I couldn't find them at first. Now, I want you to cooperate, you hear?" Sharyn declared, as she gently tied the blindfold around her husband and guided him to the edge of their bed. "This is going to be a guessing game, Michael. You'll have to deduce what item I have, and if you're correct at the end of the game, you'll get a prize," Sharyn instructed.

"A prize. Hmm. Am I going to like this prize?" Michael questioned.

"My dear heart, you're going to love it," Sharyn declared.

"Is it a prize that I've had before?" Michael asked.

"It's something that you've never, ever had before," Sharyn expounded.

"Well, in the immortal words of Marvin Gaye, 'Let's Get It On.'"

Sharyn hurried to the lamp, dimmed the lights, grabbed items out of the gift bag, and placed them gently on the bed. She caressed Michael's face as she approached him again. Carefully, she reached for the feather on the bed next to him. He smiled as she glided the feather against his face.

"Mr. Sanders, what's the item?" Sharyn asked sheepishly.

"A feather," Michael whispered.

"One point." Sharyn gently kissed her husband's lips and grabbed the pregnancy test that sat on the bed and floated it across her husband's neck. "Mr. Sanders, what is the item?"

"I don't know, baby. Do it again," he ordered.

"No second chances, Michael. In this game, you got to get it on the first try." Sharyn laughed.

"I give up. Let's get to the Marvin Gaye part."

"No points," Sharyn declared, as she grabbed the next item. "I'm not tolerating any sass." She pulled the new pacifier from its packaging. She smoothed it up and down his arms and then popped it in his mouth.

"Oh, I know what this is. A pacifier!" Michael shouted, like an elementary school student blurting out an answer. "Sharyn, are you trying to keep me quiet?"

"Something like that," Sharyn said, kissing her husband's neck. She grabbed his hand and rubbed it across her abdomen.

"That's my girl," Michael said gently.

"Or boy," Sharyn whispered, as the room fell silent.

"Or boy?" Michael questioned.

"Yes, Mr. Sanders. It's just, well, you know, earlier my stomach was tripping. I think it was the baby." Sharyn looked down at the floor, awaiting Michael's response.

"I'm sorry, sweetie, did you say what I think you said?" Michael shook his head. "I must've heard you wrong. What did you say?"

Sharyn removed his blindfold, lifted his face with her hands, and looked him straight in the eyes. "I said it must be our baby." Michael's hands trembled.

"Our baby is inside your stomach?" Michael yelled. "Sharyn,

Sharyn, oh my God." Michael enveloped her in his arms and squeezed so tight it hurt Sharyn's. They stayed on the edge of the bed and held each other as Sharyn wept.

"I love you, baby," Sharyn mumbled between sobs. Michael kissed her cheek.

"I love you so much right now. I don't think I've ever loved you more." Michael released Sharyn from his arms as she stumbled to her feet.

"This is the most wonderful thing that could've ever happened to us. I'm happy!" Michael yelled, as his hands flew in the air like he had crossed the finish line. He picked Sharyn up and swung her around. "We gonna have a baby, we gonna have a baby, we gonna have a baby."

"Michael, please put me down. After all, *I am pregnant!*" Sharyn laughed.

"Okay, okay. I'll be right back." Michael put Sharyn down, and in one leap he headed for the door.

"Where are you going, mister? What happened to let's get it on?" Sharyn asked.

"I'm going to the other room to thank the Lord for one of the best blessings. We've been praying a long time, and now the season of trial is over. Like Zechariah, I received the blessing, but God didn't send me an angel, He sent me you." Michael danced out of the bedroom.

"Wait for me, knucklehead. You haven't been the only one praying."

Angela

The sunlight burst into the room, sneaked through the blinds, and trickled underneath her eyelids. Angela squeezed her eyes tight, pulled her bedspread up over her shoulders, and turned toward the wall. She hated being summoned to the office, especially early in the morning, but Angela knew she'd better get up or she was going to be late. Her client, Tyra, and her family's case had come across her desk again after the police were called to her home during a domestic disturbance.

Angela rubbed her feet together. The warmth of flannel sheets cradled her toes. Sliding down deeper toward her footboard, she imagined sharing her bed with Martin. Being relegated to a single side of the bed, fighting for the blanket in the middle of the night, and cuddling the next morning were all she desired. The thought of belonging to someone caught in her chest. She sighed.

Angela threw the bed covers back as her body heat rose like a loaf of baking bread. She could feel anxiety building in her body as her aloneness permeated the bedroom. Angela sat up, refusing to be held hostage again. She had everything to be grateful for, including a good job and a family of her own. Unlike her, Trevion had nothing.

Angela knew she couldn't keep working his case and diverting her other job duties; she had to find answers and find them fast. The satin slippers stationed by the side of the bed welcomed her feet. Angela leaned over, pulled the flat sheet, and tucked it underneath her mattress while mulling over the details she'd gathered. Piecing together the puzzle of Trevion's life still provided more questions than answers. Angela glanced at the clock and realized she was never going to make it to the office on time. Frustrated, she reached out for the telephone and dialed her office.

"Hey you, I hope I didn't wake you, but I need to know if we are still on for lunch today," Sharyn sang out cheerfully.

"What? Hey, Sha," Angela responded in a dry, grumpy tenor. "I was calling my office. I guess you were already on the line."

"Guess so, now what about lunch? Michael wanted me to stop by his office and bring him some papers, but if I go to lunch with you, I won't have time to do that. I have so much to do today. First of all—"

Angela abruptly interrupted Sharyn. "Sha, I've got to get ready for work, and talking about your day could last all morning. Yes, we're supposed to go to lunch today, but if you have some other things to do, I understand." Angela reached over and turned off the lamp perched on the round nightstand next to her bed.

The lamp had remained a fixture in her room since she was in elementary school. There was something special about her grandmother's lamp that made her feel safe. Angela couldn't count the number of times she had overheard Big Mama tell her father that she was just a phone call away. So when Angela hadn't been able to sleep after watching a horror film, Big Mama had been the only person she knew to call.

Angela had snuck down to the kitchen and called her grandmother, and within the hour Big Mama was ringing their doorbell. Angela had recognized the lamp she held in her hand immediately. It was always stationed on the side table near her grandmother's rocking chair along with a magnifying glass, a Bible, and a glass of water. Angela had refused to take the gift at first, but her grandmother insisted. Big Mama plugged the lamp in after setting it on Angela's dresser and made Angela recite Psalm 18:28. She'd scooted in bed next her, and Angela had never been afraid of the dark again.

"Someone woke up on the wrong side of the bed. No Jonathan last night, huh? Look, that's okay. I'll meet you at Charlie's Seafood Shack at 12:15. Bye."

Angela hung up the telephone, stood upright, and took a long stretch. She snatched her red silk robe draped at the bottom of the bed and inhaled deeply, as the smell of Jonathan's cologne still lingered. She shook her head, wishing it smelled of the sandalwood and vetiver that Martin wore. She jostled to the bathroom as her foot caught on her handbag. "Ouch." Angela grabbed her stubbed toe and eyed the contents of the purse scattered about all over her white throw rug. "So much for being on time."

Angela laughed as she eyed Martin's business card, which had landed atop her organizer. Printed in bold letters under his name was *In God We Trust.* Angela shook her head; she'd stopped trusting God a long time ago. She loved Him, but her trust had left the day her mother abandoned their family home. She'd heard the arguments, the slammed doors, and the apologies, but she hadn't seen the divorce coming. Angela's most vivid memory burned in her mind.

The flu had ravaged her body in seventh grade. It was around two o'clock in the morning when she first started calling out for her mother. She called her name, but her mother never came. Angela dragged herself out of bed, stumbled to the kitchen to grab some water, and then she saw it. Her father lay facedown on the floor, praying. He petitioned the Lord for reconciliation and begged for His help. Robert wanted his wife back, and Angela didn't even know that her mother had gone. She listened to her dad appeal to the Lord for over a half an hour and then decided to sneak back up to her room. She'd had enough. The next morning when her mother wasn't at breakfast, her father broke the news. Anger was the only emotion she could clearly recognize that day, and like the glass she threw against the wall, her heart had shattered into a thousand pieces.

21

Kevon

Kevon sauntered out of his room and headed downstairs toward the kitchen. Greeted by the scent of fried eggs and burnt toast, he walked through the dining room with his nose turned up. His biceps tensed as a chill moved up his arms, his robe and basketball shorts barely warming his body. The anxiety about approaching his father turned his stomach, but he knew it was something he had to do. This was his day of reckoning.

He tiptoed into the kitchen and eyed Robert lounging in plaid fleece pajamas, reading the newspaper and drinking coffee. Robert glanced up from the newspaper. Kevon immediately lowered his eyes like a funeral director ushering a wake.

Kevon knew their relationship had sustained irreparable damage, and he was unsure if it could be revived. After their last argument Kevon had given up, left home, and headed to the liquor store for a pint of gin. He'd broken the bottle's safety seal before he made it to his car. He had to silence his father's voice. Halfway through the bottle, the alcohol hit him. Nearing a neighborhood park, he noticed the red-and-white lights shadowing his car. Luckily, the bottle he'd purchased fit under his seat.

The police officer was kind and didn't even realize he was under the influence. Kevon had learned the art of adhering to authority from pledging his fraternity. Yes sir, no sir, a bowed head, indirect eye contact, and seeking permission had saved him on more than one occasion in his father's house. A simple warning to never drive without headlights accompanied by a smile was a tune Kevon would not soon forget. When Kevon turned his headlights on, he realized he'd been maneuvering in the dark for too long.

"Daddy, I know you're reading the paper, but could I talk to you for a second?" Robert neatly folded the paper, placed it on the kitchen table, and looked directly at him. Kevon could not hold his father's stare. Sensing the cold emanating from his father's glare, he closed his eyes.

"I've been thinking, Daddy, I have." Kevon swallowed hard, trying to wet the back of his throat. He was ready to put his life back on track, and this was the first step. Step one, face his father; step two, apologize to Niche; and step three, quit drinking.

It was the fifth time Kevon had decided to quit drinking, but this time he was serious. The first time he had been a kid. Sophomore year he'd found himself stooped over the toilet at Mustang High, wishing he'd stayed away from Larry Townsend like his mother had instructed. He wished he knew then what he knew now: sometimes parents do have wisdom. Kevon leaned up against the refrigerator to steady his feet, bracing for his father's response.

"Thinking?" His father asked, gruffly pushing his coffee mug to the side.

"I now grasp, wholeheartedly, that I was headed down the wrong path. I wasn't the guy on the street corner, or the one doing time, but I was locked up." Kevon tried to communicate to his father the insight he'd gained last night. Kevon went to church sometimes, sang the songs, heard the Word, but he'd never given it a chance. Church was something his parents wanted him to do, while he'd rather be home in bed. "Daddy, I know what I was doing was wrong."

"Wrong?" His daddy said sarcastically.

"Daddy, I'm sorry. I've been selfish and only thinking about myself, and I know it's not right. You guys taught me better than that. You are right, it's time for me to stand up and be a man." Kevon fumbled with his belt, feeling the lack of alcohol in his body.

"And what do you think a man is?" Robert rolled his eyes, leaned back in his chair, and crossed his arms.

Kevon clenched his teeth as he tried not to get irritated. "I've lived my life entitled, and maybe this is what I needed to see, now. You cannot ride on another man's coattails." Kevon walked to the table, pulled out a chair, and sat down directly next to his father. "A man stands up, Daddy. He stands up."

"That's right, Kevon. When things get tough, a man has to stand up on his own two feet."

"That's what I'm going to do, Daddy. I plan to stand, but I can't do it alone." Kevon knew he needed Niche more than he needed anyone. He couldn't imagine his life without her, and he didn't want to. She was the only one who saw something good in him.

"See, that's the problem, son," Robert said, interrupting. "You young kids . . ."

"Let me finish, Daddy. I mean—I'm going to stand with Niche. I plan to take care of my child, like you did for me." Kevon inhaled deeply, happy to see his father's shoulders relax.

"Well, son, that's what I wanted to hear."

"I thank you, Daddy, for helping me recognize that I needed to step up. I don't want you to ever think that my friends and party-ing is more important than you. I love you and Mom more than you could ever know," Kevon said, as tears welled in his eyes and this truth resonated. He did love his parents, he did love Niche, and he loved his sisters, but he struggled finding love for himself. He'd tried to grab ahold of the light that flickered when Big Mama was alive; but most of the time, after she died, he'd only caught ahold of darkness.

"You are important to us too, boy. We want the best for you. That is why we've stood by you all this time."

"From this point forward I make a promise to you. I'm going to stand up and be a good black man, a Lovelace man. I'm going to be a good father *and* ace my finals. I want to make you guys proud of me. I love you, Daddy." Kevon leaned over toward his father and attempted to hug him. Robert extended one finger in the air and stopped Kevon from coming closer.

"I wanted to say that. I love you too, son." They both hugged each other, and as Kevon headed back upstairs to his room, he leaped up the stairs two by two.

Angela

Angela barreled through the double doors as the dark, damp restaurant sheltered her from the cool breeze outside. Charlie's Seafood Shack had more empty seats than filled. The lunch rush had taken their business elsewhere, and Angela was grateful. She hated waiting idly for a buzzer to ring.

Angela loved Fisherman's Wharf. She treasured the smell that lingered in the air, the bark of the seals, and the pace. The bustling crowds, sounds of distant cable cars, and the street entertainers made the wharf a unique treasure. This was her favorite restaurant, filled with local yokels, fresh seafood, and their signature excellent service.

Angela scanned the restaurant and looked for a comfortable booth as the warmth beckoned her further inside. She took off her coat, draped it over her arm, and curtsied to acknowledge the best part of her day.

Social services had been a mad house. Angela's client, Tyra, had arrived at her desk before she did. The scheduled disposition hearing she had cleared her afternoon for had been cancelled. Her favorite attorney called and challenged her recommendation for a family to be reunified, and her other client had been returned to foster care. Angela fielded calls the rest of the morning, and no one had called back regarding Trevion. Lunch with her sister was the rainbow in the cloud.

Angela's smile widened; her favorite table was empty. The scent of fresh clam chowder enticed her senses; her growling stomach applauded the culinary delight. Scanning the restaurant, surprised, she spotted a familiar haircut sitting at a table stationed on the wooden deck of the restaurant. Angela shook her head in disbelief. The fog had blanketed the bay, and the cold came with it. No way was she going to sit outside.

Angela eyed Sharyn looking up a waiter, giggling. Her sister's smile warmed her heart as she felt her irritability melt away. With her coat in tow she marched toward the deck. Her black slacks and bronze shirt displayed small coffee stains as a result of her brick wall anxiety. Her hair, initially curled tight, had loosened courtesy of the wind, fog, and her constant twirling. Angela shook her hair out of her face and licked her lips. "Now, you know I don't want to sit outside." Angela knelt down and kissed her sister.

"And hello to you, too." Sharyn smiled. "I had the waiter save us your favorite table inside. I was hot and wanted to sit out here until you arrived, is that all right with you?"

"I'm sorry, boo, I thought you'd lost your mind for real. What's up? We haven't had lunch together in the middle of the week in what, about a year?" Angela and Sharyn walked inside the restaurant toward the empty table. Sharyn plopped down into the brown wooden chair and Angela followed.

"Angie, you're always investigating. What's up with you and that attitude lately? I couldn't help but notice you cut our conversation short earlier. Did you have to cancel an appointment with Jonathan to meet me today?" Sharyn stuck out her tongue.

"No, nosy, I didn't." Angela grabbed her napkin-wrapped silverware. "We aren't meeting again for a couple of days, but I've got news of my own that I want to share." Angela smirked.

"Like what?" Sharyn blurted out. "What news?"

"Who investigating now?" Angela rolled her eyes.

"Good afternoon." The lanky waiter appeared at their table. His notepad stood at the ready. "Can I get you ladies something to drink?"

Angela danced happily in her seat. "I've been looking forward to your mint tea all day."

"Make that two," Sharyn seconded the order.

"Now, what were we talking about?" Angela grabbed the large menu stacked behind the napkin holder.

"We were talking about the fact that I'm pregnant, and I wanted you to be the first to know, after Michael, of course." Angela dropped the menu, and rushed across the table, and gave her sister a hug.

"Praise God! Finally. Sharyn, I can't believe it. I can't believe it, after all this time. I'm going to be an auntie. Congratulations, love. I'm happy for you. Pregnant! What? We gonna have us a baby!" Angela squealed.

"Yes, we are." Sharyn blushed while grabbing her sister's hands.

"I can't believe we're going to have another Lovelace." Angela smiled as the waiter returned and placed their drinks on the table. "Sharyn, when did you find out? It must've been this morning, since I'm finding out this afternoon. How did you know?"

"Well, it's a long story," Sharyn mumbled.

"And what did Mike say?" Angela grabbed the lemon slice dangling from the side of the glass and dropped it in her tea.

"I'm fine and Mike is ecstatic. He cried more than I did—can you believe it? I found out last week, but I told Mike on Sunday. I had to let it register with me first, that's why I didn't tell you sooner."

"I understand." Angela nodded, surprised at the ping of jealousy welling in her. Sharyn always got to the finish line first. She was the first to leave home, graduate college, and get married.

"But don't tell anyone else, even Mom. Mom does *not* know yet, I repeat. I'm going to wait until the first trimester is over to announce it. I don't know exactly how far along I am, but I think about seven weeks. I go to the doctor on Monday for more tests."

"Wow, Sharyn, this is wonderful." Angela raised her hands to heaven. "My own personal Sarah."

"Okay, girl, I'm not that old. Now you said you had some news, too. What is it?" Sharyn questioned.

"Well, I'm dating Jonathan, as you know, and I think that, well, I'm going to invite him over for the holidays," Angela said, deciding momentarily to speed up their romantic relationship like a quarterback calling an audible.

"Oh, good. I like him, Angie, but Mom and Dad are going to have a coronary when they don't see Martin, the MVP." Sharyn poked her lips out.

"I know, but I can change the players anytime I want. Besides, I'm the one who manages the equipment." Angela laughed.

22

Angela

Angela swallowed the last bite of spaghetti from her discolored plastic container. The red remnants reminded her of the permanent damage that was sometimes left behind, no matter how many times she tried to clean it up. She had no time to waste. Her father wouldn't let her talk about work, and asking her mother about Trevion was simply out of the question. Angela stuffed the dirty dish into her briefcase and checked the clock as she decided to make one stop before heading home. She could still exert some after-hours effort on Trevion's case, and this afternoon she'd discovered a fresh lead.

Harvest Community Center opened at three and served meals until eight. Angela had received a call from their director, Ms. Bates, who said she knew Trevion and his mother. Ms. Bates heard Angela was the social worker on the case that was scouring the city looking for information about them.

Angela grabbed the loose papers on her desk and stuffed them in her bottom drawer, pushed her mouse to the side, and shut down her computer. The coffee cup stationed on the corner of her desk still needed cleaning, but she didn't have time; the faster she left the office, the quicker she'd make it home.

Angela hated traffic and dreaded the congestion on the way to

Harvest Community Center in the San Francisco Civic Center, but she had to get to the bottom of this case. She slid off her black pointed-toe pumps, glided into her flip-flops underneath her desk, and loosened the belt on her dark blue skirt dress in an effort to get comfortable. She had a long drive ahead of her.

The mood inside the community center matched Angela's fatigue. The air seemed heavier, the people walked slowly, and the faces looked somber. The modern, remodeled building stood in stark contrast to the worn couches that lined the walls inside the lobby. People loitered about and didn't even glance in her direction as she searched for her destination. Angela let out a deep breath as she finally eyed the cafeteria sign illuminated on her left.

Angela accidentally bumped into an unsuspecting victim on the other side of the double doors leading to the cafeteria.

"Oops. I'm sorry," Angela said as she backed up from the door.

"Come on through." A handsome gentleman appeared from behind the door. "I think my wrist is broken," he said, as he wiggled it in front of her. "No, it's fine but will probably be a little tingly for a few minutes," he said, grinning.

"Geez, I apologize for the mishap. I should've been more careful. Nice to see a smile, though. I was rushing in, trying to visit Ms. Bates before you closed."

"I was kidding. I'm fine. How can we help *you*?" The stranger raised his eyebrows and looked Angela up and down. "By the way, I'm Trivell, the volunteer coordinator. You are?"

Angela stared at the man's extended hand. Angela outstretched her free hand and firmly grasped. "My name is Angela. Pleasure to meet you. Once again, I'm sorry for the mishap. I must speak to Ms. Bates."

Trivell frowned. "It's okay. I understand. Pretty lady like you must be busy." Trivell pointed toward the kitchen area.

"Thanks." She followed his lead.

"Ms. B, an Angela is here to see you," Trivell yelled, as he headed past her.

"That so," Ms. Bates said, as she entered the dining hall. "You must be the social worker." Ms. Bates grabbed a kitchen towel from next to the serving line and wiped her hands.

Angela was startled by the woman's beauty. She reminded her of Lena Horne. "Thank you for seeing me on such short notice and at this late hour."

"My pleasure, child. I hope I can help you one way or the other. Let's take a seat back in my office." Ms. Bates led Angela through the revolving service doors and toward the back of the kitchen, past several staff members who seemed to hardly notice the two women. Angela could still smell hamburgers when Ms. Bates closed the office door. "Now, what would you like to know 'bout Trevion and his mama?" Ms. Bates sat down slowly in her office chair.

"Something," Angela laughed. "Trevion is a delightful boy and he's in a great home, but I cannot find anyone related to him or his mother. I'm trying real hard to piece together their story." Angela sighed, taking a seat on the opposite side of the metal desk, the only furniture in the office besides the two chairs. Angela had never seen an office so plain. Two dirty windows set in the wall sat curtainless behind Mrs. Bates. A metal trash can sat alone in the corner, and a small digital clock hung above the door.

"Well, I don't know if I have all the pieces to that puzzle, but I reckon I may have some."

"Any information will be greatly appreciated." Angela's eyes lit up.

"You know that Trevion, he's a good boy. His mama, now she was, well, not meaning to speak ill of the dead, but she had problems. It was hard to help her, you see, on account of that anger. She had an angry spirit. Full of foolish pride, you know. Look like she'd been let down her whole life. I'd seen that spirit pass through here. Nothing one person can do about it, you know. Prayer. Prayer is only thing that can change a heart been broken like that."

"I suppose you're right," Angela agreed, desiring to know more about Samantha's history than her personality. Angela smiled broadly, reminded of her mother's teaching: nobody likes vinegar, but we all love honey.

"I began to serve homeless people when I moved to this here Bay Area. Always had a heart for the hungry. Never thought I'd see so many broken, though. That child, she was broken. She kept to herself. Like to give me a heart attack one day when she wanted to try her hand at serving. That's how I got to know her better. She served here for a little over a month or so. Ate here first, helped here second." Ms. Bates leaned forward.

"She volunteered here?" Angela was surprised.

"Sure did. I believe she was trying to get herself together at that time. Keep herself busy. Told me she was adopted. Told me she loved her adoptive parents, but then they up and died, and back into the system she went. I was sad for that child."

"Ms. Bates, that's heartbreaking." Angela shook her head.

"I know. Child said both adoptive parents died in an auto accident. Same time too. She said life was never the same after that."

"Ms. Bates, did she say she had any other family around after losing her adoptive parents?" Angela quizzed.

"No, she said she was on her own and learned to make it that way. That's where that foolish pride came from, I suppose. Said she looked for her birth parents, but stopped talking about it after that. I couldn't get that child to talk about that hurt anymore."

"Did she give you any information about Trevion's father?" Angela's heart raced.

"She did say he was a deadbeat. Said he denied Trevion from the start so she left him back in Seattle."

"Seattle?" Angela said, writing notes frantically.

"Oh, sounds like you didn't know that the girl lived in Seattle. She said she lived there for a while. Child so tormented by the loss of her parents that she fled to Seattle. I think she said she lived there for two or three years. I'm pretty sure she said Trevion was conceived there. She told me that was the reason she came back to the Bay Area. Said she did not want to be in Seattle all alone and pregnant. It gets depressing up there."

"Oh, I see. I can understand that." Angela's heart relaxed. As far as she knew, her father had never even set foot in Seattle. "Scary situation for a young mother. Pregnant and alone. Seems like that's the way she spent her entire life. Alone."

"Well, she did love that boy, though. Unfortunately, that addiction got the best of her," Ms. Bates said, glancing down at her watch.

"I'm glad she did love Trevion. He is a kind, good boy."

"She sure did. She hated to come in here and eat at first. Embarrassed, you know? She would hide her face so much, he began to hide his. Child shouldn't be ashamed, trying to get something to eat. She eventually came round though. Especially when she stopped using."

"How did you know she stopped using?"

"Well, honey, I've been round here a long time. I can almost always tell. Plus, she was clean and clearer. That's when she said she wanted to help round here. She said somebody got her in a program."

"What program?"

"I suspect those drug programs, honey. Said she was going in the day and come by here at night. A friend was keeping her child."

"Did she say the name of the friend?" Angela's pen stood at attention.

"Naw, never said. Whoever it was, they helped that child. She stayed clean for about a whole month or so. Then those demons came right back." Ms. Bates shook her head.

"They can sometimes."

"Sure can. Darn shame, though. I hate to the see the light in someone's eyes go out. Seems like her light and Trevion's went out right at the same time."

"He can be a sad boy," Angela agreed, remembering the only time she saw a real smile on his face was when he was talking about his toy snake.

"Sure, can't help it, I suppose. But somehow she always seemed to take care of him. He always had on clean clothes and shoes. I suppose I understand why she kept ahold of him tight. Being adopted and all."

"I wish things could be different for him." Angela meant every word. She never got used to seeing children in foster care. She did the best she could to help them, but the instability alone broke her heart.

"No sense in wishing, honey. God knows. He cares. Pray for the child. All's we can do is pray. Prayer changes things, you know." Ms. Bates clutched her heart.

"That I do know, Ms. Bates. That I know for sure," Angela declared. She had all the information she needed. She had another nugget, another clue to help her put the pieces together. Angela thanked Ms. Bates for her time and the information. She headed back to her car full of glee and a bounce in her step. Looked like her father was not *the* father.

Angela grabbed her cell phone recorder as she headed onto the interstate. "Note to self. Call all day treatment centers in the city by week's end. Also, send Ms. Bates a dozen roses and make a sizable anonymous contribution to Harvest."

Kevon

Kevon secured his feet on the floor and pushed with all the strength he had. The bed inched slowly across. He'd only moved his full-size bed two times since he moved into this bedroom—once when he'd wanted to redecorate his room and the other when he'd accidently scraped the hardwood flooring.

The room was a small space and not large enough for a crib, but he had to make it work. He kneed the bed an inch closer to the wall, trying to make space in his life for fatherhood. He glanced at the clock, turned up his music, and headed toward the closet to pick out his clothes. He needed to be ready for round two. He had already faced his father, and now Shameka was on her way over.

Kevon didn't hear the doorbell, and the rapping on his room door startled him. He opened his door, still in boxer shorts.

"Kevon, that girl downstairs." Robert's eyebrows raised.

"Don't worry, Daddy. I meant what I said. I have to clear the air with a lot of people," Kevon declared. "I'll be down in a second." Kevon grabbed black sweatpants and a dirty T-shirt off of his floor. He took a deep breath, dressed, and grabbed his cell phone. He scrolled to a recent picture of Niche. "I love you, baby."

Kevon had been avoiding Shameka, but he knew he had to face her. He entered the family room in silence as he avoided her eyes. Shameka sat erect on the love seat, a place his mother always used to occupy. Kevon nodded his head in acknowledgment and searched for the words to say. She gazed at him as if she'd found her prey. Kevon forced a smile.

"Thanks for coming, Shameka." Kevon plopped down on the couch and swung his leg over the armrest. "I asked you to come over so we can talk privately. There's something that I have to tell you, and it's not going to be easy." Shameka rolled her eyes as her cynical laughter filled the room.

"I already know, Kevon, it's all around campus. Niche is pregnant. But believe me, that doesn't bother me. I ain't trying to be your wife, and I don't care if you're a daddy, as long as you keep being mine, you feel me." Shameka shot Kevon a look that he knew well.

"How'd it get around?" Kevon avoided her glance and focused on the family portrait that hung above the love seat.

"I don't know. I only know what I heard. Besides, I knew what I was getting into when I first met you, you know I'm not tripping. We don't protect ourselves all the time either."

Kevon shook his head, displeased. "No, Shameka, I know you ain't tripping, but I wanted to tell you in person *and* to let you know." Kevon sat up straight.

"Kevon, I know you didn't mean for her to get pregnant, this situation doesn't change nothing." Shameka giggled, sashayed over to Kevon, and wrapped her arms around his neck. "I enjoy your company, and I know you enjoy mine."

"No, Shameka, you don't understand," Kevon snapped, as he pushed her arms away. "Let me finish. Listen, it ain't cool for us to hook up anymore. I'm going back to Niche, *for good*. I have bigger responsibilities now."

Shameka threw up her hands. "Oh, like that, okay Kevon." She pointed directly in his face. "It's all about whatever you say, right, Kevon? Do you want to know what I think? I think you're feeling it right now. But keep my number when you get over this father thang."

"Father thing?" Kevon's confusion registered in his face.

"Yeah, it's all sunshine and roses now. I mean, don't even trip, I'll be there when you need someone whose belly isn't poking all out. Believe me, you will be . . ." The sound of Kevon's cell phone interrupted Shameka midsentence. Kevon stood up, pushed past her, and pulled the telephone from his side pocket.

"Hello," he said, flustered. "Hi, baby, what's wrong, why you crying? What's wrong, Niche?" There was a long pause and darkness clouded Kevon's eyes. Shameka jumped when the phone hit the floor.

23

Angela

Angela sat down, looked around the office, and smiled, grateful for the agencies that helped her families. When she met clients at drug treatment centers, she left with a greater appreciation for the staff and the work they did on the small amount of funding they received.

The reception area was small, warm, and cozy. The smell of sandalwood immediately relaxed her. Throw pillows were placed on chairs, and each wall had a picture of concrete roads surrounded by different landscapes. The punching bag mounted high in the corner seemed out of place.

Angela rose to examine the leather boxing staple, but the small pulsation in her pocket stopped her short. She fought the urge to look at her cell phone again. The small device had vibrated incessantly since she'd last glanced at the display. Jonathan had called six times.

"Angela?" A petite woman with blond, spiked hair flew into the reception area like a strong wind.

"Hi, thanks for meeting with me." Angela shook the calloused hand of the energetic worker. She couldn't help but notice her creased blue jeans and T-shirt emblazoned with *survive* in bold red letters.

"Follow me," the small woman ordered as she headed behind the reception counter into an adjacent office. Angela parked herself on the opposite side of a large wooden desk. The woman grabbed a water bottle and took a drink. "Look, I don't know how much help I can be to you." The drug and alcohol program director hunched her shoulders. Angela scooted forward to the edge of the seat.

"As I mentioned over the phone, maybe none, but I owe it to my client to do the best I can. I'm trying to put the pieces together in his story, and I have a little guy who knows nothing about his family except the name of his deceased mother. He's stuck in a foster home with no prospect of a relative placement, or any other placement for that matter. Any help you can give would be a blessing." Angela smiled.

"I do have a small file on her," the woman conceded, and opened a small manila folder on her desk. "It has limited information though. I have no next of kin listed and no emergency contacts. There's not a lot here."

"Well, can you tell me more about her?" Angela's heart deflated like a tire that had gone flat. She knew she was losing traction.

"Samantha was quiet and angry. She hated to be called Sam and would be ready to fight if you called her that. I do remember her well. She spent hours in our office laying into that punching bag out there. She had mountains under the surface. Shoot, I thought she would've been one of our clients who'd make it, take one of the alternative roads, like in those pictures out there. Her determination, you know. I was sorry to hear of her passing."

"It's a tragic story, but she left beautiful Trevion behind."

"Oh yes, I remember now. Trevion, how she loved that boy. He came to visit her a few times. Cute as can be. I think that was part of the hope I had for her. I hoped she'd do well for that kid."

"He's a special boy. Now you can understand why I'm working hard on this case. Let me ask you though, if he came to visit her while she was in residential treatment here? Who was he staying with?"

"Oh, I don't know her name. He came with an elderly woman each time. Beautiful woman too. She reminded me of Lena Horne in ways

I couldn't put my finger on. Real regal, you know. I don't think that was her mother though. But as I recall, those two were close. As close as anyone could get to her."

"Do you suspect Trevion was staying with the elderly woman?" Angela quizzed, as Ms. Bates flashed in her mind.

"Suppose so, but I don't know who kept the boy. It may have been her, because, come to think about it, Samantha was a private-pay client. She didn't have any insurance, and we don't take Medi-Cal patients. This is not a government-funded or court-mandated rehab program. Motivated, not mandated is a key component of our program."

"Private pay? How on earth could Samantha afford a program like this? She must have had help—for God's sake, she was living in a shelter prior to coming here. Do you have scholarships?" Angela scratched her temple.

"No, we don't have anything like that here. Each client pays for their treatment, either with help from family and friends, or private insurance."

"Did she complete the program?"

"She was discharged clean and sober, as far as I know. She worked the program and was someone we would consider a success. However, this program does nothing for most without outpatient treatment. It's about learning to live outside these doors without using. Some can have great success here, but when they discharge to the larger community they fail. Sounds like that is what happened to her."

"Sounds like it. I don't know of any outpatient treatment programs she was involved in. Did your agency refer her someplace?" Angela now had more questions than answers.

"Let's see." The counselor turned to another tab in the folder and peered directly into Angela's eyes. "Looks like we gave her several options and even set up some meetings for her. That can be your next step. Just forget that you stepped in here first."

"Can I ask where she was referred to?" Angela asked sheepishly, careful not to let her desperation show.

"She was referred to Second Time Around and Clean Lifeline. They are two wonderful outpatient programs right here in San Francisco. Second is in the Castro, and Clean Lifeline is in the Mission. I don't know if they'd be willing to share some of her personal information. Those programs are different than private. I would certainly let them know she is deceased. And Angela, good luck."

"Thanks for your time." Angela stood to leave.

"I hope you find something, that's why I talked to you. Samantha deserved better than overdosing on her living room floor, and that kid does too."

Angela left the office more confused than ever. Private pay? Who could've paid for her program, and why would they? Trevion's mother would've been considered a castaway. Nobody ever foots the bill for a castaway, or at least, not on purpose.

Angela slid into the driver's seat with hardly a thought of her dinner date with Jonathan. She felt like a fish caught in a net, able to see what was all around her but unable to grasp it. Angela started the car engine with renewed energy because she knew exactly where Clean Lifeline Recovery Center was, and she planned to start there.

Angela drove quietly as she turned onto Highway 101. The radio was turned off, and her case file was ajar on the passenger seat. She didn't want any distractions as she went over each detail of this case. The beautiful elderly woman? She knew Ms. Bates had more answers to this story, and Angela was determined to get them.

Clean Lifeline's parking lot was empty, but that wasn't going to stop her. She jogged up to the old elementary school building and yanked open the front door to the office. Silence greeted her.

"Hello?" Angela walked toward the worn counter that once stood as a barrier between the staff and the students. She eyed the dated surroundings, a drastic difference from the previous program she'd visited. Tattered walls were covered with relapse prevention material and flyers for class offerings, and pictures of the staff were hung over a rundown copier tucked in the corner. Worn plastic chairs lined the walls.

"Hello?" Angela's voice echoed louder this time, as she stretched her neck toward the abandoned principal's office. Snatching up a nearby pencil, she decided to leave a note for the nonexistent staff. She grabbed the discarded canary flyer off the desk, turned it over, and scribbled her name at the top. She was startled as the door opened behind her. Angela recognized the secretary from her picture on the wall. The secretary nodded in her direction.

"Hi. I didn't see you walk up, or I'd have gotten here sooner." The burly woman smiled. "Welcome to Lifeline."

"No problem. I was leaving a note," Angela said, extending her hand. "The parking lot was empty."

"Yes," the woman replied, skirting behind the counter. Her black combat boots echoed loudly against the floor. "We park in the back— car burglaries. What can I do for you?"

"I'm Angela Lovelace, a social worker for San Francisco County, and I stopped by to see if I can talk with the director."

"Oh, I'm sorry, she's leading a group right now. Can I help you?"

"I don't know. Is there somewhere we can talk? All the information I need is confidential."

"Yes, there are places to chat, but I'm not at liberty to discuss matters not related to the program. Do you have a release of information?" the woman asked.

"No." Angela's body stiffened. "I do have specific information that I need. Is there a time when your director will be available?" Angela reached into her purse and grabbed a business card.

"We're short-staffed this evening, so she'll be running a couple of groups. I'll give her your card and ask her to call you when she has a free moment, but make sure to get that release."

Angela smiled in an attempt to hide the disappointment that welled inside her. "That would be great," she replied, handing the woman her business card.

Back in her car, Angela fought the desire to give up. She needed answers. Angela glanced at her clock. Driving to the program in the Castro could take an hour in traffic, and she definitely didn't have all night. She whipped her car around the center island. She knew where to go. Her heart swelled. *Jonathan!* She had forgotten all about dinner and was already late. Angela grabbed her phone and dialed frantically. "Hi, baby." Her voice danced as his message machine beeped. "Sorry, got caught up at work again. It's right before the holiday, and I needed to finish up some things. I'm not going to be able to get there cause I'm across town. You want to meet me at my house later, around ten? I'll make it up to you." Angela felt horrible as she disconnected from her phone and personal life. Work was her priority tonight. Her time on this case was running out.

Angela parked her car right in front, and this time she knew her way around. She jogged inside the building with renewed purpose. Ms. Bates looked beautiful but concerned. Angela knew she was surprised to see her back at Harvest.

"Hello, Angela . . . Lovelace, right? What, you come back to help us out this time? We can use all the help we can get with Christmas coming." Ms. Bates smiled and stood up from behind her desk for a more formal greeting.

Angela shook the woman's brittle hand. "Not this time, Ms. Bates, but one day I'll get down here and lend a hand."

"We sure could use it. Our lines seem to get longer and longer. What brings you by, then?"

Angela decided to jump right in. "Well, I got some news at the rehab. I was told that Trevion's mother had company from time to time, and she also had a private benefactor. Any ideas on who that could be?" Angela eyed the old woman suspiciously.

"Private benefactor?" the old woman questioned, while avoiding Angela's direct gaze.

"Ms. Bates, I know you were there, and for whatever reason the truth is not coming out. I didn't come back here to start any trouble. I want to get to the bottom of this. I'm not trying to disturb this woman's history or anyone else's, for that matter. I'm trying to help this boy. I want to help him, Ms. Bates, and I'm sure you do too."

"I've done all that I can do for that family. I have other families around here," Ms. Bates argued.

"Yes, Ms. Bates, you do, and I'm sure if you don't help me, you might have Trevion's family too. You see, the more answers I get, the more I'm able to give. He'll want answers, and when he doesn't get them, he will go looking. God bless him when he doesn't find them, and God keep him when he finds what he thinks may be the answers," Angela pleaded.

"Trevion's a good boy," Ms. Bates countered.

"God knows being a good boy or girl doesn't keep you off these streets." Angela looked Ms. Bates directly in her soft eyes. "Let's keep him off these streets, Ms. Bates."

"Look, chile, all I know is that the girl had a connection. It wasn't a drug dealer. It wasn't a boyfriend, a family member, or a pimp. It was some old guy who cared about her. She cared about him too. Called him her *beau-père*. Never seen him around here though. He did call to see if she was here. He also asked if there was a way he could put some money aside for her, but I told him no. I run a community agency, not a bank," she snapped.

"I understand, Ms. Bates." Angela nodded.

"Besides, she didn't want it no ways. I also know he always offered her money and tried to come see her, but she said no. He paid for her rehab though, and sent packages to her. I think he loved her. That's all I know, chile." Ms. Bates dropped her head in silence.

"Ms. Bates, why on earth wouldn't you tell me that? Lots of people have a sugar daddy."

"This was no sugar daddy, honey. I done seen plenty of those. Run them out of here plenty of times. This was a Good Samaritan. He still donates here."

"He does?" Angela exclaimed, readying her notebook. "Who is it, Ms. Bates?"

"He donates anonymously, and he's generous. That's why I didn't want to share this info with you. I'm also gonna ask that you keep it private. When she first arrived here, so did his contributions. They've never stopped either. And chile, if he wanted it to be known, there are avenues for that. This man wants to help and to be left alone while doing it!"

24

Sharyn

Sharyn pointed at the small empty space sandwiched between two sedans. "Right there," she said, directing Michael to park the hybrid across the street from her mother's home. Finding a place to park near Rose's at Christmas was like finding an empty department store on Black Friday—impossible.

"Why can't I park in the driveway?" Michael snapped. "We have tons of bags."

"We need to save the spot for someone else. Mom is expecting a full house." Sharyn eyed the home where she spent her teen years. Two new potted plants had arrived on the porch along with a parade of poinsettias. No matter how much greenery her mother outfitted along the outdoors, it could never substitute for suburban green grass. The concrete drive and walkway were the mainstays that had resulted in her endless childhood memories of scraped knees and elbows. Sharyn had vowed to never again plant roots in San Francisco.

"First come, first serve," Michael argued, backing up the car into the driveway. "I don't want you walking though, so let me let you out."

"Michael, park the dang car before you lose that space." Sharyn rested her head back on the seat. "It's already nine thirty in the morning, and people are going to start coming soon." Michael stomped on the gas. Sharyn's head jerked as Michael hit the brakes, barely missing the Christmas wreath that hung from a sedan's trunk. "Break my neck, won't you! Please be more careful! My stomach is already dancing." Sharyn elbowed his arm.

"I retreat. Sorry, honey." Michael reached over and patted her stomach.

"Thank you." Sharyn glanced toward the back seat and winked at Reverend Broussard. "See there, Martin, happy wife, happy life." Sharyn had been shocked to find Martin standing at her mother's front door that morning when she first arrived. Sharyn thought her sister had mentioned she was inviting Jonathan to dinner.

"Here, Sharyn, let me get it." Martin jumped out of the rear seat and opened Sharyn's passenger-side door once the car stopped.

"Thanks, Martin." Sharyn exited the car and trailed behind him up the walkway toward the brightest house on the block. The eight-foot noble fir took up the entire front window of the home, and the Christmas lights were on even though it was daylight. Decorative wreaths hung in the windows, and white flocked garland adorned the porch railings. "And thanks, Martin, for riding with us back to the store. I can't believe I forgot the chicken broth."

"No problem, I was locked out anyway. I was sure your dad told me to meet him here at nine." He moved to the side and waited for Sharyn to open the grand double doors.

"I'm sure he did because he told me he'd be here at nine too. I hope everything is okay." Sharyn walked into the house and immediately hung her tan wool jacket on the coat rack. "Mom isn't back yet either, and I'm glad because that gives me a chance to lie down." Sharyn patted her stomach.

"After all that food! Honey, you need to walk a bit, especially after breakfast." Michael skirted into the house behind them and released several shopping bags onto the small area rug.

"I'm sleepy, too, Sharyn. I had a long flight last night. Is there any place that I could rest for a sec?" Martin asked, interrupting a potential conflict.

"Sure, Martin, I'll lie down in my old room, and you could take Kevon's." Sharyn shot Michael an evil eye and pointed Martin upstairs toward the bedrooms. "It's the far door on the left." Martin headed up the stairs, out of earshot. Sharyn looked at Michael and raised her eyebrows.

Michael smiled knowingly. "Angie's got them coming and going."

"That girl is crazy, she goes through men like a dehydrated athlete goes through Gatorade."

"She's definitely thirsty," Michael snickered.

"She needs to get some of that living water then, because she is headed for trouble. Speaking of trouble, mister, I'm not going to go walking in this cold weather. I'm going up to my room to lie down. Stop policing me, and call me when my mom gets back." Sharyn's body stiffened. Michael reached for her hand.

"How am I going to do that? After I put away these groceries, I'll be lying in the bed right next to you," Michael replied, eyeing the steep staircase.

"Okay, Mr. Walk, come on and help me upstairs, I'm sleepy," Sharyn ordered, feeling exhausted.

The door to her old bedroom creaked loudly as it opened. Walking into the room was like entering a high school reunion; the space was familiar, but the landscape had changed. By the time she reached her bed, she felt guilty. She'd been curt with Michael lately, and he'd done nothing but love her. He was the ruler by which she drew a straight line; without his support, she knew she'd be off track.

Michael encouraged her to scale back when she took on everyone's problems. He helped her to relax when she tried to control outcomes. He told her she was smart even when she didn't feel like it. He loved her right down to her soul, and she had forgotten that in her quest for pregnancy. He wanted what was best for their family and had no problem sacrificing himself in the process.

Sharyn squeezed his hand, pulled him close, and wrapped her arms around his neck. "I need you," she whispered, as she looked him directly in the eye.

"Right now?" He grinned.

"No, silly." She shook her head and released him. "For life." Sharyn kissed his cheek and plopped down on her full-size platform bed, draped with a rose-tasseled duvet cover. Faux fall berry wreaths hung high on the walls, and reclaimed barn wood paraded as an accent wall. "*Mom.*" Sharyn pulled the accent pillows from atop the bed and tossed them onto the floor.

"You heard the garage?" Michael questioned.

"No, but look at this room. If she put as much time and effort into her children as she did her decor, we'd all be better off."

Niche

Niche's eyes still burned from crying most of the night. It had been a couple of days since she'd passed the tissue, and she still couldn't help thinking about her dead baby. Her thoughts were filled with caskets, funeral programs, and gravesites, which were things she'd never get. Nothing to acknowledge the death of her unborn child. She'd never get to formally say goodbye.

Niche moved slowly about her bathroom, trying to look her best. She grabbed her Denman brush and pulled her hair back into a ponytail. She snatched her skintight black-and-red sheath dress that she'd purchased for dinner last month off the door hook and slunk it over her small frame. Her stomach had a small pooch. She hoped people would still think she was pregnant instead of bloated. She wasn't ready to have *the* conversation. Niche glided her hand over her abdomen and cradled the flesh underneath that would never distend.

She hadn't seen anyone except her physician, Kevon, and Therie since being diagnosed with a missed abortion. Dr. Bateman had written her a note for the university, but forgotten to issue her one for life. She didn't want to die, but a leave of absence would be nice.

"Niche, I'm about to head out!" Therie called through the bathroom door. "Merry Christmas."

"Merry Christmas," Niche mumbled.

"Girl, you okay in there? You been seeing Dr. Bateman a lot lately," Therie inquired.

"Routine tests, don't worry," Niche lied. Niche had seen Dr. Bateman the day after her telephone call to discuss her diagnosis. Her trustworthy physician had flooded her with information on statistics, her HCG level, and birth control options, imparting confidence about her ability to conceive again and even offering to enroll Niche in a support group after giving her several contact numbers for crisis support to help handle the diagnosis. Her next couple of visits had been for emotional support.

"Well, as long as you're okay."

"I'm hanging in." Niche lowered her eyes.

"Girl, why don't you come on out with me? I'm going to check out that Christian lyricists' concert in Oakland at Jack London. Your favorite, A Brook, is going to be there," her roommate offered.

"No, you go on ahead. Kevon is on his way here." Niche's voice lifted as she tried to quell the anger that welled inside her. Kevon had shut down. He wouldn't say anything about the baby, and his behavior was starting to frighten her. She didn't know what to expect from him. He might be in a good mood, or a bad mood, or no mood at all. He seemed depressed and at times angry at the world. Other times he seemed in denial, like nothing had even happened. He flat-out refused to discuss it, unwilling even to inform his parents what had happened.

"You been in that bathroom for over an hour, *and* I heard you guys fighting last night, Niche," Therie said pointedly.

"We okay, girl, I'm finishing up my makeup and then we're headed to his mom's," Niche assured her, as she moved from the toilet and positioned herself in front of the door. "Have a good time."

"Okay, but you take care of yourself and call me if you need me."

Niche sank to the bathroom floor, and a half hour later she barely heard the doorbell ring. She scrambled to her feet, took a glance in the floor-length mirror, straightened her dress, and strolled to the door. She hesitated opening it, knowing it was Kevon.

Niche gathered her breath, closed her eyes, and opened the door. Kevon stood in the doorway, dynamic in a dark gray suit and a teal shirt. As soon as Niche looked in his eyes, hers filled with tears.

Without hesitation, Kevon clutched her in his arms as they both collapsed onto the floor, weeping. He extended his right hand into the air.

"Lord, why?"

25

Angela

Angela jogged up the walkway to the front door. She removed her black leather gloves and grabbed the keys deep inside the pocket of her red trench coat. The doors groaned as they opened and the warmth collided with the outside air. She shuffled in to escape the cold. The sound of forced air coming from the vents grabbed her attention as she closed the doors. She wished she had central heating like her mother. The old grate wall heater barely worked in her condo.

Once in the house, she dropped the bag of presents on the floor and shook out her hands, sore from the weight. The house was warm like her mother always kept it, and the familiar scent of pine made its way to her nose. Angela inhaled deeply. There was no way she was going back outside to haul in the other bags.

"Kevon, Mike!" she yelled. "I need some help down here, I have tons of bags." Much to her surprise, no one answered. "Hello, anybody home?" she yelled louder. Still no response. She peeked out the arched door lite window and eyed Sharyn's hybrid. Confused, she headed to the kitchen. "Where's everybody?" Angela pouted.

The kitchen was cluttered with groceries. Flour, sugar, and salt canisters were aligned on the counter next to bell peppers, onions, and celery stalks. Her mother's finest cookware was positioned from smallest to largest on the island. Angela headed to the stove and noticed the dual oven was on. Her peek inside was met by a foil-covered roasting pan. She breathed a sigh of relief, knowing her mother would never leave her precious home with the oven on. Before heading to the foyer she opened the refrigerator and grabbed an apple juice.

Angela trotted to the family room and removed her quarter-length coat. She tossed her covering across the love seat, plopped down on the couch, and adjusted her dark red batwing off-the-shoulder sweater as Trevion immediately took over her thoughts. Angela wondered how he was doing on his first Christmas without his mother. "The heart is in the chest and not on the sleeve," she reminded herself as she grabbed the remote control neatly placed in the caddie centered on the coffee table. Angela flicked through the channels, finding nothing but football games. She stood and hiked up her red floor-length maxi skirt.

The oak movie cabinet was stationed in the corner of the family room. Each shelf was filled with movies her mother had spent years collecting. "Ooh, I love this one." Angela shook the Blaxploitation film in her hand. She jumped as she felt a light touch graze her bare shoulder. "I knew you guys were here, about time y'all lazy butts showed up," she said, turning her head. Her eyes widened.

"Surprise!" Martin embraced her.

"Martin, what are you doing here?" Angela pulled away and retreated back to the couch.

"C'mon, sweetheart, you can't still be mad. You know I couldn't spend Christmas without you," Martin declared. "I mean, I *was* upset when you didn't reach out. But you know your father, he invited me over anyway. We both figured that you were upset, so I figured I'd surprise you. Forgive me?"

"My dad called you?" Angela bit her lip.

"Of course he did, what better day to reconcile than on Christmas? I flew back in last night. Now, we can celebrate two things, making up and the birth of our Lord and Savior, Jesus Christ. I missed you, Angela." Martin knelt before her and grabbed her hands.

"Martin, I'm surprised. I didn't know you were coming." Angela's voice intensified. "No one told me." Her face exposed her discomfort.

"What's wrong? You're looking at me crazy, girl." Martin's face contorted.

"Well, I mean, this is difficult for me." Angela pulled her hands back and lowered her eyes. "You guys put me in a predicament. I'm sorry, but I invited someone else over for dinner. I mean, he's not here now, but he'll be here later," Angela explained, as guilt welled in her throat. She shuffled uncomfortably in her seat. Her eyes lingered on his, searching for his feelings. She reached out to touch him.

"Is that right, Ang?" Martin moved backward. "I was here on Thanksgiving, and already, *less than a month later*, someone else is with you, and on Christmas nonetheless. You didn't even let the turkey get cold. Were you scared to have an empty seat next to you?" Martin's face reddened.

Angela drew her hand back, stunned by his rejection. "Look, Martin, it's not about that." Her voiced cracked. "I don't want you to feel uncomfortable."

"Well, I'm not! I was invited here today, I didn't just show up. Oh, I see, I get it now, you want me to leave, is that it?" Martin barked.

"What?"

"You want to kick it with your new little boyfriend." Martin paced the floor.

"Martin, let's be adults here."

"Well, excuse me, Sister Lovelace, I think *you* are the one feeling uncomfortable. I didn't mean to mess up your thing, but I'm not going anywhere."

"I didn't say you had to leave, Martin." Angela turned off the television and tossed the remote back onto the table. "You can stay right here." She leaned back and crossed her legs. She refused to let him intimidate her. She tilted her head to the side and waited for him to take another jab.

"Good, because you're not the only person in this family that I care about. I'm not going to be pushed out by some guy that you just met! We're all going to have to be uncomfortable then. Who is this dude, anyway? Some of my old competition?" Martin threw his arms up.

"Oh, okay, you want to go there." Angela cocked her head to the other side, readying for the fight. "Well, excuse me, Martin Broussard, but you never had any competition. The opposition was, and is, always you. Like I told you, I don't have time to be waiting on you. Believe me, there are plenty of sisters at the church who are willing to do that, but I won't. I gave you plenty of opportunities to step up to bat."

"Well, my love, my agenda was different from what you're used to, I didn't want to just hit it." Martin crossed his arms.

"I can't believe you!" Angela stood up, placed her hands on her hips, and scowled.

"Wrong again," Martin objected. "I'm probably the only one you can believe."

Sharyn

Sharyn leaned forward on the bar stool and hovered over the kitchen island. She grabbed a cracker out of the small box stationed in front of her, stuffed it in her mouth, and swallowed hard. The gourmet cleaver served as a mirror to check her reflection, and she looked well rested. She wiped the sides of her mouth with the back of her hand. "What are you going to do, girl?" Sharyn returned the clever to the block, grabbed the chopping knife, and passed it to Angela before she made the request.

"I don't know why Daddy took it upon himself to invite Martin." Angela rolled her eyes and grabbed a handful of okra from the center of the island. "I don't know what to do. I guess I'll hope for the best." Angela carefully placed the okra on a chopping block. "Daddy overstepped this time. And speaking of overstepping, Sharyn, hand me those crackers. You done had enough."

Sharyn reached over and gently touched her sister's shoulder in an effort to settle her down. "As they say, Father *thinks* he knows best." Sharyn tossed the cracker box toward her sister, slid off the stool, and headed toward the skillet on the stove. She noticed gliding off the seat was much easier than getting on. She doused the skillet with olive oil, turned on the stove, and grabbed the chopped onions from the refrigerator. Cooking succotash was one of her favorite activities. She'd inherited the recipe from her mother-in law, and her husband beamed when she served it. Unlike her sister, Sharyn wanted her man to know how grateful she was to have him in her life.

"In this case, Dad definitely does not. Jonathan is starting to grow on me, and he has no idea that Martin was in my life. Jonathan is turning out to be someone I enjoy." Angela scooped the severed tops of okra into the garbage.

"I know. It's a new relationship. When Michael and I were first dating and went on that College Students for Christ Retreat, that time together was magical. He couldn't do no wrong." Sharyn smiled, remembering the first time she kissed her husband.

Angela looked directly into her sister's eyes. "Sharyn, I'm *really* starting to like him."

"Sounds like it." Sharyn winked. She'd seen that look in her sister's eyes before.

"I mean, don't get me wrong. I still care about Martin, but I'm trying to move on. I think Jonathan is the type of man that can help me move forward."

"What's great about him?" Sharyn grabbed a spatula, turned down the stovetop, and stirred the onions.

"He's charming and attentive. I think if Jonathan discovers who Martin is, we'll sink before we have the chance to set sail." Angela shook her head.

The translucent onions reminded Sharyn of her desire to be more transparent with her sister. "Ang, remember you just got into the boat. I want you to find someone special who loves you *and* the Lord. That takes time." Sharyn grabbed the okra from underneath Angela's hands and tossed them into the pot.

"Martin isn't the only man who loves the Lord. Jonathan is pursuing me, and it feels wonderful. He was serenading me last night."

"Well, all right, that's cute." Sharyn gave in; she knew when her sister was digging her heels in.

"Martin *never* did anything like that." Angela slammed her fist on the chopping block.

"Girl, you know Martin is not that type. You can get a hallelujah though." Sharyn simulated a microphone and swayed in front of the stove.

"Can he sing?" Rose asked, entering the kitchen from the adjoining dining room. Sharyn jumped.

"Mom, where'd you come from?" Sharyn asked, wondering how much her mother had heard.

"He can sing, but not like you, Mom." Angela smiled.

"I know that's right. He sounds like he's fond of you, and if he likes you, things will be all right. What God has for you is for you," Rose replied. "Now move over, Sha, I got to get my pie started."

"My pleasure." Sharyn removed the skillet from the stove, hopped back on the stool, and motioned for the cracker box.

"Where are Kevon and Niche? Did they head to her mom's?" Angela tossed the crackers back to Sharyn.

"Was that the doorbell?" Sharyn interjected, as her hands glided over the final remnants left in the cracker box. She could barely make out the voices coming from the other room.

"Yes! Finally, it must be Kevon and Niche. I can't wait for them to see what I bought for the baby." Rose headed out of the kitchen, her golden chandelier earrings glistening as she skipped toward the front door.

"Who is she fooling? She's anxious to get to Niche." Sharyn smiled. "She has no clue that she has a grandbaby right in front of her."

"Angela, you have company!" Rose yelled from the foyer. Angela raised her eyebrows, hopped off her bar stool, and winked at Sharyn.

"Good luck," Sharyn echoed after her, because the yams weren't the only thing being tossed into hot water today.

26

Angela

Angela smoothed her tongue over her teeth to eliminate any lipstick stains. She stood up straight and swayed her hips purposefully as she slunk toward the door. Angela eyed Jonathan smiling broadly next to her mother at the front door. He looked handsome standing under the mistletoe that adorned the home's entry. His fresh haircut matched his newly coiffed goatee, and his black pinstriped suit complemented his royal-blue collared shirt. She curtsied as she caught his eyes.

"Hi, baby, you're early. It's only twelve-thirty." Angela tried to grab Jonathan's hand, but he opened his arms wide to greet her. Angela dived into his arms, wanting to kiss his thick lips shiny with Vaseline, but she restrained herself. "I'm sure you remember my mother."

Jonathan grinned. "Yes, pleasure to see you again, and your home is beautiful. The decorations are the best *by far* on this block." Jonathan knelt down and grabbed a large silver gift-wrapped box. "For your family. Merry Christmas."

Rose winked at Angela. "Thank you, that's thoughtful. I'll put it under the tree for later. Now, if you'll both excuse me, I have to finish up some things in the kitchen. Make yourself at home."

"Sure, Mom." Angela nodded as her mother walked out of the foyer and back toward the kitchen, leaving Jonathan and Angela alone.

"Your mother is *fine*! I tell you—if I wasn't with you!" Jonathan gently patted her bottom. Angela elbowed him in the side.

"Stop that," Angela instructed, as they headed toward the family room arm in arm. Angela observed Martin's eyes widen as he saw her approach. The Seahawks football game held the attention of the other men gathered, who hardly noticed them walk in. "Excuse me, I'd like to introduce you to my friend Jonathan. Michael and Daddy, I believe you've met when he picked me up from the movies."

"Oh yeah, I remember, on Sharyn's birthday." Michael nodded, glancing away from the television.

"Nice to see you again, young sweet back," Robert said, pointing at him. Angela walked Jonathan over to Martin, who sat staring at the end of the leather couch.

"This is Reverend Martin Broussard, an associate minister at my church." Martin stood to his feet and shook Jonathan's hand without pleasantries. Angela felt a dip in her stomach as the two men stood shoulder to shoulder.

"Good to meet you, Reverend Broussard," Jonathan said. "I can't call a minister by his first name," he confessed. Martin nodded and shifted his gaze to Angela.

"Okay, now you've met everyone, I'm going to get my coat, and I'll meet you in the hallway," Angela said, pulling Jonathan's arm toward the foyer.

"Oh, we don't have to leave right away, baby. I know I'm a bit early, and if these gentlemen don't mind, I could catch some of the game," Jonathan countered.

"Yes, Angela, he could sit down and relax with us," Martin offered.

Angela's jaw tightened. "No problem, I'll be in the kitchen if you need me. Whenever you're ready, yell. Do you want something to drink?" Angela asked Jonathan, as she reluctantly released his arm.

"No, baby, I'm fine for now, thank you." Jonathan kissed Angela on the cheek and gently squeezed her elbow.

"Ang, I'd like something to drink." Martin interrupted their brief show of intimacy.

"Sure, Martin. What can I get you?" Angela asked, harshly throwing her hand on her hip.

"You know what I want." Martin leaned back in his seat, placed his hand behind his neck, and leaned to the side like a reckless driver behind the wheel.

"That's right," Angela enunciated in a robotic tone. "I think I do remember, apple juice, right? However, sometimes you tend to be indecisive, Reverend. You know how uncertain you can be." Angela exited the family room without awaiting his reply.

Angela popped another saltine cracker in her mouth. She'd finished half the sleeve without even noticing the taste. She was not an emotional eater, but her anxiety had provided stomach upset. She gazed out of the bay window at the white peeling paint curling from the neighbor's house.

"Girlfriend, it's been an hour. When are you guys leaving?" Sharyn inquired.

"I better check," Angela replied, "but I'm scared to go out there." Angela shoved the box toward the middle of the island as the doorbell rang. She scooted off her stool, flipped her hair, and bowed to the inevitable. "I'll be back." She hated to head toward the land mine. "And I'll get the door." Angela wiped cracker crumbs off her sweater, adjusted her skirt, and walked toward the foyer. Peering through the peephole, she recognized a familiar face. "Hey, it's about time, Mom was starting to get worried." She opened the door and kissed Kevon on the cheek.

"Merry Christmas," Niche and Kevon said in unison. They both scooted past her and headed to the living room, where the second Christmas tree stood with bright, flashing holiday lights.

"Hmm, no smart remark, Kev?" Angela yelled after him.

"Not today, sis," Kevon replied. Angela noticed Niche's bloodshot eyes. She knew not to ask since they always had drama; she barely had enough time to troubleshoot her own problems. Angela shut the door and headed toward the family room. Jonathan had positioned himself next to Martin, and the two were chatting energetically. Angela could hear their laughter as she edged closer to them. She stopped short in the entryway and swallowed hard. "Jonathan, you ready?" Jonathan met her eyes, smiled, and rose to his feet.

"Yes, baby, we'd better get going." He turned, shook Martin's hand, and offered an explanation. "Were on our way to my mom's." Jonathan turned toward the other men huddled around the television. "Pleasure meeting *all* of you, but I can't keep my beautiful woman waiting. Hey, nice talking to you too, Reverend Martin. Is it cool to call you that?" Jonathan walked toward Angela and snaked his arm around her waist.

"No worries—it's cool," Martin replied, as Angela's jaw clamped down, resisting the desire to call him something else.

Kevon

Kevon placed the last of his gifts under the ornate Christmas tree in the living room. He'd hardly had time to shop, but he couldn't arrive at his mother's empty-handed. She had expectations, and no one ever veered from them. The noble fir was set atop a plush red rug with embossed silver reindeer galloping along the edges. Small silver angel ornaments were placed carefully about the tree from top to bottom. An enormous angel sat atop the tree, adorned with red faux fur and wings fashioned from crystal. Candles were strategically set about the room, adding the fragrance of cinnamon spice to the natural aroma of the Christmas tree.

Kevon sat back in the upholstered armchair and looked at the love of his life staring off into the distance, her puffy eyes were a reminder of the pain. He hadn't expected things to get out of control. Speaking to his mother might help; she was the master of control. Kevon stood and headed toward the kitchen. "I'll be right back." He skirted through the adjoining door, and immediately the odor of onions scratched at his nose. "Hi, Mom." He surveyed the kitchen and eyed two freshly baked apple pies placed on cooling racks on the counter, several unopened cans of chicken broth on the island, and a half-severed onion in his mother's hand.

"Hey you, I was wondering what happened to my baby boy, baby girl, and that grandbaby of mine." Rose laid the onion and knife on the chopping board and walked toward her son. Kevon felt soothed by her embrace. He wanted to tell her right then. Confess that his baby was dead. Confess that it was his fault. He'd wished it away. The power of death rested upon his tongue, and he had spoken it into existence.

"We were missing you," Sharyn chimed in. Kevon saluted his sister like a cadet acknowledging an officer.

"We had some other things on the agenda today. Busy, you know." Kevon looked around the kitchen; it still looked different without Big Mama standing amongst the women. It'd been years, and he still missed her presence. "Where did Ang go?"

"She's spending some time at Christmas with her friend's family."

"Where's Daddy?" Kevon asked.

"Where else?" Rose replied.

"I'll be back." Kevon headed toward the family room, knowing he'd have to wait until later to get some time alone with his mother.

"What's up, y'all?" Kevon greeted the men and turned back toward the living room, making no excuses for not watching the game.

"Boy, where you going?" Robert yelled behind him.

"Oh, I'll be back, Daddy. Niche and I are going to spend time together, you know how it is." Kevon needed to keep Niche away from his family. She'd been crying uncontrollably, and Kevon could hardly keep up with her mood swings. At any second she could come unglued.

"I'm back." Kevon plopped down on the floor next to Niche, looked around, and then pulled a flask from his inside pocket.

"Kevon, what are you doing?" Niche pulled away from him.

"I need to take the edge off a bit," Kevon explained, as he glanced over his shoulder to make sure no one was around. A little brandy was sure to quiet the voice in his head.

"But you promised, no more drinking," Niche reminded him.

"Calm down, baby. I'm not drinking again, I'm gonna have a sip, that's all. Nobody is gonna get wasted at my mom's house, okay?"

"Okay," Niche grumbled, "one sip."

27

Angela

The light from the visor lit up the car as she checked her makeup. Angela wished they were headed to her condo instead of back to her mother's. She reached in her handbag and grabbed her lip gloss. The red stain accentuated her lips.

"Give me some of that," Jonathan ordered, as he turned the corner near her mother's street. She reached over to hand him the lip gloss vial. "You know what I mean." Angela half smiled and leaned in until her lips met his. She took in a deep breath, enjoying the familiarity of his flesh. He was a man who was fully capable of making her feel like a woman. He wanted her, and not the other way around. She knew Martin wasn't going anywhere; he was imbedded in her family like a stain on the carpet, and the only way to get rid of it was replacement. The only problem was he felt like he was meant to be her permanent covering. "I had a wonderful time, Angela. I think my parents fell in love with you." Jonathan glanced in her direction.

"You think so?" Angela smiled broadly.

"I can't believe how you started joking along with my crazy family. Sometimes I get embarrassed by my parents. They don't know when to stop, but you fit right in." Jonathan placed his hand on her knee. "You know, baby, you don't know when to stop either."

"How so?" Angela batted her eyes.

"You won't stop taking up residence in my heart." Jonathan squeezed her leg.

Angela avoided his gaze, uncomfortable with his response. "You're sweet, and your parents are so easygoing. I hope I didn't embarrass *you?*"

"Naw, baby, you could never do that." Jonathan pulled up in front of her mother's driveway. "I'm sorry we're later than we intended." Jonathan frowned. Angela glanced at the clock and her heart leapt, happy that they were later than planned. She wanted to keep Jonathan as far away from Martin as possible.

"No big deal, the cars are still here. Besides, I wasn't in a rush tonight." Angela eyed Martin's truck still parked on the corner, occupying a space in her life.

Angela and Jonathan's joined hands swung in unison as they walked into the house unannounced. It seemed as if they'd never left. The men were still in the family room watching television, and Niche and Kevon were still in the living room talking.

"Hello, we're back!" Angela yelled out. Rose burst out of the kitchen, shaking her finger at the two of them.

"You know dinner started at six o'clock. Now, come on here, take off those coats. Angela, you have work to do in this kitchen." Rose turned on her high heels and returned to the kitchen in a huff.

"No easygoing around here." Angela shook her finger playfully at Jonathan and walked toward the kitchen. She entered the kitchen and began dutifully cleaning the dishes leftover from dinner. Her mother stood watch over her shoulder like a security guard.

"How was his mama's food?" Rose asked hurriedly.

"It was a great dinner, Mom. Sorry I missed ours, but I was in no rush to get back here," Angela confessed, trying to keep the peace.

"Why is *he* still here?"

"Angela, Martin is welcome here. I don't know why this is

bothering you so much," Rose declared as she pulled a clean glass from the dish rack and examined it.

"Cause she loves him," Sharyn teased, as she wiped down the island.

"Love is fleeting." Angela stuck her tongue out at her sister. "Now, let's get this show on the road. Time to open some gifts."

"Now that's an idea." Rose headed out of the kitchen, yelling, "Present time!"

Angela wiped her hands on a dish towel and headed toward the living room. She found a seat on an accent chair as her entire family flocked in to open up Christmas gifts. She refused to look at Martin, standing alone in the corner near their family portrait. Angela pointed to the floor adjacent to her when Jonathan approached. "Let's draw numbers to see who goes first," she suggested.

"That's corny. Let's go in alphabetical order like we always do," Sharyn replied.

"Fine then, that makes Angela first." Rose nodded.

"Fine by me!" Angela grabbed a giant blue square box near the bottom of the Christmas tree. "Let me see . . . this one is from Daddy."

"This is going to take forever if we open each gift individually. Let's all open Mom's and Dad's simultaneously, then we can open family and friends," Sharyn proposed. Angela knew her oldest sibling felt it was her responsibility to keep the family organized.

"Now, that sounds like a plan," Robert agreed. "I don't want to be sitting here forever. My back hurts and I want some of that sweet potato pie."

"Okay, okay. Daddy, this might take a while, go get some pie." Angela winked at her father and then passed out all the gifts that were from her parents. Kevon received a silver watch. Niche loved the matching baby-blue mother and baby T-shirts. Sharyn received a beautiful cashmere sweater, and Angela her favorite perfume. Michael was gifted a gray pullover, and Martin a tie.

Angela's pride bustled when her father reached in his wallet and pulled out a twenty for Jonathan.

"Merry Christmas, Jonathan," Robert whispered.

"No, thank you, sir." Jonathan waved off the cash. Rose pulled out a small black box from underneath the tree and handed it to Jonathan. He opened the box delicately.

"Thank you much, Mrs. Lovelace. I needed some new handkerchiefs." Angela shot her mother a knowing glance. She was delighted her mother kept extra gifts under the tree.

Angela's leg shook with anticipation as it was now her turn to open her other gifts. "Sharyn, I hope you paid attention to all the hints that I was dropping."

"What hints?" Sharyn snickered.

Angela gathered all her presents from under the tree and plopped back into the chair. "What's with these small boxes, people?" Angela laughed as she grabbed the first box from Sharyn and Michael. Angela tore open the small black box and squealed with delight at the crystal teardrop earrings.

"My earrings! I love them." Angela danced in her chair. "Thanks, guys."

"No, thank you, my dear, for making your hints so subtle." Sharyn rolled her eyes.

Angela opened up a green gift bag from Kevon and Niche. "Right on, y'all, this is exactly what I needed for the upcoming year." Angela fanned the tan leather organizer over her head.

"Let me take that from you." Jonathan removed the organizer from her hand and pulled a small red jewelry box from his pocket.

"Well, thank you, sir." Angela offered her best southern drawl. She opened the box slowly and almost dropped it when she saw its contents.

"Oh my God!" Angela exclaimed, as she pulled the box up to her chest.

"What is it? Let me see." Rose hopped to her feet, and Angela handed the small box to her mother. Rose eyed it suspiciously and passed it around the room. Silence filled the room as eyes fell to Jonathan.

"Well, I guess I'm on the spot." Jonathan giggled and wiped his brow. "So." Jonathan hesitated. "I'd like to take this time to say what I've been wanting to express for a while now." Jonathan knelt before Angela.

"Should I grab the camera?" Kevon asked.

"No camera needed, it's a little too soon for an engagement ring, but I wanted to convey to you *all* how much I care about this woman." Jonathan laughed nervously. "Angela, I can't tell you how much I've enjoyed each moment we've spent together." Jonathan took a deep breath and clasped his hands like he was going to pray. "I wanted to buy you something this year that expressed the way I truly feel about you. I tried to express to you how important you are to me, but I don't think you understood what I was getting at. I am outing myself in front of your entire family. You're a wonderful woman, Angela Lovelace, and we all know that. And I wanted to make my commitment to you known. The ring is a promise ring, and baby, I promise to be there for you as long as you need and want me to." He leaned in to kiss her.

Angela jumped to her feet and nearly pushed him over. She wanted to spare Martin from having to watch any more. Although she was tired of Martin's games, she still respected him. She smiled at Jonathan, knelt down, and kissed him on the cheek. "Wow! Thank you, this is too much. It's gorgeous, and I must say I'm floored *and* embarrassed." She giggled. "Let's talk about this later tonight in private, okay? Now, family, *mind* ya business." Angela winked at him, feeling sweat form on her back. She hoped panic was not at her doorstep.

"Whatever you want, baby." Jonathan winked back.

"I wish I could be a fly on *that* wall." Kevon smirked.

"Shut up, Kev," Sharyn scolded.

"Here, Ang." Kevon placed his finger over his lips, then shoved the next box toward his sister.

Angela grabbed the next gift. "Finally, an enormous box." She threw her hands up toward heaven. "Hallelujah." Angela knew this box was from Martin. She had avoided him all evening, and now she sat face-to-face with their signature pastel-green wrapping paper. They'd started dating when he taught a Sunday school class that she volunteered in, and their first art project had been outfitted with pastel-green cherub-embossed paper. It had been their wrapping paper ever since.

Angela looked him directly in the eye. "Thanks, Martin." Her eyes softened when he patted his hand over his heart.

Angela ferociously ripped through the wrapping paper, already expecting the comforter she'd hinted to him about. He had initially refused to buy her bedding for her birthday, citing it was too forward, but she knew he'd purchase it for Christmas. Inside the large box sat a smaller green box followed by another box. Each box decreased in size until Angela pulled out the last and smallest green box. "No comforter?" she whined.

"I hope you like it." Martin spoke to her for the first time that evening. Angela stared at the box for a long time.

"Will you open it already?" Kevon leaned forward in his seat.

"Well, it certainly isn't the comforter I told you about," Angela reiterated, peering at the box, hoping it wasn't the engagement ring she'd longed for. She shot her brother a menacing glare. "Give me a second, Kevon. This *is* my last gift, you know." Angela took a deep breath and decided to dive into the pool headfirst. She frantically ripped off the wrapping paper. Angela raised her eyebrows as she held the box up to display the two-carat, pear-shaped diamond. "It's a diamond ring!" she howled, leaping out of her seat and taking a step toward Martin. Angela stopped short as she saw Jonathan staring at her from the corner of her eye. "Wow, how exciting," she said, carefully controlling her intonation as she waved her hands in the air like a dancing Temptations singer and then plopped back into her seat.

"Not any diamond ring, Angela," Martin said, gazing at Jonathan.

"It's a pre-engagement ring." Martin shifted his eyes to her parents. "Mr. and Mrs. Lovelace, I too have enjoyed the *two years* that Angela and I have spent together. And as both of you know and she is also aware, I plan to eventually make her my wife, but only when the time is right. I believe I've found my rib, but 'wait, I say, on the Lord.'" Martin swallowed hard and approached Angela's chair. "You know you're my sweetheart, Angela, and the two carats are for the two wonderful years we've been together."

"Martin." Angela lowered her head as tears filled her eyes. Emotions flooded her body. Her leg began to shake uncontrollably. Martin stooped down, grabbed her hand, and lifted her face.

"I love you, and I never want to lose you." He stood and turned back to address her parents.

"Mr. and Mrs. Lovelace, this year I thought it wasn't wise to propose, obviously, based on the circumstances at hand, but I want you to know that I do love Angela. You know God has designed it so that the man should be in charge of his household. Taking on the role of a husband is a responsibility that I don't take lightly. The Bible says in Proverbs 18:22, when a man findeth a wife, he finds a good thing. I know I've found my good thing in your daughter. And for my years of prayerful preparation, we'll obtain favor in the Lord. Prayerfully, on Valentine's Day, we can make it official." Martin looked directly at Jonathan.

"Amen," Robert declared, wiping away tears.

Angela couldn't lift her head again. She gripped the sides of the chair as she felt panic rising in her chest. She could only hear her own breathing as tears flooded her eyes.

"Excuse me." Jonathan broke his silence. "I don't know what's going on here or what to say right now. Umm, Angela, could I speak to you outside for a second?" he asked, as his head motioned toward the front door.

"Sure. Excuse me, please," Angela whimpered, coming out of her daze. Weakened, she pushed herself up by leaning against the chair and headed toward the front door.

"Whatever you have to say, Brother Jonathan, I hope you don't mind if I come along, since I have a vested interest in the outcome of this conversation. Believe me, I don't want this situation to be any more uncomfortable than it already is," Martin declared.

Jonathan turned on his heels and headed back toward the living room. "Excuse me, Mr. and Mrs. Lovelace, I've had a wonderful time in your home, and I thank you for your hospitality. It's best that I go now." Jonathan peered directly at Martin. "And you, Reverend whatever your name is, I don't know what's going on here or what's up with you, and why you keep coming at me, but you're disrespectful. Why would you even sit here and pull this stunt?" Jonathan threw back his shoulders and stuck out his chest. "Reverend or no reverend, you're *way* out of line. Before things escalate, I'm gonna be on my merry way."

Angela's body began to tremble. Jonathan was right; Martin had planned this all along. She raised her hand high in the air, incensed. "No way, this is *not* going to happen on Christmas Day in my mother's house." Angela walked over to Martin in disbelief, squaring off with him. "I don't know what you were thinking, and anything Jonathan has to say to me doesn't have anything to do with you. He is my guest. You know, Martin, I've told you several times that it's over between you and me. You're too late. Like I told you before, I'm moving on, and you for some reason can't seem to understand that."

Martin grabbed her hand. "You don't care about me? Is that what you're saying?"

"Yes, I do care. Heck, I was there for you for two years." Angela shook her hand loose as she could hardly see his face through her tears. "I waited on you for two whole years, but you didn't want me on my terms."

"I always wanted you, Angela," Martin insisted.

"You wanted me on your own terms. Well, I'm sorry that it's come to this, but you brought this on yourself. Two years is too long to wait for anyone—even you." Angela shook her head as tears continued to flow. "I'm leaving, I'll call you guys later. Come on, Jonathan, let's go."

28

Sharyn

The room was quiet, like an athlete was laid out injured on the field. Sharyn didn't know what the next play was. Should she hand Martin his ring or not? This was Angela's mess and she'd left everyone else to clean it up, along with the wrapping paper and boxes crumpled about on the floor. Sharyn knew she'd have to be the first to act. Kevon loved chaos, her father wasn't adept at handling emotions, and her mother refused to tolerate drama. Besides her, no other Lovelace was left in the room. Sharyn cleared her throat loudly and broke Martin out of his stupor. He looked around the room.

"Well, I guess I made a fool of myself. Won't be the first time, though." Martin chuckled. "I'm not the first man to be a fool for love."

"Hey, Rev . . ." Robert stood.

"No, Deac, it's okay. Truly, it'll be okay. Besides, God knows my heart for your daughter. He'll work it out. As always, thank you again for opening up your home to me. I'm sorry how things turned out. I do love your daughter, and I thought she loved me too." Martin swallowed hard as tears started to form in his eyes.

"I'll walk you to the door, Martin," Rose said.

"No, I will," Sharyn interjected, knowing her mother wanted to clear out the debris.

"No, that's okay, Sharyn. I'll see myself out. Hold onto that ring for your sister, okay? I do apologize for all the trouble I've caused, but when a man is in love . . ." Martin's words trailed off. He stood up straight, lifted his head up, and walked toward the front door.

"Dang! Was that a trip or what? All this over fathead Angie," Kevon said as they heard the front door close.

"I do feel sorry for Martin though." Sharyn picked up the diamond ring.

"You guys, it was an eventful evening, but out of respect for your sister, we're not going to discuss it. We will not gossip in my house. Next person to open presents, please," Rose said.

"Yes, let's keep the family tradition intact." Sharyn rolled her eyes.

"Amen!" Robert shoved a present toward Sharyn. She looked down at the small red box from Michael and batted her eyes.

"It's not a diamond ring, is it?" Sharyn laughed and opened the box, smiling when she saw its contents. She pulled from the box two bibs that read *I love my Grandma and Grandpa*. Sharyn handed them both to her parents.

Rose eyed the yellow bib. "I thought this gift was for you."

"What's going on here?" Robert asked.

"Mom and Dad, Niche is not the only one pregnant in this family. I am too." Sharyn smiled. Rose dropped the bib on the floor, ran over to Sharyn, and grabbed her.

"Move now, I want to hug my baby too," Robert said, tapping Rose on the shoulder.

"Join in, why don't you?" Rose barked. Both hugged Sharyn.

"Enough," Michael shouted, "I'm here too!"

"Oh my goodness, sorry, Michael, but you kids are going to give me a stroke this Christmas. Kevon, do you have anything else you want to add before I pass out?" Rose asked, as she wiped tears from her eyes. Kevon smiled broadly at his mother.

"No, Moms, nothing at all," Kevon mumbled, staring at Niche. "Way to go, Mike. I'm happy for you guys. Congrats, sis."

"Okay, let's get this show back on the road, I'm going to need to lie down soon." Rose pushed another present toward Sharyn while tears still rolled down her cheeks.

Sharyn looked down at the tag labeled *Niche and Kevon.* "Oh guys, you didn't have to get me anything." Sharyn opened the flat white box and was shocked to see a baby picture of Kevon. Her brows furrowed as she shot Niche and Kevon a suspicious glance. "Thank you, guys," she said, wondering why they would give her an old picture of her brother.

"What?" Kevon pursed his lips and threw his hands up in the air. "That's not what I bought."

"Let me explain, Sharyn," Niche said, as she tightly held Kevon's hand. Niche paused.

"Why does she need a picture of me, Niche?" Kevon's voice rose.

"Because you're all they get, Kevon. No new baby. No baby at all, because our baby is dead."

Before anyone could comprehend what she'd said, Kevon bolted out of the living room and slammed the front door.

Robert

The energy inside St. John's Church was high as a joyful noise was being made throughout the congregation. Praise and worship time lasted so long that the chorale director stood to announce that the choir would skip their second selection. "Who's on the Lord's Side" seemed to envelop the spirit of worship, and the pews were filled with parishioners dancing on their feet. The congregation swayed back and forth as lifted hands resembled the wave being carried out at a local sporting event. The organ crescendo was heightened by the drum's high hat. The celebration honoring the Lord and Savior Jesus Christ was in full swing.

Despite the overhead fans swirling at the highest speed, Robert still felt too hot to stand. He was one of the few members that remained seated. His white dress shirt dampened from the tears flowing from his eyes. He wiped his face and dried his hands on his black slacks. An usher dutifully brought him facial tissue and asked if he needed water. Robert respectfully declined and leaned back into the pew, weighted with his newfound reality. He would have to start this year without her. Two untimely deaths in one year, like Big Mama and his brother.

Robert sat quietly with his family, looking distraught like a lone Republican at the Democratic National Convention. He hadn't stood up, clapped, or waved his hand the entire service. He didn't know what to think, but he knew what to do. Casting his cares on his God because He cared for him was the only route he knew to take. Robert scooted forward, slid off the pew, knelt down, and prayed. He'd lived through a crisis before, and this one was no different. God hadn't failed him yet, and Robert knew He would make all things new.

Sharyn

Sharyn sat between her father and her husband. She gripped Michael's hand tight, like holding onto the reins of a horse so as not to fall off. Her other hand lay secure on top of her black slacks across her abdomen. A miscarriage. The news that had devastated their family on Christmas Day played over and over in her head. Nothing like this had ever happened to them. Christmas had always been a time of joy.

The guilt overwhelming Sharyn was palpable. How could she be the one still pregnant? Why? She was the one that had aborted her baby. Getting pregnant was a different battle than staying pregnant.

She inched closer to her husband. She needed to feel safe now more than ever before. Michael leaned in and kissed her cheek.

Sharyn glanced at her father, who'd been crying throughout the service. She sat surprised when he sank to his knees. The news of the miscarriage had impacted him more than she'd imagined. Sharyn wished she could help, that she could provide him with reassurance, but she couldn't give what she did not possess. She was all out of strength; someone else would have to hold this family together. God could take her baby too. She nodded at the usher heading away from her father and signaled for a fan.

Angela

Angela's leg hopped up and down like a seamstress directing the pedal of a sewing machine. She didn't want to unravel, but she knew something needed to bind her family back together again. Her houndstooth pencil skirt had moved well above her knee, and the sweat on her thigh had started to dampen the pew. Her father had placed his hand firmly on her leg several times to steady it, but it wouldn't stop shaking. Angela gazed straight ahead and tried to focus on the choir, but she couldn't restrain her thoughts. She'd been plagued by panic attacks almost daily since Sharyn told her about Kevon's baby. The reality of being given a gift and having it snatched away hit too close to home.

Angela gritted her teeth to will her mind not to scan the faces of the many men with whom she'd become one. The more she tried to forget them, the more she recalled, including the multiple times she had ended up taking the morning-after pill. Sure, it was her choice, but what about Niche? Niche hadn't had a choice.

Angela glanced up at Martin's empty seat in the pulpit. He was right not to have slept with her, and she was wrong to have rejected him. Her life had been empty since Christmas. Martin would've been the first person she called to get perspective about miscarriages. She constantly checked her phone, hoping he'd call, but was left disappointed. The vacant chair reminded her of the loneliness that had crept up deep inside her. Her social life was the exact opposite of *Alice in Wonderland*. At her table was a host of men but no true friends.

Sharyn

Sharyn could barely hear over the roar of her own thoughts as the pastor read the Lovelaces' name off the prayer list. Her stomach dropped, and she gripped her husband's hand tight, like a pregnant woman in labor.

"Sharyn," Michael whispered, as his eyes darted toward the rear of the church.

Sharyn followed his gaze and couldn't believe it. Her eyes enlarged as she lifted her torso, ready to run toward the rear of the building. She spotted her mother's hat swaying haphazardly over the top of the crowd. Before she could walk over to her mother, Sharyn realized Rose had moved past the congregants assembled in her row and stomped toward the front of the sanctuary. Clearly her mother was more moved by the loss of her unborn grandchild than Sharyn had thought. Sharyn knew each step her mother took was more determined than the previous one, and it was impossible to stop her. Sharyn nestled back in her seat and elbowed her husband. Her father attempted to grab Rose as she passed their row, but his effort proved fruitless as her violet silk sleeve slipped right through his grasp.

"God has spoken, let the church say amen," Rose bellowed repeatedly as she headed up to the choir stand. The church clapped emphatically as the strongest alto grabbed the microphone. The church body knew what was to come, and so did Sharyn. Despite the earlier proclamation by the chorale director, the choir stood at attention and awaited the songstress.

Rose's voice swam high above the sanctuary. It seemed to lift the church off its foundation. The dance of happiness was exhibited in the congregants as the divinity of the Lord was proclaimed. The pastor stood in the pulpit and lifted his hands as the praise to the Lord magnified. The church knew that Jesus was alive and His spirit enveloped His people.

Rose collapsed as ushers and nurses surrounded her. The door-keepers for the Lord lifted her high off the ground and headed toward the choir room. Sharyn stood to her feet and shouted, "Hallelujah!" Her tears wouldn't subside as the pastor rose to preach and the congregation waited for their cup to continue running over.

Angela

Angela fanned herself furiously as sweat trickled down the sides of her face. Her heart swelled like a water balloon filled to capacity as she watched her mother carted out of the sanctuary. She faced the pulpit, trying hard to keep her tears from falling. The pastor took a sip from the hidden water glass, and the church silenced as he cleared his throat.

"Word Up" rang out from the pastor's microphone. Bibles were strewn high in the air as the congregation stood to honor the King of Kings. "Wasn't the Lord magnified in this sanctuary today, but oh, is He magnified in your life outside of the sanctuary? Are you on the Lord's side?" The pastor's voice rang loud with emphasis. His passion was felt all over the building.

Angela lowered her head. A tear dotted her patent leather shoe as she tried to swallow the unknown feeling that rose inside her.

"Matthew 23, verse 23–26," the pastor instructed, as Bibles opened all over the building. "The Word of the Lord says 'Woe to you, teachers of the law and Pharisees, you hypocrites! You give a tenth of your spices—mint, dill, and cumin. But you have neglected the more important matters of the law—justice, mercy, and faithfulness. You should have practiced the latter, without neglecting the former. You blind guides! You strain out a gnat but swallow a camel. Woe to you, teachers of the law and Pharisees, you hypocrites! You clean the outside of the cup and dish, but inside they are full of greed and self-indulgence. Blind Pharisee! First clean the inside of your cup and dish, and then the outside also will be clean.' Church, let's clean up," the pastor roared.

The congregation sat down like fourth-graders in an assembly.

"Tell it, Pastor!" yelled one of the deacons in the front pew, as he stood to his feet.

The pastor preached God's word, and the church swelled as rapid hallelujahs rang out from among the crowd like bullets. Angela closed her eyes and surrendered. She couldn't stop the tears from flowing. "Thank you!" she sniffed, as an usher placed a box of tissues in her hand.

"Take out the trash, disinfect the tongue, and sanitize the body. Offer yourselves before the Lord. He forgives. He forgives. Glory to God, He forgives," the pastor proclaimed from the pulpit.

Angela stood and lifted her hands as the pastor exposed her life. *Forgive me, Lord.* She could feel her feet jumping alive again with revival. Hallelujah escaped her lips as restoration blanketed her soul.

29

Angela

Angela tried to untangle the telephone cord. Clasping the receiver up against her ear, twisting furiously, and yanking seemed to finally yield progress. The cord seemed to be a metaphor for her life, and she was determined to straighten out the kinks. She tired of spinning around men, getting tied up, and then breaking off communication. She vacillated between wanting Jonathan, loving Martin, and being alone. Her feelings, like her future, remained uncertain.

"Did he call?" Sharyn inquired. Angela could hear the tinge of judgment in her voice. Her anger rose like flames doused with lighter fluid.

"No, and I don't care either, Sharyn." Angela grabbed the loose papers off her desk and shoved them into her desk drawer. She pushed her keyboard off to the side and wiped the crumbs from this morning's donut onto the floor. "How dare he spring a ring on me like that! Doesn't he know that I've been waiting years for some sign of exclusivity?"

"What if he was desperate, Ang? Like Niche was at Christmas. It's not like he has a lot of relationship experience. I think he was afraid of losing you," Sharyn offered.

"I can't even deal with Niche right now." Angela rubbed her temples. "And Martin, how dare you make excuses for him? You can't lose what you never had." Angela leaned back in her chair and closed her eyes. Sleepless nights had now become her norm, haunted by what could've been. Between worrying about Kevon, Trevion, and Martin, plus Jonathan's incessant texting, she'd taken to watching novelty sitcoms instead of resting.

"Please, Angie, he had you from the gate. You're the one who said lately he was starting to heat things up. Maybe this was his natural progression."

"Why are you on his side, anyway? Forget Martin and your agenda. Are you in cahoots with Mom?" Angela had fielded calls from both of her parents begging her to have an open mind. She didn't need to hear from anyone except for Kevon.

"My agenda is to see you happy. We know you're in love with him. I don't want you to shoot first and ask questions later."

"I'm happy, Sharyn," Angela barked, shuffling Post-It notes on her desktop in order of importance.

"I understand *you* more than you think I do, Angela," Sharyn proclaimed. "Speaking of understanding, we have to talk about Kevon."

"I gotta go," Angela declared, desiring to stay anxiety-free.

"I bet you do," Sharyn said sarcastically.

"Yes, I do. I'm at work, you know." Angela sat up in her black office swivel chair, dropped her shoulders, and admired her clutter-free desk. She had finally achieving organizational success.

"So am I," Sharyn noted defiantly.

"Working from home is not the same." Angela shook her head. Her sister was probably still in her pajamas and fuzzy slippers.

"Whatever, girl, I earn my keep," Sharyn reminded her.

"Touché, I'll talk with you later." Angela grabbed her pen, her notepad, and her cup of cold coffee and headed toward the staff meeting in the conference room. As she left her office, she recognized the faint tenor of Trevion's ringtone. She stopped immediately and listened closely. Her eyes widened as she heard it again.

Angela carefully placed the coffee back on her desk and grabbed her cell phone out of her top drawer, relieved that she'd assigned each client a ringtone, a tactic she'd learned during graduate school when the instructors gave their students personal numbers for classroom assignments. Ringtones helped her organize cases and screen calls she didn't want to answer. "This is Angela," she asserted, waiting for a response from the unidentified caller.

"Hey, this is Ray, you called me?" Angela recognized his name immediately. She'd been waiting weeks for his call. As one of only three contacts in Trevion's mother's phone, hopefully he could help her find some answers. Trevion had begun to trust her, and she'd begun to grow fond of him. Frozen yogurt had become their tradition as she'd made multiple unsanctioned trips to Dublin to play baseball, go to the movies, and eat burgers with her new client. Angela knew she had to protect her heart, and the sooner she was off this case, the better.

"Hello, Mr. Ray, thanks for returning my call. I was phoning about a case I'm working on."

"I know why you were calling. I heard about you," Ray snarled. Angela's shoulders tensed as hostility permeated through the telephone line.

"I'm the social worker for Trevion. I was trying to speak with people who had experience with his mother, Samantha, in an attempt to better serve him."

"Is Tre in a foster home?" Ray snapped.

"Yes, he is currently in foster placement." Angela returned to her seat, placing her pen back into the pencil cup.

"So, 'currently' must mean he may get out soon?" Ray pressed.

"No, Mr. Ray, unfortunately not. Trevion doesn't have any other potential placements at this time." Angela wondered about his genuine interest in the child.

"You mean to tell me that he's out there all alone and gonna *keep* staying with some strangers?" Ray questioned. Angela sat erect. She'd dealt with hostile people in the past, but she refused to lose him. She needed to get into his good graces. Angela's voice softened.

"Sadly, we have no next of kin," she clarified.

"No next of kin. No one is coming forward to claim Tre? Well, I'll be darned, and some people call themselves Christian."

"Well, sometimes even Christian people find it hard to take in strangers," Angela explained.

"Tre ain't no stranger," Ray retorted. Angela pursed her lips. She had made a misstep.

"Sorry, Mr. Ray, I'm unsure what you're referring to." Angela grabbed a notepad.

"Nothing. Forget it." Ray clammed up. Angela could feel her heart beat faster with excitement. Ray had something to hide, and this could be the answer that she had been looking for. Finally, she suspected Trevion's father had come forward.

"Believe me, Ray, Trevion is in a stable home. Yes, we would like to see him in a relative placement, and there is compensation for that. We don't seek child support or anything like that. We want him out of our system and with folks that care about him. He is happy despite . . ." Angela purposely stopped midsentence. The bait was set.

"Despite what?"

"Forgive me, I've spoken too candidly," Angela lied.

"Well, speak on it, lady. What's wrong with my boy?" Ray grilled.

"Your boy?" *Hallelujah!* Angela rejoiced at Ray's revelation.

"Yeah, that's my boy. He's a good boy and smart too," Ray confessed.

"He's smart. But I'm confused, Mr. Ray, you mentioned that he was your boy, but no father was identified on his birth certificate. Are you?" Angela asked innocently.

"Oh no, that's none of my doing. I have three sons of my own. I meant my little homeboy. Somebody else is responsible for that one."

Angela's heart sank as the picture of her father glided into her mind.

"I see." Angela's heart thumped in her chest. She was scared to ask the follow-up question. She could see her father sitting on a talk show with an open envelope detailing his DNA. She jumped in. "Do you know who his father is?" she asked half-heartedly, as the words she dreaded escaped her lips.

"Sure don't. I mean, his momma and I were friends, but she never mentioned no daddy. We went through rehab together, you know. I tried to help her, but she didn't want no consistency, like a sponsor. She told me things, but she never mentioned Tre's daddy. Granddaddy maybe, but no daddy," Ray said.

"Tre has a grandfather?" Angela asked.

"Sort of, I guess you can call him that. Surprised he ain't come forward, thought he would have showed up by now. Hey, can you hold on a moment?" Angela held the line, anxiously waiting for more revelations. "Hey, I gotta go, Angela, my hardheaded boy done got into it at day care. What you need, anyway?" Ray asked.

"Help, Ray, I need some help. I need help to aid this boy. Is it possible we can meet for coffee?" Angela crossed her fingers and closed her eyes.

"Can I see Tre?" Ray inquired.

"Not yet, Ray, but I'd be happy to get a letter, note, or message to him. Meet me over coffee, and I can assure you of that."

"That sounds like a plan."

"All right. I'll be the lady in the red scarf." Angela threw her head back against her chair. She had another lead.

Sharyn

Sharyn's orange ruffled top lifted high above her blue jeans as she danced to one of her favorite songs. Her bulging stomach cascaded over her belt as her hips rocked back and forth with the vacuum handle as her dance partner. Ever since Sunday, a joy resonated within her. She knew for certain this time God was going to work it out. Sharyn grabbed the vacuum and pushed it over the beige hall carpet one more time. The scent of gardenias magnified with each swipe over the carpet deodorizer.

"Sharyn, where's my black-and-red tie?" Michael shouted from down the hall. Sharyn pulled the plug from the wall and headed toward their bedroom.

"I don't know. I saw it earlier on the bed, but I haven't seen it since." Sharyn entered the room, approached the bed, and dragged the brown goose-down comforter off. She still didn't see it. Ever since she'd become pregnant she no longer had the energy to clean, but this week had been different. She didn't even feel pregnant. "Get another one because you're going to be late," Sharyn ordered, replacing the bedding. She plopped down on the bed and unbuckled her blue jeans, feeling the imprint of the grooves from the waistband crinkling her skin.

"I'm hurrying!" Michael snapped. "I wanted to wear that tie, Martin gave it to me last year."

"Michael, I'm sure he won't even notice. It's a sweet thing you're doing, meeting him for coffee. I love our alone time while you're on vacation, but he could use your ear more."

"I'd need dialogue, too, if I got my engagement ring handed back to me. Have you been able to reach Kevon?" Michael rummaged through the dresser drawers.

"No, but I will. He needs to burn off some steam. He was frantic *and* crazy the way he ran out of Mom's. Did you see Niche almost trip running after him?" Sharyn hadn't talked to Kevon, but she knew to give him space. Worried that he'd fall into one of his funks, she'd called several times, but his voicemail was full. Sharyn knew he didn't handle loss well, ever since Big Mama, and walking a fine line with him was paramount. Lean into him too much and he'd fall, but leaning back too much often yielded similar results.

"Niche almost fell?" Michael turned around and leaned against the dresser. "That porch was slippery."

"I haven't talked to either of them since Christmas, and it's not like I haven't been trying." Sharyn walked over to her husband, snaked her arms around his neck, and rested her face against his chest. "Did you smell alcohol on him?"

"The only thing I smelled was smoke, he was out of there fast," Michael said, rubbing her back.

"Thank God I was able to calm Mom down. In some weird way, it calmed me down too. The Holy Spirit was working in that house and then again on Sunday. It's like the Spirit came in and set up an emergency break."

"Yeah, honey, but I don't think all this is going to stop anytime soon."

"Not an emergency b-r-a-k-e but an emergency b-r-e-a-k." Sharyn squeezed him tight, pulled back, and looked him directly in the eye. "It's like God is allowing all to break apart before putting it back in its rightful place. God had to remind me that sometimes He allows us to break so He can align us back to our rightful place."

"Like when a bone is misaligned, the doctor has to break it first, then set it, so it can grow back correctly?" Michael winked.

"Exactly. I'm grateful that God brought back to my remembrance one of my favorite scriptures on Sunday. 'Come, and let us return to the Lord; for He has torn, but He will heal us; He has stricken, but He will bind us up.'" Sharyn laughed. "It's easier to submit when you're already on your knees."

Michael patted her protruding stomach. "Now let's prepare for the latter rain."

30

Angela

Angela could smell the nutty, bold aroma of freshly brewed coffee as she entered her favorite coffee shop, Panaderia, on the corner of Mission Street and 24th. Mission Street was always busy, and she loved people-watching through the large storefront windows. The coffee house was filled with patrons, and both window booths were taken. The hum of laughter danced about the establishment as two groups of teenagers hovered over laptops.

Angela eyed an empty corner booth as she passed the large assortment of pastries at the counter. She hurried and placed her empty notebook on the table next to a hand-painted wall mural in an effort to save her spot.

"Hey, Johnny," Angela greeted the young man stationed behind the counter.

"Hello, Lovelace," he said, winking in her direction. "What can I get for you?" Angela knew what she wanted, but she wanted to get Ray something prior to his arrival. Her eyes scanned the pastry case.

"I will have six conchas and two caramel lattes," Angela said, happy with her choice.

"I do have some maple cakes left today also. They're in the back," Johnny informed her.

"Well, don't forget to give me one of those. I deserve a special treat for working during the holidays." Angela smiled, surprised he still remembered her favorite.

"Two lattes coming right up. I saw you stake that booth in the corner. Juan will bring your pastry order out to your table," Johnny said, returning her credit card.

"Thanks." Angela headed back to the empty booth balancing two coffee cups. The red scarf Sharyn had bought her last Christmas would be used for easy identification. The scarf slid out of her purse with one quick tug, and she looped it around her neck. She opened her empty notebook and wrote Trevion's name at the top, as she planned to add to the existing case file.

"Hello, social worker."

Angela lifted her eyes, surprised by the tall, thin man greeting her in pleated khaki pants and a collared shirt. She'd expected a burly brute by the tone and inflection of his voice on the telephone. She stood to her feet, wiped her hands on her gray slacks, and half smiled, careful not to alarm him with a phony grin.

"Ray, thanks for meeting me here. I took the liberty of ordering some coffee and pastries. Have a seat." Angela extended her hand toward the empty side of the booth.

"I don't have a lot of time. I have to pick up my wife from work, and I don't do sweets. I'm three years clean, but I still stay away from temptations," Ray explained.

"No problem. I wanted to meet with you to talk about Tre and how I can better serve him." Angela spoke softly, examining his eyes for the unspoken.

"What you need from me?" Ray questioned.

"I'm looking for some more of his mother's history. I want to make things more comfortable for Tre, as comfortable as I can, anyway. Sounds like you talked with Samantha quite a bit."

"I did. Did you know she was adopted?" Ray asked.

"I read she was, but Samantha's adoptive parents died in an

auto accident, and she was placed back in the system," Angela said, shaking her head and wondering how much she should share. She searched his face for any resemblance to Trevion. His nose was too narrow, and his square face stood in contrast with Trevion's round appearance. His hooded eyes varied from her client's deep-set ones.

"I think Samantha started using shortly after that. It broke her up, and I think that was her way of dealing with that grief. Truth be told, I think she wanted to go to heaven to be with her adoptive parents. I told her she had a death wish."

"Unfortunately, Samantha got her death wish." Angela lowered her eyes.

"Unfortunate for Tre, prayerfully his mama is in 'Glory' now. You know, Sam loved that boy. She got up and took him to school almost daily, high or not, and when she couldn't, she called me to." Ray smiled.

"He loved her too," Angela declared, noting that he called her Sam, a name she had forbidden at the rehab. Maybe they were more than friends.

"Sure did. Sam didn't have much, but she had that boy," Ray said, eyeing his coffee suspiciously.

"Sounds like she lived a lonely life," Angela noted.

"A lonely life, full of people. I think she learned about that in those group homes," Ray explained.

"Did Samantha spend a lot of time in group homes after she went back into foster care?" Angela asked.

"She told me she gave a hundred foster homes a try, but after having loving parents, it was hard for her to be a temporary. Sam would die if she knew Tre was in a foster home."

"Foster homes can be difficult." Angela took a sip of her latte, familiar with the gripes of temporary living arrangements, bitter-sweet like her coffee. She'd placed hundreds of children in the foster care system and had heard double the complaints. Angela wished the system worked better, but it was out of her control. Encountering loving foster parents was as common as engaging with horrible foster parents. They were like any other government system, highlighted among a continuum of imperfections.

"Those homes were definitely difficult for her. She said after a while she gave up and started running away and ran right into a slew of group homes."

"All kinds of stuff happens in those," Angela said, as horrendous group home complaints danced in the back of her mind. She shuffled uncomfortably in her seat.

"You telling me. Some of the stories she used to tell me. Crazy. Just crazy. She did say that not all were bad. Sam liked one, but she ran away before she could really settle in, she was scared she was gonna disappoint the director. He believed in her. It's hard to have someone believe in you when you don't believe in yourself," he recounted.

Angela swallowed hard as this truth resonated within her. Martin also saw purpose in her, but she wasn't able to identify it herself. She changed the subject. "Samantha only had three numbers in her phone. Yours was one, and the other was someone named 'Studebaker.' You know him?"

"Baker. Shoot, I'm not surprised. He was no good for her. That dude met her one time at church. Church! Who does that? But the snake was in the garden, what can we expect? She there trying to get her life right, and here he comes."

"Sometimes it can be like that. I call them thorn bushes."

"That sounds like a perfect name for Baker. He was definitely a thorn in her side. I don't know him, though. All I know was that he was no good for her. She tried, you know. Rehab didn't stick. We both fell off, but I was able to stand back up. Difference is, I had a family. I grew up with two parents. No single mama or poverty-stricken stereotype for me. My dad was a senior vice president at Francisco Bank and Loan," Ray divulged proudly.

"Sometimes family can make all the difference," Angela agreed, wondering what she was doing there. She closed her notebook, accepting it was time to let the investigation go and focus on her own family. The Lovelace family was what she knew for sure.

"You sure right about that. Family was good for me, but God saved me. He's my family. Praise God, He appeared so He might take away my sins. He picked me up right out of the muck and mire. Shoot, picked me up from a pit of hell on earth. Once I realized that God was for me, how could I be against my own self?" Ray said, reveling in his salvation.

"Sounds like you sure turned your life around." Angela smiled.

"God and me. It was hard work, too, but anything worth doing takes some hard work. Speaking of work, am I gonna get my letter to Tre? I wrote him something." Ray pulled a tattered paper from his back pocket.

"Yes, of course. I'll be sure to get it out to him this week," Angela said, as she eyed their pastries making their way to the table.

"Sorry, Lovelace. Juan sold the last maple cake earlier. I didn't know. I put a couple of extras here to make up for it. I got you next time too," Johnny said, placing the tray of pastries in front of them. Ray laughed and looked at Johnny conspicuously.

"No problem, Johnny, next time though," Angela said, as Johnny headed back to the register. "Happy I didn't get my sweet treats, huh?" Angela poked fun at Ray.

"Oh no, that's not it at all. I just thought your nickname was remarkable," Ray replied.

"Lovelace is unusual, but no, I'm not a former lingerie model." Angela smiled, recalling her high school taunts. "It's my surname. What, I look like a Jones or something?" Angela said, shaking her head.

"It's unusual and ironic too," Ray answered, looking down at his watch.

"Ironic?" Angela queried.

"Yeah, Tre related to some Lovelace person, and here you are his social worker by the same name. The irony."

"He is?" Angela's eyes widened.

"Well, that's what his mama said, anyway. Sam found her real parents after her third group home stint. Said she was tired of her life and wanted to find out if something else was out there for her," Ray divulged.

"Her parents? I thought you said Tre was related to Lovelaces," Angela said, confused.

"Yeah, through her. She said she found her real mama, some Lovelace woman. I can't remember her first name though, but who can forget that last name. Say her mama gave her up for adoption cause she was a teen mom or something like that. Too young for a baby, anyway." Ray nudged the tray of pastries.

"How did she?" Angela said, trying to keep her focus as her heart raced.

"It's hard for teens to raise a child, but the lady gave her up and never looked back."

"Oh, that's how she was adopted." Angela picked at a pastry and looked around, trying to find something to ground her. She had sat through uncomfortable interviews before, careful to maintain her poker face, but this was different. Ray was talking about her own mother.

"Sam said she was glad her birth mama gave her up after all. She found the old hag and told her that her adoptive parents died. Sam assumed the lady would take her in or at least love her. Well, the lady broke her heart all over again. Abandoned her for a second time. Can you believe that?"

"Abandoned her?" Angela asked, trying to fit the pieces together as she sneaked her hands underneath the table and started progressive relaxation exercises. "What about her father?"

"Naw, no daddy in the picture. Stepdad though. Sam said her stepdad was appalled by her birth mother. The dude wanted to take her in, but her mama wouldn't allow it. She told me they divorced some years later because of it. You know, she kept in touch with that dude until she died. Called him her Beau Pierre."

"Beau Pierre?"

"Weird, right? He loved her, I think. She said he was the dad she never had. Someone who wanted to help her. She found her real dad six feet under years later. But that Pierre dude paid for a fancy rehab and made sure she had what she needed. Kept her rent paid and Tre's stuff together. He wanted to help her more, too, but she wouldn't have it. Truthfully, I think she loved and hated him at the same time. You know, cause his association with her birth mom."

"I can understand," Angela mumbled, as memories of her mother's rigidity overcrowded her mind.

"I thought he would've come forward for Tre, though. Get him out of that foster home. You never know people, though," Ray said, pushing the plate of pastries closer to Angela.

Angela could feel the tears welling in her eyes as she pulled out the tattered picture from her purse. "Is this Samantha's stepdad?" she inquired, as her stomach dipped.

"Yeah, that's the cat. That's the old picture from her place! Wait— you okay?" he asked, as a tear fell into her coffee cup.

"I'm good. Such a sad story. That poor woman, so lost and alone. Abandoned. True, Ray, you never *really* know people."

31

Robert

Robert opened the door all decked out in Golden State Warriors gear. He'd been waiting all day for the basketball game. Robert had been a fan of the sport since he played in high school, and the game never disappointed. The curve of the ball and the gritty leather felt like power in his hands. Each time he dunked the ball he defied the odds, something he had tried to do all his life. Coaches had instructed, no matter what came at him, it was his job to make a play. Dribble, crossover, pass, hesitate, it didn't matter, as long as he could see the court and anticipate his next move.

"Come on in," Robert said, as he turned on his heels and headed toward the living room, plopping down on the couch and refusing to leave room for her to sit near. He half smiled in her direction in an effort to investigate the playing field. "You want something to drink?" Robert still tasted the resentment from their last conversation.

"No, thank you. Now, what's this all about?" Rose said sourly, securing a seat on the love seat. She clutched her black leather handbag on her lap as her black leather block-heeled boots tapped against the hardwood flooring.

"Listen, Rose, we need to come together here. I've tried to talk to you about this, but you shut me down. We can't ignore things any longer," Robert declared, trying to stave off another argument, appealing to her reason. He knew meeting with her was like rolling dice; he never knew what combination he was going to get: loving and caring, or resistant and hostile.

"Robert, I don't have time for this." Rose pursed her lips like she had ingested a sour lemon. Disappointed, Robert shook his head. He had rolled and crapped out.

"You make time, then. Our family is falling apart, and once again you refuse to deal with it. Stop running away, Rose."

"Running away. Please, not this again. I'm not running. That same old song has been played, this is why we didn't work. I won't compete with your ghosts."

Robert's nostrils flared. "Don't, Rose. This is not about my mother." He scooted further away from her. Although she was occupying the love seat, he wanted to keep as much distance as he could. She had thrown a curveball, and he refused to get hit.

"It's always about your mother. I'm not her, Robert, and I don't behave like she did." Unclutching her handbag, Rose extended her arm and flippantly examined her fingernails.

"This is not about my mother. My mother was a drug-addicted prostitute who committed suicide. *You* are the mother of my children. I'm clear about who you are. But I'm also clear that you avoid and run away from issues." Robert shifted his torso and looked directly toward her to ensure his fastball made contact. "Like you ran from Samantha. My mother didn't care about her life or ours for that matter, but you care too much. Your perfect family and our perfect image. There is no room for blemishes. Samantha was a blemish, Kevon is a bruise, and only God knows what is going on with Angela."

"Angela is fine. She's confused." Rose stared at her wrist and fiddled with her cluster of silver bracelets.

"Confused? We had two men proposing to our daughter in *your* living room while our son and his girlfriend sat a few feet away, struggling with a miscarriage, all the while, your other daughter overdosed and her child is sitting up in foster care. Who is confused?"

Robert sat straight up as he readied himself for battle.

"Robert Lovelace. Don't you dare . . ."

"Dare what? Dare to tell the truth?"

"Your truth, Robert, not mine. My daughter is confused about how to spend the rest of her life. My son is supporting his girlfriend, and the *only other* daughter I have lives with her husband, Michael. That is the truth!"

"Rose, we can still help Samantha's son." Robert moved to the love seat and sat next to her. "He needs a family."

"This is not television, Robert, and there isn't happily ever after. This girl who you keep throwing up in my face had parents. True, I birthed her, but I loved her enough to release her. God does not hold me to my past, and you shouldn't either."

"I never said you had to be her mother, but you could've been her friend. I wasn't her father, but I *was* her friend. I tried to help the least of these, and that, my love, is what God does hold us to."

"That's your problem, Robert. You're always trying to help, and look where your help has gotten us. It helped us right into divorce court." Rose stood and headed toward the front door, never looking back.

Angela

Angela ate every single pastry. She shifted the crumbs off her lap onto her plate and took a deep breath. The crumbs reminded her of the debris her mother had left behind, but there was no cleanup. Angela couldn't go anywhere to avoid this wreckage. She couldn't go back to work, and she definitely couldn't go home.

The cold emanating from the booth sent a chill down her spine. Angela pulled the red scarf tight around her neck, leaned back, and closed her eyes. The loud rings of laughter had stopped when the group of young adults left, her anticipation had given way to anger by the time Ray exited the coffee shop, and when Juan turned the lights up at sunset, an unfamiliar bitterness had entered her atmosphere.

"More coffee, Lovelace?" Johnny touched her shoulder, awakening her to the present.

"Thanks, Johnny." She lifted her cup toward the young businessman.

"*Cómo estás?*" He met her eyes.

"I'm good, but it's been a hard day at the office," she said, taking a sip of coffee.

"I understand, Lovelace, you got yourself one hard job. I know that guy left a while ago, but you take as much time as you need." Johnny looked at her sympathetically and headed back toward the counter.

"Thanks, Johnny." Angela's shoulders slumped. She pulled out Trevion's case file from her bag and opened it to the front page. Her fingers slid across the section that outlined his family history. She couldn't take her eyes off the name that was highlighted in yellow with *deceased* written next to it. Samantha was deceased. Her sister was dead. They would never meet. Her mother could never right this wrong; no wonder she'd fallen out in church. Defeated, Angela lowered her head to the table.

"Ang?" Michael towered over her. Angela lifted her head, startled by the familiar voice.

"Michael? What are you doing here? Is Sharyn okay?" Angela panicked. She grabbed his arm.

"Sharyn is fine. She's at home hanging out. Are you okay?" he asked. Angela smoothed her shirt, trying to keep up her appearance, a trait that her mother had deeply instilled. She wasn't going to out her mother, not until she talked to her first.

"I'm good, tired is all. Unlike you guys, I have to work during the holidays. Here, sit down." She gestured to the seat next to her, closing the case file.

"Thanks, but I'm meeting Martin here for coffee." Michael lowered his head like a guilty child.

Angela clutched her chest. "My Martin?"

"Yes, ma'am. We're searching for some spiritual insights. A lot has been going on lately."

Angela's eyes shifted downward. "It sure has," Angela said, tucking in the edges around her newfound family secret. "And Kevon."

"What's wrong with Kevon?" Martin asked, sauntering up behind Michael.

"Hey, Rev." Michael smiled broadly.

"What's up, Mike?" Martin lifted his hand as their fists bumped in the air. "Angela." He nodded.

"I'll get us a table and grab a couple of lattes." Michael rushed toward the counter like a cat scurrying away from a dark shadow.

Martin looked around, briefly examining the faces in the coffee shop. "You alone?" His eyebrow raised.

Angela motioned toward the closed file on the table. "I was working on a case. How are you?" She stood, moved toward him, and opened her arms, still afraid to meet his eyes.

"I've been better." Half-heartedly, he embraced her and took a step backwards.

Angela smelled his familiar scent and immediately relaxed. Jonathan was wrong; she didn't belong with him. He was a substitute for the real thing, the thing she'd felt afraid of her entire adult life: genuine love. She belonged with Martin, the man she knew who'd safeguard her heart. "About Christmas." She lowered her voice and clasped her hands in front of her mouth, wanting him to see that she didn't don Jonathan's ring. "Martin, I . . ."

"Angela, don't." He grabbed her hands. "Michael's waiting for me. Take care of yourself." Martin released her and fled toward the counter.

Angela's eyes filled with tears as she watched her future walk away while her palpitating heart acknowledged that she was too afraid to go after it.

32

Niche

Niche was tired of waiting. She didn't want to run into traffic. New Year's Eve was one of the busiest nights in San Francisco. She could feel the heartbeat of the city pulsing into her apartment. The neighbors' hip-hop music shook the walls, and the sounds of car horns complemented the beat.

Niche heaved a heavy sigh and leaned over to her nightstand. She flipped on classical music to help soothe her jitters. Kevon was late most often but usually by no more than an hour. Niche glanced at the creases in her silk pantsuit. She stared at the oval clock in her small bedroom, the second hand keeping her attention. It was eight-thirty, and she'd been ready since six o'clock.

Niche looked stunning in her royal-blue pantsuit. Snug at the top and cinched at the waist, the Christmas gift from her mother accentuated her figure. She had pulled her hair back into a ponytail so it didn't compete with the jeweled neckline and her faux-sapphire studs.

Niche didn't realize her leg was moving until she discovered the tempo of the hip-hop beat. Eighties hip-hop was her favorite. "Hard Times" by Run-DMC blared in the background, reminding her of her condition.

She needed to keep herself calm; the last thing she wanted was another argument. *Time for refreshing*, she told herself. Niche headed to the bathroom, standing with her shoulders arched back, trying hard to muster self-assurance, knowing inside she didn't feel the part. Her reflection in the white framed mirror made her grin. Blue went well with her skin tone. She opened her bathroom cabinet. Her mini makeup bag was hard to locate amongst all the beauty products tossed about the junk drawer.

"You look beautiful, Niche," Therie announced, pirouetting into the bathroom and grabbing a red lip liner from the clutter.

"What's up, dancing diva, you think you Misty Copeland or something?" Niche leaned into the mirror and applied more eye shadow.

"More like Debbie Allen, girlfriend." Her roommate shook her hips wildly. "Besides, don't bark at me, it's Kevon who is late. Does he even own a clock?"

"It drives his entire family crazy," Niche said, glossing her lips.

"My dad was like that, he couldn't be on time for anything except for church. Now, he was going to be on time to the Lord's house." Therie fluffed her bangs.

"I wish I could say the same about Kevon. He's always late, even getting up into the choir stand." Niche rolled her eyes as she recalled the last time they attended church. Lately, they'd missed more Sundays than she could count.

"Well, that I could forgive because your boy can sing. He ain't no Luther or Legend, but he can certainly blow." Therie raised her hand and fanned her face like an overheated concertgoer.

"True, I love to hear him sing, but he hasn't done that in a while." Niche scooted past her roommate and headed toward the living room. The sound of heavy rain pummeled against the windows as Therie headed toward the front door. "Whoa, it is certainly starting to come down out there."

"I'm out, Niche, I gotta meet my mom for a late dinner. Happy New Year!"

"I'm about to leave too. You be careful, Therie, those roads are going to be slippery," Niche declared, smoothing her pantsuit, carefully avoiding her abdomen.

"Did you call him?" Therie's eyes softened.

"A thousand times, but his phone's still off." Niche glanced at her watch. "Forget this, when the clock strikes nine, I'm out of here."

"I'll see you later, girl." Her friend gently closed the door behind her.

Niche scribbled a short note at her desk, grabbed her peacoat and umbrella, and headed toward the front door. She read the handwritten note that she taped on her front door. "Kevon, I left. I'm headed over to Tony's, and then to Sharyn's. Nothing else I could do since you were super late—again! Call me if you get here before tomorrow."

Niche shielded herself under the carport, shook the rain off her umbrella, slid into her hybrid, and eyed her soaked jumpsuit. She turned the heater on full blast and pulled out of her apartment complex like a child driving a go-cart. She checked her rearview mirror for the highway patrol as she raced onto the 101. Heading toward Tony's apartment, she knew she'd find him there. Kevon had been staying with Tony since Christmas, and she suspected he was afraid to go home. He said facing his parents was too much to deal with.

Niche exited the freeway, thankful that she'd purchased new wiper blades last month. She could hardly see the street lights because the rain was coming down in sheets. She swallowed hard as the weather mirrored her life, storming out of control. Without a doubt, her revelation was like blasting the news on the front of the *San Francisco Chronicle*, but she had no choice. There was no easy way to announce you had a miscarriage, and she needed Kevon to acknowledge it.

Niche turned the corner fast and headed down Fillmore Street toward Tony's apartment. Her defrost wasn't working well. She cracked the window, leaned low in her seat, and peeked through the bottom of her windshield, eager to eyeball Tony's building.

She turned into the dimly lit parking lot and searched for Kevon's car. She knew Tony wasn't home as he'd gone to visit his parents for Christmas and left Kevon in charge of his apartment. Calm washed over her when she spotted it in Tony's stall.

Niche double-parked and exited her car with one swift move of her hips. Headed to the second floor, she hurried up the stairs, careful not to slip on the soaked concrete. However, knocking proved fruitless; banging on Tony's door only stung her hand. Her heart filled with disappointment. Thoughts of deceit ran through her mind, and her stomach dived. Niche tried the knob of Tony's door. Surprised, she twisted it open.

Niche tiptoed into the quiet apartment and was greeted by a horrible stench. The darkened apartment reeked of alcohol, marijuana, and dirty gym socks. Her mouth watered from the sour pooling in her stomach. She stepped over a pile of cigarette ashes on the floor. As she walked toward the bedroom she spotted Kevon, passed out on Tony's stained upholstered couch. He wore the same white tank and blue Levi's he'd worn yesterday. Niche rolled her eyes, walked over to him, and shook him hard.

"Kevon!" Niche yelled. "Kevon, baby, it's me." Kevon lay motionless. Anger began to clog her throat, reminding her of the last time she'd traveled this road with him. "Kevon, get up!" Niche pinched his cheek. There was no way she could lift him into a cold shower alone again. Picking up Kevon's hand to slap him in the face with it, she noticed a piece of notebook paper that slipped to the hardwood floor. Niche grabbed the paper. Her face crinkled; the small print of Kevon's handwriting was barely legible.

I'm sorry. I'd rather take my own life than be responsible for taking someone else's.

Niche screamed, sinking to the floor as his note fell from her trembling hands.

Sharyn

Sharyn opened the front door. Tasha and her husband, Roy, were smiling like Cheshire cats. Sharyn inspected her lifelong friend from head to toe and winked with approval. Tasha looked stunning in a black sequined off-the-shoulder cocktail dress, looking like she belonged to the southern half of the Golden State.

"Hey, Queen to Be, where you headed?" Sharyn asked, laughing, equally as beautiful in a silver cocktail dress that swayed asymmetrically at the knees. Tasha and Sharyn exchanged knowing glances as they kissed each other's carefully constructed cheekbones.

"To the kitchen." Tasha patted Sharyn's stomach as she walked past her. "Fix your eyeliner," her best friend mumbled in the crossing. Sharyn smiled at her friend's candor. They were almost the final party guests in attendance. Sharyn peeked through the window, eagerly awaiting her last two guests. Kevon and Niche still hadn't arrived.

Sharyn closed the door, grabbed her flute of apple cider, and strolled toward Jonathan, surprised he had finally left Angela's side. "Beautiful, isn't it?" she proclaimed, noticing him perched under her stairway gazing at the family portrait that the Lovelaces had taken many years earlier.

"Yes, it is. You guys haven't changed one bit. My family has had pictures taken of us, but it seems like we are constantly changing." Jonathan rubbed his abdomen. "Spreading, that is."

"We've changed, too, but mostly on the inside. The outside looks different too," Sharyn said, stepping back to admire the photo. Her parents, arm in arm, stood over their brood of teenage children.

"Well, it's the inside that matters, isn't it? I have a feeling about you guys, your sister, especially." He tipped his flute in Sharyn's direction.

"Yes, I know, that was clear on Christmas." Sharyn snickered.

"She's a good woman, even though she can be challenging." Sharyn glanced at her sister in the photograph, still remembering the perfume Angela had soaked herself in that day, after her sister discovered the photographer was a bachelor.

"Yeah, I got that, Angela is a firecracker, but I'm taken by her. Who doesn't love fireworks, right?" Jonathan said, glancing over at Angela, decked out in a backless floor-length red dress.

Sharyn observed him eyeing her sister. She was sure he was in love with her like the other men Angela had brought home. He was just another face in a parade of others stepping behind Martin, the grand marshal.

"I'm starting this year off right, you know. With Angela on my arm, I feel like I can do anything, I've even started looking for a piece of property. She has been distant lately, but I want to show her that I am not gun-shy."

Sharyn's eyes widened. "A home?"

"Yes, my parents have been bugging me for years to buy something, but the time was never right. Everything has a season. A big old home for one person, the fit wasn't right, and I wasn't ready to change things."

"So, you had some changing to do, huh?" Sharyn poked his shoulder, not able to place the look in his eyes, but it made her uncomfortable.

"Sure did. I had to change my mind about my future. I live in an apartment, and it was always enough for me. But the sooner I buy, the better. It's funny how things can change overnight with the right woman." Jonathan grinned.

"Well, call me surprised," Sharyn said, distracted by the sound of the telephone ringing for the third time. She knew that if she didn't grab it, it wouldn't get answered. "Excuse me, Jonathan, I'll be right back."

"No problem."

"Can I get you something?" Sharyn rushed toward the telephone stationed in the kitchen as Jonathan shook his head no.

Sharyn placed her flute on the countertop and grabbed the cordless handset off its base. "Happy New Year! Hi, Daddy. You're where?" She paused, her face turning pale.

"Kevon did what? Oh my God!" Sharyn's knees buckled.

33

Robert

The double doors of the emergency department parted automatically as if they expected their arrival. Robert barreled through, kicking over the yellow wet floor sign stationed beside the portable floor dryer. His ex-wife marched closely behind him, navigating between empty gurneys. Robert, still in his pajamas, had rushed to the home of his ex-wife en route to the hospital.

The facial expression on the thin nurse behind the information desk changed when she located Kevon's name. She rushed them to the intensive care unit waiting area. The nurse disappeared shortly after instructing them to wait, leaving Robert to field his own questions. He paced the dimly lit waiting room as Rose sat silent. "When is someone going to come and talk to us?" Robert demanded loudly.

"I'm going to go find that nurse." Rose stood up and marched toward the emergency entrance. Niche stepped out of a side door labeled *Staff only*.

"Hi," she murmured.

"Is he okay?" Rose rushed over to Niche and hugged her tight. Her silk lilac pajamas were still damp from walking in the rain from the car to the hospital.

"I don't know," Niche reported, tears streaming down her face. "Let me take you . . ." Niche's voice trailed off. She signaled to the staff entrance. Rose clamped her mouth shut and shook her head frantically, like a toddler refusing vegetables.

Robert peered at Rose's bloodshot eyes, a mirror image of when she had contracted conjunctivitis years before, knowing she couldn't stand much more. He walked up behind her and rested his hand on her shoulder. "Stay here, I'll handle it," Robert insisted, and walked toward the staff entrance. He knew he had to manage this as he glanced back at the woman he'd met so long ago. She was fragile then and even more now.

Sharyn

On the way to the hospital, the silence in the car was deafening. The smell of fresh rain couldn't relieve the fear that lingered in the air. Sharyn cracked the window and looked down at her slippers; she didn't recall putting them on or even getting into the car. All she remembered was her best friend, Tasha, holding her sister while directing guests out of the party. Sharyn grabbed another napkin from the glove compartment as tears dripped onto her cheeks. No matter how hard she tried to shut off the valve, the flow wouldn't stop. She didn't even notice the receipt from New Horizons fall to the floor. Her jaw moved in a familiar motion as she began grinding her back teeth. She bit down hard, trying to stop the stress from undoing years of dental work. The fate of her baby brother was still uncertain, and so was she. How was she going to fix this?

She could hear Michael praying softly from the driver's seat. Sharyn shook her head, wishing she had his faith. If there was a God, they needed Him now.

Angela

The surreal feeling of freezing started to overcome Angela again as she scooted forward in the back seat. The numbing of her hands and feet. The sound of her heart pounding in her ears. The stiffening of her torso. She wasn't at work this time, but she knew she had to push past it. Like trying to wake from a nightmare, this was going to take a fight. Angela cradled her forehead and squeezed, massaging her temples to keep her in the present. She kicked off Sharyn's running shoes and pushed her feet down into the floor. She began tapping her fingers against her head to practice the emotional freedom technique she'd learned in therapy. Breathing in deeply and steadily, she could feel her anxiety start to wane.

Kevon was her only brother. The one who'd followed her around when she was a girl. The boy who'd put her lipsticks in the trash because he didn't want any boys looking at her. Her brother who'd rushed over to her condo when she was sick and brushed her hair all night to make her feel better. Angela tried to remember the last time she'd talked to him besides the holidays. Was it weeks or a month? She touched Sharyn's shoulder from behind. She couldn't see her sister's face, but she knew the pain in her heart.

Angela drew in a deep breath as Michael barely missed the car next to the empty parking stall he'd found. Hasley Hospital had greeted her multiple times throughout her career, and she knew the nurses by name. She'd taken babies out of its doors, never again returning them to their families, but this time was different. Kevon was her baby, and he was coming home. She grabbed her purse, opened the door, jumped out of the car, and led the way as they funneled into the lobby of the intensive care unit.

The sterile white lobby was illuminated by the shadows on the freshly waxed floors. The smell of antiseptic stung her nose. Sharyn and Michael trailed behind her as they tried to keep in step. Angela fought the familiar feeling of loss. When she entered this hospital, it was usually to remove someone from their family.

Angela saw her mother first, sitting alone in the corner. She beheld her mother's frail frame as she slowed her jog to a snail's pace. Angela refused to embrace her mother after what she'd done. Anxiety turned to anger as Angela tightened her jaw. Tears began to form, and she could hardly view her mother clearly. A thin black raincoat covered Rose's shaking body, and her dull hair lay lifeless on her shoulders. A picture of Samantha's discolored face flashed through Angela's mind as she was finally able to identify the resemblance, the unmistakable likeness of her mother and dead sister after the light had been sucked out of both their bodies.

Sharyn

Sharyn power-walked to keep up with her sister. Angela's red silhouette seemed to get farther away with each step. The long corridor leading to the waiting room was endless. Sharyn glanced back at Michael when she finally saw a row of chairs. Immediately, she spotted her mother, draped in Niche's raincoat. Rose, sitting near the staff door, was alone in the midst of the empty green seats, her hands covering her bowed head as if she had a migraine. Sharyn walked right past her sister, who had stopped short. Her protruding belly was the first part of her body to reach her mother.

"Mom, what happened?" Sharyn questioned, taking a seat next to her mother. Rose's head lifted slowly. Her face was empty, like someone had stolen her hue.

"I don't know, baby. I don't know," Rose said, as tears streamed down her eyes. Sharyn instinctively wrapped her arms around her mother, and they cried together.

Angela

Angela pushed back the anger that fought to rise in her chest. Her shoulders squared, she had to put the past behind her. She glanced at her mother, pale, her lips chapped from constant biting. The agony was apparent in her bloodshot eyes. Angela unclenched her fists and willed herself not to abandon a family member like her mother had years ago. No matter the circumstance, it was never acceptable to leave the broken behind. It was time for her to model the Christ she had learned so much about. She refused to cast the first stone in judgment. Maybe she was like Joseph after all. Angela headed toward her mother and extended her arms. The three women grasped onto each other like life rafts, crying their uncertainties. Angela's arms tightened around the shell of her mother and sister in an attempt to stop the waves from crashing.

Sharyn

Pain held a presence in the waiting room like a thick band of smoke. Sharyn pulled back and watched Angela and Rose weep together. *Suicide!* The word pounded like a steady clap in her mind. She looked away from her family and forced herself to focus on something tangible. Her eyes shifted to her husband staring blankly out of the window. She wondered what he was looking at. His mouth moved silently.

Sharyn bowed her head slowly after she recognized the muted language spewing out of her husband. He was praying. "Amen," she heard herself whisper in agreement with her devoted spouse as she heard a small voice creeping up in the back of her mind. *He has made everything beautiful in its time.* Sharyn jumped to her feet and headed to the window. She wrapped her arms around Michael's waist and nuzzled up to his back. His shoulder blades pressed firmly against her cheek. She smiled because she'd finally realized they were never alone.

Robert

Robert stood frozen in the doorway, watching Kevon's chest rise and fall as he had the day of his birth. The curtains were closed, the rickety chair in the corner was vacant, and the silver tray table lay empty, a stark contrast to the day his only son was born. But like that day, he still couldn't bring himself to enter the hospital room.

The tubes in Kevon's nose, arms, and taped to his chest frightened him. The last time he'd seen someone hooked up to machines, death had come. Robert turned toward the hallway as vomit spewed violently onto the floor. The bile pouring out of his body was like hot lava erupting out of a volcano. He didn't want to play Pac-Man, his mother's ghost moving in on one side and Big Mama's on the other, death passing through him and changing him at his core. The devastation suicide leaves in its wake had gutted him once, but he had hoped never again. The desire to rejoin Rose in the waiting room surged in him.

"Are you okay, sir? Can I help you?" The beautiful nurse in pastel scrubs gently touched his elbow. Her resemblance to Big Mama startled him.

"No, thank you. I'm sorry about this," Robert said, pointing to the puddle on the floor.

"No worries. I'll send someone right up. You okay?"

"I've had better days, but I'm okay."

"Well, okay, but we are just a phone call away." The revelation hit him out of nowhere as he watched the nurse shuffle down the hallway.

Robert was certain then, like years before, that God had the ultimate plan. He'd learned that from Big Mama. It was no coincidence that this nurse had come to his aid. It was a reminder. Robert rested on his heels, hummed the chorus to "We Shall Overcome" and confronted the truth that his son also had a mental illness, and with the Lord's help, they could conquer anything.

Angela

Angela heard his footsteps before he entered the waiting room. His cadence was seared in her memory like a familiar film score. Her heart pulsed as his scent alerted her senses before he did. She could feel their connection before she'd even laid eyes on him. He was faithful, loving, and the man she needed right now. Like some birds, Martin mated for life, and he was returning to the nest he'd spent two years preparing. He touched her shoulders softly as their eyes met, both knowing that apologies weren't necessary. He sat down next to her and enveloped her in a familiar chenille throw, and she leaned into his arms.

"I thought I'd bring the better blanket Big Mama gave you," he said, wrapping his arms around her. She closed her eyes and let go; it was so nice to be finally covered.

Robert

Robert headed through the disinfected hallway back to the waiting room, his footsteps lighter. Kevon unintentionally exhumed Robert's corridor to the past, but this time he'd decided he would leave it in the hands of the Lord. He was tired of carrying the burden all by himself. Mental illness was not a choice, but getting better was. His mother had made a choice, his son had made a choice, and now he was going to make a choice. He could give his son something his mother never had—support.

"Mr. Lovelace?" The short, portly physician called after him from behind. Robert turned and headed back toward the man outfitted in black scrubs. "I wanted to inform you, Kevon is recovering nicely and should make a full recovery."

"Thank you, Dr. Leslie." Robert extended his hand and shook vigorously.

"Kevon's physical health is stable, but his mental health is more of a concern. He will require intensive psychotherapy, coupled with strict supervision for the next couple of weeks."

"I understand." Robert nodded.

"When he wakes up we'll be able to obtain additional information. In the meantime, I'd like to set up a family meeting with our staff and Kevon's support system. Our mental health liaison is in office first thing tomorrow morning."

Robert thanked the physician and provided his availability. He knew lots of work lay ahead as he mumbled a quiet prayer thanking God for a second chance.

"I have good news!" Robert shouted, as he opened the door to the waiting room and looked directly at Rose. "Kevon is going to be fine."

"Hallelujah," "Praise God," and "Thank you, Jesus" echoed loudly.

"What did the doctor say, Daddy?" Sharyn stumbled to her feet and looked deep into her father's eyes.

"It's not what the doctor said, sweetheart. It's what the Doctor that made the doctor said. Now, let's sit down. We have to talk. There is work to do, and we need every one of you." Robert walked over to an empty chair stationed along the wall. His family crowded around him.

"You okay, Daddy?" Sharyn patted his shoulder.

"Where's Niche?" Angela asked.

"I sent her to get something to eat," Robert replied.

"Should I get her?" Sharyn inquired looking toward the hallway.

Robert grabbed Rose's hand securely and held it tight, looking directly into her puffy eyes.

"No need. Now Rose, our baby has serious issues. Problems I never recognized. The doctor said a meeting will be held tomorrow and we *all* have to pull together." He squeezed her hand. "The doctors won't relay any more information, but the nurse shared that he took some pills and alcohol." Robert looked at the floor and paused, thankful Kevon hadn't used a gun like his mother.

"I know it's hard, Daddy, but we need to talk about it," Angela assured him.

Robert's eyes met hers. "He needs to be observed. They have someone coming in to assess him tomorrow. He wrote a note."

"A note. What?" Angela snarled. Martin moved closer to her, slunk his arms around her waist, and squeezed tight.

"The note is addressed to us. Niche gave it to me when I got here. I haven't read it yet," Robert said.

"Read it now, Daddy. I need to know why he did this!" Sharyn said eagerly.

"I don't think now is the time," Robert said, keeping silent about his concern for his ex-wife.

"Read it, Robert. We have a right to know," Rose insisted, squeezing his hand.

Robert pulled the note from his front pajama pocket, cleared his throat, and read. "The pain is inevitable." He crushed the note to his heart and took a deep breath. Tear-stained blue ink testified to his anguish.

Robert gently unfolded the crumpled paper. He looked at his ex-wife as tears saturated his cheeks. "Rose, it's hard to face another suicide." Robert groaned, feeling his resolve melt away. "I may be weak, but Your Spirit is strong in me."

"What are you talking about, Daddy?" Sharyn shook her head, confused.

"Like David, encourage yourself, Doc." Martin stood up straight. "Your grace is all I need, and Your power works best in my weakness. In my time of trouble, You shall hide me." Robert sat up erect, reciting God's word.

"It's okay, Robert, that was a different place and time." Rose arose, knelt before him, and wrapped her arms around his neck. "It all was."

"But it feels like yesterday, Rose." Robert shook his head, trying to ward off the pain.

"Daddy, *what* exactly are you talking about?" Sharyn grabbed her heart, trying to interrupt her parents' private yet public conversation.

"Robert, we have to clean house like the pastor said. We have to tell our truths. God will restore us," Rose whispered in his ear. He could feel her strength radiating toward him, something he'd never known. Robert pulled away from her and sat up straight. He wiped his tears and looked her directly in the eye. He nodded tenuously. Rose stood up straight and faced her children. "Your father and I have some information to share with you all."

"What information?" Angela exclaimed.

"Rose, don't!" Robert instructed, changing his mind.

"No, it's time to tell my children the truth. I was afraid they'd see me differently, but not anymore. Now I want them to know. I've almost lost another child to the grave. The truth has to be told."

"Please, tell the truth," Angela beckoned.

"Not now!" Robert begged.

"Why not? Would they no longer love me if they knew I was raped? And would they hate me if they knew a child was born as a result? Would they no longer love you if they knew your mother killed herself? And Samantha." Rose buckled at the knees. "Samantha," she whispered.

Robert knew he had to do something. He guided Rose into a chair and decided to let God have control. He sat next to Rose, lifted his head, cleared his throat, and hoped the truth would set them all free.

34

Robert

Robert sat at his kitchen table and beheld the tear-stained letter. He grabbed his mug and sipped his morning coffee. So much had happened since that dreadful night. The family had grown much closer since Kevon had tried to take his life.

Today, he'd decided his usual coffee wouldn't suffice, so he'd made the special trip to Ollie's in Russian Hill to grab specialty beans. He wanted to ensure the richness of his coffee matched the fullness of this day. In therapy, he'd learned to be mindful, taking in every moment.

He took another sip and placed the note back in his robe pocket. It had been a year since Kevon's suicide attempt, and Robert read the letter monthly as a reminder of what he could've lost.

"Uh, Daddy? We have way too much to get done today. You can't be sitting around reading the paper. Hop to it!" Angela marched into the kitchen, her manicured fingers gently smacking his strong hand. "It's nine o'clock already. We need to be dressed and ready by noon."

"I know." Robert looked up and kissed his daughter's cheek.

"We're already rolling, Daddy. Kevon's upstairs taking a bath. I think you better get to doin' the same. Mom is set to be here at ten, and I know you don't want her walking in and seeing you still in your pajamas."

"You're right about that. I refuse to take on your mother today." Robert rose from his chair, walked over to Angela, and wrapped his arms around her shoulder.

"I love you, Daddy, and I'm glad that you modeled for me what a man should be."

Robert smiled, slowly exited the kitchen, and walked up the stairs toward his room, leaving the steaming coffee on the table.

Angela

Angela peered up the stairs until her father was out of sight. Her ponytail danced at the nape of her neck as she pranced back to the kitchen. Underneath her white cotton gown and terrycloth robe, her body shivered. She sat down in her father's chair, grabbed his mug, and sampled his coffee.

Her eyes surveyed the kitchen where she grew up, nostalgia pulling at her heartstrings. She studied the artwork her mother had framed years ago that Angela, Kevon, and Sharyn had drawn as children. She smiled brightly when she noticed a newly framed masterpiece completed by her nephew Trevion.

Angela was now grateful that God had allowed her to be the on-duty social worker who responded to the complaint of the absentee student. Finding her half-sister dead would always stay with her, but God's tender mercy had placed her at the opportune place to unite Trevion with his family.

She twirled her engagement ring around her finger and relished in her new understanding of sacrifice. Anger toward her mother no longer resided in her heart. She understood why Rose hadn't wanted a relationship with her estranged daughter. For some, it was easier to try to forget than to forgive, a lesson Angela had learned early in her career. Unlike her mother, Robert had cared, provided, and loved despite Samantha's demons, like he said Jesus did on the cross.

Sharyn

Sharyn turned the fire off on the stove and removed John Alexander's bottle from the pot of steaming water. She hated the bottle warmer. It never got his formula warm enough. She shook the bottle, squeezed milk on her wrist, and winced. It was too hot for her infant son. Sharyn placed the bottle in the freezer for a quick cooling, grabbed a tumbler from the cabinet, filled it with ice, and poured some apple juice.

"Is it ready yet?" Michael called toward the kitchen from the family room. Sharyn shook her head in disbelief. Her husband was more impatient than their child.

"No, not yet. Why, is he fussing?" Sharyn replied, echoing her husband's tone.–

"No, but he's hungry," Michael retorted.

Sharyn added some cold water to the milk, walked to the living room, and handed him the bottle. She placed the apple juice on the table in front of her husband and smiled. "Bottles for both my babies."

Michael propped John high on his shoulder and patted his back softly. "Thank you, sweetheart." He winked. "Sorry I was snippy, but my son—"

Sharyn cut him off. "Our son." She smiled as she marveled at her son and his father. Michael was a natural. He was a loving, attentive father, and since the birth of their son, he'd spoiled them both.

"*Our* son was hungry." Michael laughed. "Are you? I could fix you something?" he offered.

Sharyn shook her head, declining. She didn't need her husband to take on any more. After Kevon's suicide attempt, her whole outlook on life changed. Her career no longer occupied first place. It took her a while to acknowledge that self-sacrifice wasn't healthy for her or her family and neither was being selfish. In family therapy, Sharyn was able to identify that by taking care of others' needs she found her importance, but when family didn't meet hers, she became angry.

"Here, give him to me," Sharyn said. "You'd better go get dressed before we're late. The photographer's coming at eleven." John looked handsome in his white tuxedo, and Sharyn had to be extra careful today in an effort to keep him clean. She eyed the clock centered on the wall. If they headed out the door within the next thirty minutes, they might be safe from traffic. "Upstairs, please." Sharyn scooped her arms around John and pulled him to her chest. She sat down, shook the bottle, and fed her son. Sharyn watched her baby take in only what he could handle. By three months old, he'd already learned that if he drank too much, he'd throw up. Sharyn was glad she'd learned this lesson right along with him. Codependency was what their family therapist called it. "Lesson learned," was how she'd replied.

Niche

Niche's living room was in chaos. She had received so many gifts from her family and friends that the blue-and-white packages over-took the small living space.

"His tuxedo is in the garment bag on the bed, and his T-shirts and socks are in the top drawer. Don't forget his shoes on the dresser."

"I won't." Therie winked as she cradled two bottles of lotion in her hand.

"Try not to pack too heavy this time, please," Niche said, as her friend rolled her eyes and headed toward the bedroom.

"You want to be ashy?" Therie said, swinging the lotions in the air.

"When is Kevon coming? Did he lead the church group this morning?" she asked.

Niche headed to the kitchen to pack her snack bag. "Living Victoriously was cancelled today, he's still at his dad's," she explained, stuffing two bags of potato chips into a blue lunch sack. "I'm going to start putting my stuff in the car, then we can head over there."

"Yes, let's get this show on the road!" Therie yelled from her room.

Niche leaned onto the counter and beheld her small apartment. "Let's. I feel like I am crossing over into the promised land. It took us a while, but I'm glad we've finally made it. You have to climb uphill to the mountaintop." Niche grabbed her hairbrush off the counter and tossed it into the bag.

"Now you sound like Kevon that Sunday he rededicated his life to Christ. He meant that thing."

"He has certainly been changed since he became more active in the faith. We all have. The depression support group he started at St. John's and the anger management group have made such a difference, plus the family therapy has brought us all closer."

"Hallelujah, girl, God is good," Therie acknowledged.

"Yes, He is." Niche's eyes welled with tears. She grabbed a paper towel, then fanned her face to save her makeup. "Yes, He is."

Kevon

Kevon and Martin stood near the altar, looking like orchestra conductors in black-and-white tuxedos. The blue-and-white flowers cascading around them matched the ribbons tied at the edge of the pews. It was four o'clock, and guests were still filing in.

"Are you nervous?" Kevon asked Martin, glancing at his watch.

Martin straightened his tie and leaned in next to Kevon's ear. "I want to get this thing started. The wedding was supposed to begin an hour ago," he replied, as the piano music interrupted him. "And I have a plane to catch."

Kevon smiled, patted Martin on the shoulder, and faced the center aisle. He winked at his fraternity brothers sitting in the front row. The two ushers in the rear of the church closed the sanctuary doors as the last guest was seated, and Kevon stood at attention.

Angela

The dressing room was full of flowers, lace, and laughter. Angela, Niche, and Sharyn sat gathered in front of floor-length mirrors adding final touches of makeup. Angela grabbed her lipstick and applied heavily. "I love this color," she professed. She put her hand down and tried on several different smiles to be camera-ready.

Angela was stunning in an ivory dress adorned with lace and beading. The A-line gown complete with formfitting corset accentuated her well-toned physique.

"We look beautiful. I think I'm going to cry!" Sharyn exclaimed, fanning her face furiously as Angela's coworker Jeannine stood behind her, adjusting the curls in her hair.

"If you get tears near my dress, I'll have to kill you. There's a look I'm going for, and I'm going to catch that bouquet because, like your sister, I need a new ringtone." Jeannine flexed her arms for emphasis.

Angela leaned back in her chair and snapped her fingers twice, approving her coworker's confidence. Her telephone rang out loudly. Angela grabbed the phone, silenced the call, and plopped it back in her purse.

"I know that isn't who I think it is?" Jeannine said, familiar with Angela's ringtones.

"Yes, Jonathan is *still* calling and he *knows* it's my wedding day. He texted me more than forty times last night. I finally gave up trying to reason with him around seven. Anyway, I think you guys better get out there. We don't want to be even later." Angela pointed at the door.

The sudden knock at the door startled the women.

"Come in!" Sharyn yelled loudly. Robert slowly opened the door, gallant in his black tuxedo. He looked around the large dressing room and walked in with his hands up.

"Now, don't shoot the messenger. You ladies look wonderful, and I love you all, but we are running awfully late. Can we get this show on the road?"

Sharyn blew him a kiss, stood up, and smiled. "All ready, Daddy." Sharyn walked past him and exited the large room. Jeannine immediately followed.

Angela grinned as she heard the wedding march being played forcefully on the organ. She stood up, smoothed her dress, and curtsied. "Let's do this!" They walked hand in hand out of the dressing room into the foyer. Angela leaned into her father as they stood at the sanctuary doors. "I'm scared, Daddy," she whispered, holding tight to her father's arm.

Robert smiled and whispered to his youngest daughter. "It's all right. Step on that carpet and let God do the rest. Now, go in there and get your groom," Robert replied, as the double doors opened and they stepped onto the white runner. Angela's veil shimmered as its rhinestones caught the church lighting.

"That I will, Daddy. That I will." Angela beamed as she walked slowly, carefully taking in the moments that the photographer couldn't. She steadied her breathing as the faces blurred in her wake. Her heart fluttered like a car running out of gas, but this time it wasn't a panic attack. This time she was at peace. She could only see one thing clearly as she glided down the aisle—the love in his eyes.

Niche

The doors leading to the vestibule were shut again as Niche heard the wedding march playing again. Her hand glided over her flat abdomen as she remembered the life that was lost, all the while rejoicing about the one she was going to gain. She positioned herself in front of the stately doors and traced her teeth with her tongue once more to ensure no lipstick stains. Michael held Niche's arm tight.

"I'm ready," she whispered.

"You look marvelous." Michael belted out his best Billy Crystal impression. Niche giggled as the huge etched oak doors opened. "You got this," he coached, as Niche's arm began to shake.

Niche's formfitting ivory gown was equally as beautiful as Angela's and clutched the curves of her slender body. Her bare shoulders, brushed with body glitter, glistened underneath the chandeliers. Her veil was a simple crown of ivory rosettes that cupped her curly updo. Eyes admired the beautiful bride and the handsome man who stood in place of her father.

Niche could see Kevon's eyes watering as she approached him. She fought back tears underneath her veil. Kevon walked toward Niche before the pastor could address the assembly. He raised her veil and kissed her softly on the lips.

"I love you, girl!" Kevon exclaimed. He lowered her veil and linked their arms. Niche swallowed hard as she surrendered her heart directly into his hands.

Robert

Robert Lovelace beamed as he leaned back in his seat and wrapped his arm around Trevion. He couldn't stop grinning as he watched the wedding of his two youngest children. He slowly snaked his finger around his ex-wife's hand and exhaled. Big Mama was right; his latter days were greater.

ACKNOWLEDGMENTS

My God: I love, worship, and adore you. I thank you for the manifestation. Jeremiah 29:11.

My Husband: You are and will always be the love of my life. Thanks for always holding my heart.

My Children, Jodie B and Biddy: The gifts I don't deserve. You are my inspiration.

My Beloved Parents in Glory: My love and gratitude. Gone but never forgotten.

My Sister: Thanks for letting me ride on your coattails. I am in awe of you.

My Family: The Nic to my Nac, roux to my gumbo, orange juice to my ham. I love you.

My Pastors: Metters/Turner: Spiritual leaders and servants. My greatest appreciation.

My Sorors: The Headquarters, The Hard Way, and The Heroines. My love and adoration.

My Readers: My appreciation and love for each of you extends well beyond this book.

My Publishers: For kicking down doors to create value in all voices. I thank and applaud you.

ABOUT THE AUTHOR

Bobi Gentry Goodwin is a native San Franciscan. The Bay Area was where she first discovered her love for people and their stories. She has held a passion for writing since early childhood, and as a clinical social worker her mission field has been working with women and children. She is a wife and mother of two, and an avid member of her local church. Goodwin currently resides in California.

SELECTED TITLES FROM SHE WRITES PRESS

She Writes Press is an independent publishing company founded to serve women writers everywhere. Visit us at www.shewritespress.com.

True Stories at the Smoky View by Jill McCroskey Coupe $16.95, 978-1-63152-051-8

The lives of a librarian and a ten-year-old boy are changed forever when they become stranded by a blizzard in a Tennessee motel and join forces in a very personal search for justice.

Clear Lake by Nan Fink Gefen $16.95, 978-1-938314-40-7

When psychotherapist Rebecca Lev's father dies under suspicious circumstances, she becomes obsessed with discovering what happened to him.

American Family by Catherine Marshall-Smith $16.95, 978-1631521638

Partners Richard and Michael, recovering alcoholics, struggle to gain custody of Richard's biological daughter from her grandparents after her mother's death only to discover that they—and she—are fundamentalist Christians.

The End of Miracles by Monica Starkman $16.95, 978-1-63152-054-9

When a pregnancy following years of infertility ends in late miscarriage, Margo Kerber sinks into a depression—one that leads her, when she encounters a briefly unattended baby, to commit an unthinkable crime.

Shelter Us by Laura Diamond $16.95, 978-1-63152-970-2

Lawyer-turned-stay-at-home-mom Sarah Shaw is still struggling to find a steady happiness after the death of her infant daughter when she meets a young homeless mother and toddler she can't get out of her mind—and becomes determined to rescue them.

Stella Rose by Tammy Flanders Hetrick $16.95, 978-1-63152-921-4

When her dying best friend asks her to take care of her sixteen-year-old daughter, Abby says yes—but as she grapples with raising a grieving teenager, she realizes she didn't know her best friend as well as she thought she did.